Sutra of the Pearl

Lee Kaiser

ISBN: 978-1-7774577-0-9

"In a visit which I recently made to a gonpa, one of the lamas told me of a prophet, or, as you call him, a buddha, by the name of Issa. Could you not tell me anything about him?" I asked my interlocutor, seizing this favorable moment to start the subject which interested me so greatly."

Adventurer Nicolas Notovitch

"... In conformity with established custom, every disciple or lama who visits Lhassa makes a gift of one or several copies, from the scrolls there, to the convent to which he belongs. Our gonpa, among others, possesses already a great number, which I read in my leisure hours. Among them are the memoirs of the life and acts of the Buddha Issa, who preached the same doctrine in India and among the sons of Israel, and who was put to death by the Pagans, whose descendants, later on, adopted the beliefs he spread, — and those beliefs are yours."

Chief Hemis Monastery Lama

From:
The Unknown Life of Jesus Christ, original text of Nicolas Notovitch's 1887 Discovery

Acknowledgements

Parts of this novel are based on the memoirs of Russian scholar and 19th century adventurer Nicolas Notovitch without whom this story would not exist. I also owe a great debt to German scholar Holger Kersten for the impeccable research within his book: Jesus Lived in India, His Unknown Life Before and After the Crucifixion published in 1994.

The following writers and early readers gave not only their expertise but unfailing encouragement: Faye Arcand, Heather Caruso, Irene Lalonde, Jonas Saul, Kate Smith, Melody Bailey, and Una Rose. Also thank you to Alberta oilman Gary Pettit for his knowledge and humorous asides on that industry.

Sutra of the Pearl

Prologue

The Kettle, 2006

Julie Paglia was a crackerjack of a liar, just like her mother.
The pebbled shoreline below the old railway bridge looked narrow and insignificant today, the way things shrink when you haven't seen them since childhood. Twenty-seven years was a long time to carry a lie as resilient as the rattler her brother tried to kill that year. No matter how many times he whacked it, it kept bouncing back.

Buffeted by April gusts, she clung to the rickety railing spanning the Kettle River and held fast to the lump inside her windbreaker, as a mother might cradle her feverish child. On the riverbank, a dog snatched an airborne frisbee and trotted back to its master. Somewhere in his twenties, the man wouldn't remember the park's manicured lawn, which was swept away by 1979's flood waters, never to be replanted.

Sunlight flickered through pine boughs lining the shore and glanced off rivulets trickling between rocky shoals. Hardly the roiling mass that had carried Doni away.

She plucked the rubber ducky from her jacket, pressed it to her lips, and tossed it over the side. "Go to Doni, little duck. Go find Doni." It hit the water, bobbed, and righted itself, riding the waves to the rapids, where it disappeared. Downstream—in a place where currents once dragged her baby brother's face along the muddy bottom of the river—lay the truth.

Even back then, at five years old, Julie knew better. When someone hurts you and you didn't start it, that person should be punished. Slowly and painfully.

Yet nothing happened. Not in the black and white terrain of her childhood, at least.

She did what she could, never one to suffer a bad actor like Big Sara. Pinned down or backed into a corner, Julie kicked her way through childhood, sinking her foot into the soft tissue of her mother's groin, and only once did she make the deadly mistake of using her mouth instead of her foot to call Big Sara on her shit.

She mounted her bicycle. Twenty-seven years was long enough to wait for justice. What was true and right in life was sometimes as dark and unsavory as the bottom of the Kettle.

I

Cedarwood, 2002

In a life pockmarked by embellishment Julie Paglia never needed to include her activism in the charade. Years before she sent Doni's duck on its watery adventure, the twenty-eight-year-old patrolled Cedarwood's main thoroughfares, of which there was just the one in this former gold rush railway terminus.

"Can I use your bike?" Yelling above Paula's screeching hair dryer, Julie batted at the steam tumbling from the bathroom into the parched cedar beams of the cabin.

All she could see was hair the sheen of burnished copper being tossed around like storm surge. Cut blunt, show-pony style, it reached halfway down her friend's back. Because Julie believed hair dryers and curling irons to be useless, bourgeois contraptions, her own kinky, chestnut locks always fell on the gale-force end of the sexy windblown look.

"I hear you've been scaring our senior drivers with that air horn of yours." Paula's husky voice strained against the white noise. In primary school the girl with the pink hearing-aid and damaged voice box found a friend in Julie, the cross-eyed one known as Googly Eyes.

Since arriving at Paula's proxy home a week earlier, Julie had replaced the jaunty *ka-ching* of her friend's bicycle bell with the bellow of a horn used to whip ice hockey hoards into a frenzy.

"It's their own fault," Julie said, unrepentant. "Their big-ass trucks caused global warming. They killed the electric car."

Paula knew every one of the town's elders by name. She lowered the dryer a touch. "*Who* did they kill? Surely, they didn't mean to."

"Okay. I promise not to use it unless I have to. I'm going to the old house later today."

Her friend yanked open the door. Still holding the dryer motionless above her head, Paula clicked it off. "What did you say?"

"I'll lay off the air—"

"No, about the house." Paula's stunned expression had the sickly tone of an unripe strawberry. She'd heard Julie, all right. "Why now?"

"You *know* why. You're the one who told me it might not be standing when I get back from India next spring."

"I didn't think you'd care. You should wait so I can be here for you. I'll only be on Vancouver Island a week."

Julie shook her head. "I don't give a shit about the house. There's something in the garage I want."

Paula plunked the dryer on the bathroom counter and headed through the kitchen. "It's not there anymore."

Julie stared after her, unable to get her legs moving. When she caught up, Paula was on her knees inside the walk-in pantry, sifting through a jumble of mismatched winter boots piled in one corner.

"What the hell happened to it?" Julie dodged an airborne reject.

"Remember the heavy snowfall last year and the freezing rain?" Paula bounced another boot off the wall and into the discards. "The roof caved in. The town council forced your mother to haul it away. Cost her big."

"Ha. She finally had to dip into that fat bank account. Good. I hope it pissed her off." That was some consolation.

Before Julie could ask about the garage contents, Paula stood and wheeled around. She cradled a knee-high mukluk under one arm as she dug around inside it. Out came a faded photograph. "Here. Is this what you want?"

So, her mother overlooked at least one of Doni.

"I cut the chain on the garage doors," Paula said, cupping her hand to the small of Julie's back. "It's the only one I had time to find. I didn't want your mother to show up and accuse me of theft."

Julie held it to her chest but knew immediately she was mistaken. One memory, no matter how sweet, wouldn't be enough to forget her two-year-old brother's trembling blue lips. "You didn't see a plastic Flash Gordon bowl in any of the boxes, did you? It's got a big chip out of it where he nailed her in the head from his highchair."

The two women grinned at each other.

"Goddamn it," Julie said. "I wanted that."

Back then, trying to hide Doni's bowl from certain destruction after his death was no middling show of defiance. Julie counted it as her first official act of non-violent resistance against her mother.

The day after Paula left for her totem pole carving retreat, Julie cycled into town toward her family's derelict house. She didn't plan to relive the good times, those clichéd stories the neighbors had. The ones they repeated over and over at family reunions. The Paglia family anecdotes? The only place fit to tell those was inside a police detachment.

Almost there, she skidded to a dusty halt in front of the QuickieMart and stared in disbelief at the wooden bench beside the store's entrance. Other than the faded paint, this safe seat where she sat for hours after school doing her homework, hadn't changed. Casting aside the bike, she wiggled into one splintered corner, the warped boards under her thighs as familiar as the knobby elbows of aged grandparents.

"For the price of a popsicle you sure got your money's worth out of that bench." At the corner of the building, Old Dora, the clerk, gave her a sloppy grin and took a drag from her cigarette. "I haven't seen you in years."

Julie used to imagine this horn-nosed clerk lived in the basement where she spun her gossipy stories into shape on a loom and slipped them into customers' bags.

"Hey, Dora. I'm not around much anymore. Traveling and writing."

"Tapping out travel stories in moldy hotel rooms in the Third World, eh? Still can't find your name inside that *National*

Geographic magazine you work for." Her chin high, Dora stubbed out her cigarette with her heel. "Well, back to my perch at the till."

As early as primary school, while other girls played with dolls, Julie collected adventures from the pages of *National Geographic* and smuggled them out of the school library in her underpants. In bed, she peered at the faded photographs by flashlight and moved the beam to the world map on the wall for the exact location of the expedition. She dashed across the Arctic with dogs, scrambled up the Khyber Pass blocked with snow, then descended into the Lost City of the Incas.

Although Julie, the writer, had traveled rough to every continent all she'd managed to sell were watered-down snippets for in-flight magazines. Far from high adventure, they catered to the traveler looking for comfort and predictability — visits to Hong Kong's night markets, day trips down the Danube, and weekends at a dude ranch in the Canadian Rockies.

Even so, her minor scribblings massaged and cemented an aura for her many acquaintances of no consequence in Canada that she was *living the adventurer's dream*. Hard-ass skeptics like Dora got nothing but slack-jawed, mute civility out of Julie.

Via the screen door Julie overheard a co-worker ask Dora, "Who was that?"

"One of the Paglia girls. Remember? The mother used to come in here wearing that god-awful hat of peacock feathers and a fanged boa over her shoulder."

At the time Doni disappeared Julie's mother was a sixties blond bombshell in the braless seventies who blasted into a room like an icy nor'easter, leaving everyone scampering for warmth.

"She's the one who killed her kid," Dora added.

"Well, she looked capable of it. If they ever find the body, they'll know the boy's death was no accident."

At the Paglia's two-story clapboard house dry rot eclipsed any sign of paint. Julie leaned her bike inside the rickety picket fence and, out of habit, tickled the underbelly of the giant Weeping Willow. Such an oddity in dry conditions, some speculated it stood above a shallow aquifer which would explain the house's sinking foundation.

Danger! No entry by order of the Village of Cedarwood. She ducked under this yellow warning tape strung across the crumbling stone stairs to the front door.

As always, the loose brick slid out of the porch edging, revealing the front door key. Her scalp crawled as if arriving home before her older brother, Sam, or Papa. Inside, she stumbled sideways. Without furniture to mask the sloping floor, it seemed to undulate with a nauseous funhouse effect.

She propped the photo upright atop the mantle. "Welcome home, Doni … Papa."

Julie trailed fingertips down her cheek, imagining her papa's callused paws during her nightmares. "*Patatina,*" she mouthed. "Wake up, Little Potato." Dare she go upstairs to her old bedroom? Surely the threat would be gone by now.

Inside the kitchen where the stairs started, she could see the railing had disintegrated, but the steps seemed intact. She toed each one as she climbed until emerging onto the top landing.

STAY OUT! NO TRESPASSING! Scrawled like blood across her parents' old bedroom door with one of Julie's red crayons, her mother's words lashed out. Suddenly she was six years old again, peering through her bedroom keyhole at her mother, hands on hips in the hallway, standing amid strewn piles of her papa's clothes. Inside the hollow bedroom Sara Paglia's sexual angst lived on.

Returning downstairs, it was while Julie passed through the plaster archway into the living room that she spotted him tucked into the bay window alcove. Asleep on a saggy, stained couch she pegged him to be a squatter who'd broken in through a window and hauled in a cast-off

Then, the horror of the scene sunk in. He wore her father's dirty work coveralls and slippers; it crossed her mind the figure she'd seen in the casket wasn't her papa. He'd come home to Cedarwood, and here he remained. Alive or dead — until today.

The man's arms rested at his sides, the railway cap covering his face as she crept closer, leaned in, and tugged on his pant leg to wake him. The cap slid sideways, revealing a waxy, white cheek. Julie jumped and groped the wall.

"What the hell are you doing here?" The raspy voice came from far away, like inside a tunnel.

Fuck me. In two leaps she was at the front door. She yanked it open, vaulted down the first two steps, tripped over a piece of loose cement, and crashed through the yellow banner at the bottom. As she whipped her bike around, out of the corner of her eye she saw something move on the stairs. Julie peered over her shoulder. The front door swung inwards as if someone was pulling it closed.

❈ "When was the last time you spoke to my mother on the phone?" Julie asked her Aunt Dot when she came on the line.

"I haven't phoned her yet, today. Hey, aren't you supposed to be on your way to India for *National Geographic*?"

"Another week. Just waiting for Paula to get back."

"Right. I drove to Okanagan Valley yesterday and saw Sara at the house there. Why are you suddenly so interested in her?"

"I crossed the yellow tape and went into the old house yesterday." She didn't trust her aunt with info on leaving the photo behind. "Has my mother moved back in?"

"Cripes, no. And you shouldn't be in there, either. It's too dangerous."

A week later, Julie returned with Paula for the photo. It lay on the mantle, face down in the dust. Whoever she saw that day, was gone, along with the dirty couch. Did she imagine it, or what?

Either Vancouver's homeless hordes had finally arrived — or the place was officially cursed. Her papa may have called Mrs. Sara Paglia a *Bella Donna* during Julie's childhood, but the kids at school called her a witch and said she sacrificed stray cats inside the town's abandoned gold mines.

No point saying anything to logical Paula who stood framed within the kitchen doorway, staring at the floor. "Is this where the attack happened?"

Julie came alongside her and nodded. "Aunt Dot walked in and found me face down in the broken glass."

"She didn't suspect your mother, her own sister?"

"We've never talked about it, but I bet she did. I grabbed Sam's bat and locked myself in the bathroom. I heard her tell my mother, 'I'm not leaving the baby behind in this craziness.'"

Paula raked her fingers through her hair. "You should tell your aunt that she saved your life."

No free pass for Aunt Dot. Julie wanted her aunt's confession nearly as much as her mother's. "I don't owe that woman anything. She keeps the lies going about Doni."

Safe and wistful in Paula's embrace, Julie inched the photo in her fist to eye level. "Papa baked Doni's birthday cake. The two little candles look so sad, don't they?"

"Your father was a gem. That's for sure."

She lowered the image and, at their feet, the indentations left in the yellowed tile from the old table sent an ache whistling through her. Whatever paper-thin confidence Julie acquired, fermented here, sitting across from her papa at the butcher-block table. They sometimes chose silence, certainly never talking about her mother's illness and how it affected them.

Julie was not quite thirteen the night Papa nudged her quarter-cup of homemade red across the expansive table before taking a thoughtful sip out of his own tumbler of wine. With Sam at juvie again and her mother holed up inside the hospital, the house seemed hollower than ever.

"It's all up to you now, Juliette."

Already upset with something her mother said on the way to the hospital, Julie gnawed on another ice cube. Through lips as wrinkled as soaked heels her papa smoked with a disquieted interest in her habit, until she spat the half-chewed cube into the sink. "What do you mean?"

He stubbed out his cigarette. "Keep writing, Patatina. Finish your school and get away from here." This was as contemplative as Antonio Paglia ever got. She counted on little *except* getting the hell out.

Today, inside the abandoned kitchen, Julie twisted out of Paula's arms. "But I never told him about Doni. I should have, shouldn't I?" Wisely, perhaps, Paula never answered this.

"I knew he'd take her side. I don't think I could've handled that."

Paula rubbed Julie's upper arm. "We're not supposed to be in here." She cracked open the back door and edged out.

Before leaving the condemned house, Julie traced a figure eight around her and Doni's face. "I'm so sorry."

⸙ The battered daypack Julie always traveled with lay between her and Paula on a vinyl airport bench at Vancouver International—a four-hour drive from Cedarwood. The grimier the pack became, the more it reminded her of all the half-baked adventure stories punctuating her past.

"Wish me luck, why don't you?" Julie said.

The melancholy in Paula's eyes didn't seem to hold any new hope. She shifted to face Julie. "I would if I knew what you were going after. Do you have a plan this time?"

"Yeah," Julie drawled. "The scroll described in Notovitch's book, *The Secret Life of Jesus Christ.*"

Paula sniffed and nodded. "By that Russian explorer guy? The journal that disintegrated in your hands when you pulled the thing off a shelf in a Kits bookstore? Not much of a foundation for an expedition to a remote monastery, is it?"

"The Jesus scroll has got to be there. That's where it was the last time anyone saw it."

Paula lifted the backpack out of the way and slid in close. "You don't have to convince me. I'm already on your side." She rested her hand on Julie's thigh. "If you're going to get *National Geographic's* attention, stick with the stories. No more saving the seals."

"There aren't any seals in India." Julie frowned at Paula. "I'm going to show them all I'm not the piece of crap they say I am."

"What? Nobody says you're a piece of crap."

There was something ominous in the way Julie folded one arm into another.

"Okay ... but who cares about *her*?" Paula said.

At the thought of her mother, Julie hugged herself. "I've been thinking ..." She squinted at Paula. "You know ... about calling the police ... when I get back."

At first, Paula's temperate expression didn't budge.

"So-o ...?"

"Oh, heavens. Are you ready to take a woman like your mother to court? She'll say you're lying. Trying to put her away to get at her money. Think about it. The investigation has been closed for over twenty years."

"They'll let Sam out to testify."

"Sweetie. He's what lawyers would call an unreliable witness."

Okay, then Aunt—"

"Do you really think so?" The air drained from Paula's puffed cheeks. "If she wanted to turn your mother in, she would have done it by now. And you know Hank will say whatever she tells him to."

Julie refused to look Paula in the eye. To take a woman as spiteful as Mrs. Sara Paglia to task, while the *right* thing, might very well do herself more harm than good.

Life with her mother felt like an interminable shifting mirage. She could charm the pants off anyone when it suited her. Although the officer investigating Doni's disappearance might not have dropped his drawers, he fell for her lies.

Julie flicked at a tear rolling down one cheek, giving way to her friend's embrace.

"*Tsk, tsk, tsk.* You're going to make yourself sick again. See how you feel in eight months' time. I'm here for you, whatever you decide."

Paula pulled four fifty-dollar bills from a leather satchel around her waist. "Here. Take this." She fanned out the cash with the flourish of a card shark. "You'll need it."

Julie stared a touch longer than she intended. Paula made a healthy living as an aid for the deaf while Julie's writing assignments were spotty. *Why not take it?* She wagged her chin.

"Oh. Come on." Paula's eyes twinkled as she brandished the red bills at eye level. They played this choreographed game each time Julie flew out for work.

Julie reached up and pinched out one bill from the rest, then glanced at her cell phone. Her slow grin dissolved. "I should go. It could take forever to get through security."

They hugged, then Paula pulled a sad face. "Stay out of trouble. Don't go off on any tangents."

The artifact Notovitch found in 1887 had promise. If only Paula believed in it too.

⁓❀⁓It took a full hour into the flight to Kolkata, India before the suit reading the *Wall Street Journal* piqued Julie's interest. When he lifted an archeological trade journal she recognized from his briefcase, Julie all but toppled into his lap. "I read that, too," she said, with a perky rebound into her seat.

His bushy eyebrows arched with such mime-like precision, Julie took it to be a brush-off. This might become the most tedious cross-Pacific flight of her life.

"I look at it in the library," she said. "I'm not really an archeologist."

"I am."

That's all it took. Questions poured out of Julie. They didn't cease until the seatbelt announcement for their India touchdown, eighteen hours later.

In Kolkata, a familiar stench of curry mixed with urine had taken the arrivals hall hostage. As she waited for her backpack to appear on the baggage carousel, Cedarwood felt far away, indeed. What her new archeologist friend told her about a placid fishing village on the Bay of Bengal set her adventurer's imagination churning.

This is precisely the kind of lucky break great explorers depend on. Hiram Bingham and his crew slashed through miles of brush to uncover Machu Picchu. Not me. I can wrap up this one in a day. I already have a camera.

Her soil-stained Maple Leaf flagged backpack registered — and circled past.

All I'll need is a boat and diving equipment. Then, boom — fame, money, a desk of my own at National Geographic's newsroom. Maybe my own prime-time television show. Juliette Paglia's Secrets of the Ancients, every Wednesday on the Discovery Channel.

Something soft bumped into her behind. "Ready?"

Julie turned to see the archeologist with her backpack slung over his shoulder.

"Is this all you've got?" he said.

"Yeah, but how …?"

"It was the only thing left on the carousel."

The glass doors of Kolkata's international airport parted onto a wall of humidity. Another wall of humanity shouted and shook signs with passenger names on them or grabbed at prospective taxi customers. Julie stopped at the row of idling yellow taxis just as a bone-rack of a luggage tout, going for a tip, tried to yank a rigid Samsonite case out of the hands of a middle-aged tourist. The tout sprawled one way; the case bounced off in the other.

Her new friend nudged her elbow. "No, no. These are tatty and smell of tobacco. The air conditioning is too feeble. They're not acceptable for women riding alone."

"I've never had any problems in all my trips here. They're safe."

"Here's my driver and limo now." He must have seen Julie's horrified expression because he added. "It's already paid for. This is yours; I'll wait for the next one."

This particular trip was already shaping up into an experience unlike anything before. Julie climbed into a limo bound, not north to the Himalayas and site of Notovitch's manuscript, but south to a village on the Bay of Bengal called Vakkali.

While Paula's warning about tangents played in her ears, the quick, easy money from Vakkali's hidden treasure drowned it out.

II

Vakkali, India

Oh, joy. Julie sucked back a dry heave.

The damp sand reeked of mildew and the tang of cow piss; a gamey whiff of half-consumed rat hovered over the open ditch, already steamy with a soup of fish entrails and yesterday's bowel movements. High tide coming in from the Indian Ocean slapped against the monsoon run-off inching past her feet.

Three months already gone, the village's streets and shops felt as familiar as home yet never would her olfactory organs get used to this daily ambush.

The swath of sewage blocking her was wider than the others she'd already straddled that morning along the beach, but she wasn't in any mood to backtrack to Fishermen Colony Lane as a way home. From corner water pumps, the fishwives' kohl-smeared eyes would watch her every move. In Vakkali's homegrown beauty salons, news of the meddlesome foreign woman must be spreading faster than head lice.

She scanned the line of painted skiffs, their gill nets rolled beside them like rainbow-hued cotton candy spun on a stick.

First thing. Lose the flip-flops. Julie overhanded them across, almost striking two fishermen sitting amongst a mound of pink filaments, their over-sized needles weaving in and out of gaps ripped by giant crabs.

Every so often, the one with an oily yellow rag wrapped around his head flung an ocean intruder into a discard pail of seashells, sponges, and tasteless tadpoles, then turned and spat out a red wad into a second pile of chewed betel nut leaves.

This guy had surely dropped straight from his father's loins, fishing in a polyester shirt and traditional wrap-around cotton dhoti pulled between his legs and tucked in at the waist. The entire ratty outfit may have gone the rounds through generations.

Open-air turban guy jabbed the other one in the ribs when Julie cinched down her backpack and rocked on her heels.

His helper's taut, sweaty body glistened with twenty-first century India, cocky in nothing but a Speedo and sun visor. Only his cracked, sun-blackened skin hinted at a living pulled from the sea. That, and the worn-out plastic flip-flops that all fishermen wore.

She remembered the nonsensical way this one laughed like a braying donkey when she asked if he could take her to the dive site. Still, it was nowhere near as disturbing as how the others reacted — they bolted. Why give her the run-around like that? How long did the villagers think they could hide something the size of a city?

Julie ran and launched, pitching face-first into the sand on the other side. No laughter — only a cold nose nudging and licking her ear, taking in a share of the grit.

Sandy spittle hung off her lip. "Rocky. Hello, little one."

The black puppy danced around while she struggled to her feet. She scooped him to eye level and inside the leg puncture from an older beach dog, a white patch vibrated with maggots. "Doesn't look good," she told him, his stubby tail whipping the air. The only alternative was to pick them out one by one at her suite.

One minute, Rocky trotted alongside her heels after the milk biscuit bait; the next, he was gone, enticed by two fishermen carrying a rattan basket overloaded with sardines. It swayed from a pole balanced on their shoulders. Rocky poked his muzzle into the sand below it and dashed off with a tiny fish between his teeth.

Using his free arm, the one in the rear launched a rock, striking Rocky in the head as he ran. He squawked, the fish fell from his mouth before he doubled back for it and took refuge behind a boat hull.

She found him crouched low, hyper-alert, his face underlined with a world-weariness far beyond his short life. He chomped on the sardine propped between his paws and his eyelids fluttered to clear away blood dribbling across one eye.

Julie sat beside him and hissed under her breath. "Dammit, dammit, dammit."

Behind her, a male voice asked, "Madam, may I assist you?"

Julie staggered up, expecting to see her archeologist from the flight, his shiny loafers caked with sand. Instead, against the adjacent hull, another fisherman leaned in a similarly bunched dhoti from which two limbs emerged no more substantial than gnarled popsicle sticks. Amidst a cratered complexion, his affable grin seemed friendly enough.

Still, Julie hesitated, expecting the usual ruse. An invitation to drink chai, perhaps, and from there the suggestion she come to his house and meet his many young children who needed money for school uniforms. She'd been a sucker for sad stories such as these, especially since they were likely all true. No more.

"No. I'm busy with this puppy. He needs medical help."

Without hesitation, the fisherman kneeled, waited for the dog to take the final swallow of fish, and scooped him into his arms.

This was the first time she'd seen any local touch a street dog.

He arched his eyebrows. "Shall I catch a rickshaw and direct the driver to a vet? I am happy to be helping if I can. Here is my boat." The fisherman elbowed the hull of the skiff behind him. Painted in typical broad stripes, a crude design of shark's teeth at the prow singled this one out.

Julie eyed him and considered. Even a puppy can seem heavy in thirty-five degrees Celsius under the mid-afternoon sun. Would the offshore breezes gusting up her loose kaftan shift be relief enough?

She gravitated to these billowing outfits for a far less practical reason—to camouflage her flat chest. Her Sicilian heritage lodged instead in sensuous hips pinching to a narrow waist. Curves suited to a stunning Greek toga. Not skinny jeans. She never wore *that denim uniform of Western imperialism,* instead donning flowing linen. Desert fatigues. Lawrence of

Arabia fare which could double as a bedsheet or tarpaulin in a pinch.

She beckoned to the man and headed down the beach to her suite.

He trailed behind, carrying the sleeping puppy in his arms.

At the bottom of the concrete stairwell to her flat, an adolescent boy thrashed through a series of jumping jacks and shouted—"Dog Doctor"—when he saw her.

It was a misnomer, of course. The closest she came to earning the title was during a volunteer stint at an animal shelter in Kolkata years earlier.

A bright-eyed, old worker, too bent over to carry the paralyzed dogs around anymore, told her, "Do this because you love them, not because you're angry or sad. It's easier that way."

By the time she hit Vakkali village she'd forgotten that bit of wisdom. She carried an aluminum mini-shovel to bury the dead puppies she came across, but it was the half-paralyzed dogs with raw hindquarters which left her the most drained.

As the teen babbled, the fisherman grunted and launched a volley of sharp words at him, then turned to Julie. "There is a problem on the beach with a dog."

Julie bounded to the fisherman and pulled the puppy from his arms.

When she was halfway up the outside staircase, the fisherman yelled: "May I ask your good name?"

While she fumbled with the key to her place, she glanced down the stairs to where he waved goodbye, a magnetic grin spread across his entire face. "You don't forget, ah? My boat has teeth."

Whatever game this freak was playing, she didn't have time to figure it out now.

She left water and kibbles for Rocky on the balcony; her own puppy scratched at the door in curiosity.

While she plowed through the sand, the panic in the boy's voice hung in the air. *Please don't let it be a beach dog being beaten. Or writhing in pain from a horrific injury.*

Ahead, a dozen men jostled each other in a broad circle. A drawn-out howl erupted. She knew, then, and took off across the sand like a racehorse; her lungs wheezing against the humidity and her own tears.

Do this because you love them … It's easier that way. Who was that old guy kidding?

The emaciated animal pulled itself around, its back legs already powerless against the rabies virus. Gnashing its teeth, it whined in distress and pain. Once the virus worked its way along the dog's spine, the brain would swell, and death would follow. But that was hours away.

A few men ranted and threw rocks at the dog, trying to stone it to death.

"Don't you dare." Julie slapped the rock out of one man's hand and pushed past him into the clearing between the dog and its tormentors. How to comfort the animal in the last hours of its life? She sent the boy to find a fisherman with extra netting for sale.

When the worthless, torn bundle arrived, she paid for it then threw it over the dog from a safe distance and showed the men how to anchor the edges with stones. In its weakened state, it barely moved. When finished, she lowered herself to the sand for the long wait.

The bored onlookers drifted away, the hour for eating dinner and watching television upon them.

Six hours later, angular shadows of couples, hand in hand, appeared at the water's edge. A crescent moon rose, smudged by the mist, and soon after a shudder rattled through her shoulders. Was it the dampness seeping from the sand or the macabre hiss of the outgoing tide locked in a seesaw with the dog's gasps?

An outline of legs appeared and a male voice asked, "Do you need any help?"

"There's nothing anyone can do for *this* dog." Too tired to look up from where she sat, Julie wrapped her arms around her knees.

The man crossed over the netting, crouched down, and leaned in close. "I can't see the chest rising, but I still hear breath. Might be awhile yet." When he returned, she felt something encircling her shoulders from behind. "You must be freezing in that top."

She ran her hand along the plush, ribbed material of one shoulder but immediately tried to slip the sweater off.

"Don't be stupid," he said, pulling it up. "I brought it from my hotel for you. The beach isn't safe this late at night. I'm staying."

Enveloped in the warm baggy folds of this man's sweater, she let out a throaty moan of relief. But even a minute can linger when paired in silence beside a stranger.

"You a tourist here?" he finally asked.

The monotonous in-out of the surf was preferable to *that* question. What would be the point in lying she was with *National Geographic* when she didn't have her damn camera bag with her? It would only lead to more questions – the kind she didn't have the answers to. Like: *Why are you here in the middle of the night with this dying dog?*

She hadn't taken a photo in over two months but continued to lug around the camera, bag of unused film, and dusty lens attachments whenever she wasn't with the dogs. Slung around her neck, the camera coaxed tourists into asking if she was a professional. Julie's line was then, "I'm on assignment for *National Geographic*."

With tens of thousands of miles between her and the truth, who would dare argue anything different? This shadow with take-charge elbows might.

"A tourist?" she answered. "Not really. You?"

"Nope."

She frowned. *O – kay. Good to have our stories out of the way and all figured out. Didn't he just say he was in a hotel?*

She opened her mouth to find out what he was doing in Vakkali when he asked, "Do you know where I can get a shovel?"

"What for?"

"Aren't you going to bury the dog?"

She thought of the shovel at her place, then the two puppies who hadn't been taken out to pee all day. "Oh my God." Julie jumped to her feet and headed toward Fishermen

Colony Lane, the sweater's arms flapping against her legs. Almost out of earshot she yelled back, "I'll bring the shovel."

Julie found both of them inside Jimi's bed in the tangled bliss of tired puppies. The balcony door swung open in the breeze above a field of cardboard bits and a dozen yellow piddles.

She slumped against the door jamb and let her eyes close … *just a few minutes*, she told herself … slipping over the edge into oblivion before jerking alert. *Shovel, shovel.* She stumbled to where she'd tossed it hours before on the balcony.

Back inside, crouching beside the puppies, she fondled the velvety soft edge of Rocky's ear. "Why am I the only one who cares? Huh?"

A sigh escaped from inside his puppy dream.

"Who will love you when I'm gone?" Tear after tear splashed across her hand until, without thinking, she wiped her runny nose along the sleeve's cashmere-weave, and snapped back, horrified at what she'd done.

It took the stranger a long time to dig a hole with Julie's miniature shovel.

"I can take it from here." She put her hand on the shovel's shaft but still couldn't make out the man's features in the blackness. "You could become infected from any open sore."

"You've been at this for hours. Let me pull it in."

She noticed his physique for the first time; how foolish to think she could do it when so exhausted.

Together with the netting, he dragged the dog to the edge of the hole where she stopped him and placed two fingers at its nostrils. "Okay, it's gone."

The limp creature fell into the shallow grave with a soft thud. She didn't recognize it. Probably wandered, delirious, into the town in the last few days. Still, as the dirt flew, she sniffled until her shoulders heaved and tears rolled off her chin.

The man stopped. "I'm sorry. Was it your dog?" She shook her head and he went back to his shoveling.

Her dogs? But of course, they were. Each morning at sunrise Julie checked the concrete bus shelter where they huddled around idling rust-buckets. Then Fishmonger Alley, usually alive with the crack of hand scythes on stone at that hour.

At the crest of the town's highest hill, she found them sheltering inside the ancient open-air temples dug out of granite cliffs. The street dogs charged at the steaming pail of chicken fat and rice slop, yelping and barking.

When the dogs were happy, so was she. The short, brutal life of India's street dogs didn't bode well for Julie.

❀ "Bopal girl, bad sick. Dog biting." A week later, Julie handed her landlord the rent at his doorstep and this was his reply.

She couldn't deny this ugly truth. The dogs carried a killer virus about to claim its third child in three months. Each time, resentful eyes followed her down every street. The more dogs she kept alive, the locals said, the worse it would be. Better to shoot them or throw them into the waves in sacks.

She trudged home, unable to stop thinking about the girl. Was the doctor there? She remembered fetching one to the house of the first dying child. And the faces of the boy's parents as they watched their son slowly suffocate on his own saliva and blood. Whether through ignorance of the symptoms or lack of medical care, the families always waited too long to act.

Julie cursed the education system.

The fishermen cursed her.

Upon arriving home, she found glass shards from her kitchen window littering the countertop, sink, and floor. The weapon, a brick, lay nearby. With the first act of violence against the *Dog Doctor*, anxiety washed over her. Had she been standing there, she might have been severely injured, if not killed.

She placed Jimi and Rocky inside her bedroom while she swept up. Rarely did she go out after dark, but tonight, a stroll along Fishermen Colony lane to her favorite hang-out might shake off any remaining jitters. Suni's off-beat la Boulangerie café and guesthouse sat waterside at the foot of the main tourist street.

The brick and stone Colonial mansion rose from the seven-mile-long beach like a fine, leather-bound encyclopedia, bookended by sterile pensions. In the upstairs hallways, which led to the rooftop bar, airy French windows and hairline cracks in the marble floors ensured a quality of decayed decadence so perfect as to look intentional. To the contrary, the guesthouse carried on in the same ad hoc fashion as the laminated menu at Julie's elbow. Merely suggestions, depending on what was for sale at the open-air market.

She flopped onto her usual, tired zebra-hide couch and slung her handbag from the snout-shaped armrest, forgetting how this taxidermic calamity made her cry the first time she saw it.

The way she sat splayed out with her head tilted back gave her a view of the second floor's stone overpass where a young Indian man stared down at her. Dressed as if he'd stepped off the pages of *Yachting World*, a cheeky pair of European sunglasses poked out of an upper pocket of his designer polo shirt. A stain on la Boulangerie, here was the kind of person who constantly tried to alert her to the dangers of clothes without collars.

The man appeared to salute someone behind her. "Ganesh. How are ya', buddy?"

Julie turned to the bizarre sight of a gleaming white limo parked in front of Suni's, a capped driver standing inside the café. "Good evening, Mister—"

"It's Sepoy now. Remember? What're you doing here?"

"Mister Musahar is in the car."

The man above her sagged against the stone parapet before trudging down to the vehicle where a tinted window in the back descended halfway.

A hand appeared clutching a piece of paper.

The man snatched it up and turned on his heels before a comment inside the limo stopped him. "I don't care if people call me Osama bin Laden," he said, lunging at the window.

"Here in India, I'm Sepoy. So whatever you're doing, leave me out of it."

At the next muffled response, he exploded. "Respect you? This"—he motioned at the limo—"is built on the blood of women and children. And you know it."

Okay, that was more than adequate introduction to Suni's new guest. Julie sprang from the couch but caught her foot on the leg of a metal chair, sending it clattering to the concrete floor and drawing a scowl from the man.

He sat on the front stoop in a haze of dust from the departing limo. Unless she wanted to climb over the broad back and gangly legs of this nefarious character who called himself *Sepoy*, she would have to wait until he finished his phone call—or moved.

"Hey, you crazy fucker," he said into his cell. "Are you the one who blew my location at Suni's?" He chuckled, a high, jolly trill which set his body vibrating. "How's the surf in Madagascar?"

"… I'll still be here. I need a long break to thaw out from that bleeding frozen Mongolia. Sad, isn't it? Twenty-four and I'm already fed up with travelling … Say what? … Naw, I think we're both too old for that now. The guests here are girls. I can't be your Indian pimp anymore. But listen, those black guys there won't like you messing around with their women."

That did it. Julie stomped forward and squeezed past the guy without so much as an "excuse me." A glance back from a safe distance revealed sultry eyes of liquid mahogany drilling into hers.

Quiet couldn't be taken for granted in India. The best place to escape the crowds was above them on the country's flat rooftops—including the thatched variety at la Boulangerie.

The massive guesthouse was built when the ramparts of its seawall supported parasols and mint juleps—not sand-encrusted surfboards and beer cans. The owner's wife, Kabitha, was so taken with its grandiose beginnings she squired guests around like a museum guide.

"Most colonials took the train north to the Darjeeling Hill Station to escape Calcutta's heat," Kabitha said during Julie's first meal there months earlier. "Apparently, this family liked the seaside. It was closer and easier to get to."

"You mean they were cheap buggers of a parsimonious inclination, living off the backs of the wretched." Julie never missed an opportunity to mock the long-departed English. She exchanged a crooked smile with Kabitha and knew she had found her first Vakkali friend.

On this morning, as soon as the raucous young travelers checked out for the long-distance buses, Julie settled at a rooftop table to resume her last session of brooding.

Even though her six-month tourist visa was about to expire, she was no closer to finding the offshore site. Not only that, people were killing her dogs and throwing bricks through her window. Anyone could see her grand plan was flagging. She needed to get back on track.

Kabitha served Julie's breakfast in her usual lumpy, knee-length shorts which would be considered too racy for rural India if not for the tourists in even more egregious versions of female trousers. Black rubber boots forced her squat Nepalese legs to clomp up and down with a cartoonish determination.

The boot habit was likely a way to deal with the muddy streets of Kathmandu, the city where Suni's wife lived most of the time while their children attended school. A childhood of serving foreign trekkers at her family's outfitting shop left Kabitha with flawless English.

"I have something to ask you," Julie said. "Do you have a few minutes to sit?"

"You mean, since you're practically the only one in here?" Kabitha smiled and pulled over a chair.

"On my way here, I met an archeologist on the plane. I said I wrote stories for *National Geographic* and he told me about underwater ruins spotted here in Vakkali during a tsunami in the eighties. When I asked the guy why he didn't check it out himself, he went all quiet and weird. Said it was probably a hoax, but I think he was covering up something. Now that I'm here … no one wants to help me."

Kabitha pressed her fist to her lips and pondered. "Sorry, but I can't do much for you, either."

Julie slumped in her chair. "I've never had a problem hiring people in India before. You and Suni have been here since before the eighties. You must have heard something."

"I spend so much time in Nepal, I'm really out of the loop. But maybe Suni knows something. If you want, I can ask him. He knows the fishermen and might be able to get a boat for you."

Oh boy, did she ever want that.

—✿—While she waited for Kabitha to bring her change after breakfast, Julie recognized the lone guy drinking an inappropriate breakfast beer as the preppy snot from the night the limo pulled up. Since then, he seemed to be everywhere. Schools of iron-hipped Malibu babes trailed his surfboard through the waves, and steamy torsos tossed beer cans from the jammed balcony of his second-floor, bongo-blasted party room.

With his legs flung out, he was either snoozing behind his sunglasses—or inconsolable. Julie stared at a disgusting yellow stain at the crotch of his cuffed white shorts. He fingered his glasses down his nose to leer at something around boob level. She could check if the strap on her bra had slipped down—if she ever wore one.

When he shoved his glasses up, it hit her who he was. Julie marched over.

"I just recognized your sweater. I mean … it dawned on me that …" Julie leaned in with both hands planted on the man's table but reared back from a stale beer stench.

He pushed himself upright and blurted out robotically, "I still have your shovel."

"Yes, exactly. Can I join you? I'm Julie."

"Ram. Uh … Musahar." He checked his bare wrist in a wooden pantomime. "It looks like I have some time."

Julie sat and cringed. Weird. The guy from the night with the rabid dog was so different—calm and organized. He threw his sweater around her chilled body.

"I was so upset. I don't think I even thanked you."

"Uh. I dunno. Maybe not. Sorry. I had a rough night and I was just heading back to my room for a sleep."

While he trudged up the gnarled staircase to the rooms, Julie gasped. Not loud, but enough to realize his waterfall of blue-black curls, gathered with a strip of leather into a ponytail, put whatever logic she had in peril. If only she could separate this irresistible hair from the pathetic man himself. *Seriously? Beer and a nap before the day has even begun?*

—❀—The next day Julie sequestered herself in a strategically dim corner of Suni's downstairs café to monitor for any sign of Ram the Loser.

The lunch crowd came. Went. She felt foolish. *What am I doing? He probably left town.*

That worry barely solidified when Ram plodded down, barefoot, from the upper story. At the bottom, he yawned, shook his head, then squinted against the afternoon glare.

She watched this performance, clenching her teeth, but her eyebrows twitched at his outfit—a faded, black T-shirt, and wrinkled, linen sweatpants. *Now that's more like it.*

She inched the newspaper broadsheet she held to nose level but flung it aside when a young Indian boy from another table wandered over to peer at the upside-down headlines. The time was right to make out like she was leaving. She sidled next to Ram. "Hello."

He slammed his forearm on the stack of light-bonded documents stirring in front of him and closed one eye as if trying to focus. "Ohhh. Y—you again." He returned to his reading.

She stepped away, then swiveled to face him. "By the way, you look much more presentable today. Burn those other clothes."

Sensing him admiring her retreating figure, she sashayed out the door.

❀By the time Julie stumbled up the solitary slab of concrete which separated la Boulangerie from its dust-swirled laneway, and ducked under the half-mast metal shutter, her jaw hung slack as a dog's panting in the gathering glare. The plan was to arrive early and grab the table closest to the kitchen to have Suni to herself for the boat conversation.

She flapped the hem of her voluminous beach shift and moaned at the delicious wind tunnel in motion between her clammy inner thighs. "Hot as hell already."

Her complaint blasted the plaster walls and fell on a sprig of black hair doing a jig along the surface of a glass display case. She followed the cowlick to find Suni squatting and scooping gooey cinnamon buns from hot baking tins onto shelves.

He darted up, smiled, and scrunched his face in welcome. India seemed to move in a constant, demoralized circumambulation, teetering on the edge of its own event horizon. Not Suni. He was rare. He was also Chinese.

Behind Julie, what sounded like a bird tangled in his metal shutters turned out to be a pair of fluttering gardening hats askew on the heads of a rotund middle-aged couple. They plodded in and collapsed onto two of Suni's equally exhausted wooden chairs.

Julie had seen aging hippies shuffling around town in their orthopedic Birkenstocks, gray ponytails tucked under wrinkle-free Tilley Hats, likely remembering the glory days. Unfortunately, these two square pegs were not of that poetic ilk. From the look of their affectations, nor had they ever been.

The man pumped the proprietor's hand and pulled two framed pictures out of a briefcase which sent Suni scurrying for a ladder.

From her table, Julie gawked as he climbed to unseat her most cherished la Boulangerie curiosities—a bedraggled black-light poster of Jimi Hendrix, and a photograph of Tibet's Potala Palace—and hung two hideous watercolor paintings of surfers in their place.

Staring up at the defaced wall, the man thumped Suni on the back while the woman's jowls quivered with delight.

For over ten minutes, Julie stamped her feet, sighed dramatically, repeatedly dropped her utensils on the concrete floor, and even sang along with *Margaritaville*, inserting her own offensive lyrics.

Nothing. The three of them were too busy yukking it up over a jolly good cup of tea to notice *her* misery. Suni liked to see people smile and Julie expected to soon be on the receiving end of that.

When the couple left, he poked his head out from behind the kitchen door. "Israeli?"

As she pushed off the couch, Julie held his gaze. She steered him by the elbow until the kitchen door swung shut behind them. "Did Kabitha talk to you? Do you have a friend with a boat?"

He perked up and cocked his head to one side.

Damn, he probably thought she was talking about the Israeli breakfast falafels. "Boat. You know." She thrust out her elbows and mimed pulling on oars.

Suni surveyed her charade with due diligence before taking up his own fictitious oars. They rowed together awhile, Suni barely at a crawl while trying to lubricate his memory, until— "Hai!" He slapped his palms together as if to dive and shouted. "You Water City. Yes?"

So much for it being a town secret. All that mattered was Suni had come through.

Fresh from his charade triumph, he bounced around on the balls of his feet with the energy of a schoolboy, pulling ladles out of drawers and hoisting pans onto the gas stove. She could've hugged him. "So, about this friend of yours—"

Rounds of sparks flew from the lighter Suni held to the burner. As the flame jumped to life, he poked the device in her direction and cut her off. "You like eat falafel?" He bounded to the fridge and disappeared behind the open door.

Not the brush-off from him, too? Whatever was spooking the locals only made her more determined.

Suni slammed the fridge door shut and stood holding a bowl of dough. He looked at Julie, who hadn't moved, and his grin dissolved. "Sorry."

She waited, but when he said nothing further, Julie trudged out and stood in front of the zebra head. She felt numb. A discovery of this magnitude came around only once for a no-name explorer. Without a guide, she wouldn't know where to begin.

Suni flashed a wan smile after he set her breakfast down, but his eyes had lost their sparkle. He was her best hope, and Julie could tell it broke his heart.

It soon became a daily thing. Julie joined Ram at his usual table near Suni's open-air entry on the pretense he was hogging all the English language dailies. Turned out he was every bit the avid debater as Julie, even during the afternoon heat and noise of the street when she wanted to retreat to the breezy rooftop.

"They put up another one." *The Hindustan Times* Ram held vibrated with staccato pokes. "That's exactly how India is going to move ahead. Why is this weather satellite important, you may ask?"

Julie's eyebrows arched in comical gyrations at his boyish enthusiasm.

"Because it's *that* design which will take us to the moon. Then we can tackle Mars."

Her light mood shattered. "Why in hell does India want to get to the moon, or fucking Mars, when it hasn't even figured out how to remove sewage? Get some drinkable water in here for more than two measly hours a day. The school needs books. A teacher who shows up."

From Ram's pursed lips came a spurious *hmm* as if Julie were a child entangled in twine.

"Yes, I went there," she said.

"You sure swear a lot. I like that. Look. I agree about the school, but that doesn't mean we can't become a world leader in aerospace technology. Bring in foreign investment so we can train the youth of today to be the scientists of tomorrow."

"W—what? Did you fish that propaganda from a waste bin at Bangalore airport? Doesn't it strike you as strange one boy can become a scientist but another has to dig through garbage for survival?"

"Well, yes, if you put it that way. All I'm saying is we may need Mars someday."

"India doesn't want to be caught short when the time comes to nuke Pakistan, does it?" Julie leaned closer. "How about it, Ram? I bet you'd like to wrap your legs around one of those intercontinental ballistic missiles. Long. Steel-hard. Powerful."

Ram looked at his watch and smirked. "A little early for dirty talk. Not by much, though. It reminds me of a time in ..."

It's so true, she thought. As much as they joked, their debates filled her loins with fire. Yet she knew nothing of real importance about him. He evaded questions on his background, deflecting instead to tales of the exotic places he'd had sex: Chinese sloops in Hong Kong harbor, a sacred Buddhist temple in Burma, the stairwell of a Muslim minaret in Morocco, and stretched out over the sacrificial stone at the top of an Aztec pyramid in Mexico. She doubted the Alpaca in the Andes story.

This suspended-in-time world of his felt like a vivid movie clip in which one has no idea what's happened, nor where it's leading. She considered herself *street smart* — in the void, unsettling theories were forming. He was a pervert or even a good con involved in sex-slave trafficking. Or a terrorist awaiting orders.

When Ram's phone rang, he rose and turned his back to Julie. "Alana? ... Don't cry." His voice pitched above the late-day din of motorbikes and three-wheeled auto-rickshaws tearing along the dusty laneway.

After Julie folded her newspaper and set it aside, she leaned in, straining to catch the words.

"Please. I don't know right now. I promise I'll call you later when I'm back in the room."

He returned to his seat and said, "Tell me, why are women obsessed with babies?"

Dumbfounded by his frankness, Julie said nothing.

"That was my Swedish girlfriend. She's making me crazy. She wants a baby. We've been together six years, and now this comes out of nowhere." He swilled his coffee and placed a hand on the table in front of her. "You don't have children. I admire your freedom to do what you want."

Nobody ever told Julie they admired her for being childless. Quite the opposite. Still, when it came to a family and marriage, she was willing to let time and the laws of probability make the decision for her.

"What do I tell her? She travels for work. I travel. We hardly see each other anymore. Shit, I haven't even been laid in six months."

Julie batted her lids. His boasting about Rockin' the Kasbah was nothing but a lie, but what bothered her more was the salvo to his manliness. That a young man would be forced to go without sex for six months was downright sad. Right then and there, she decided to help him out of his dilemma at her earliest convenience.

"Where does she live?"

"New York. She's a translator for the United Nations. We met at Oxford."

Now we're getting somewhere. He went to Oxford. "You could fly to New York. That would help."

"I love her. I just don't want a baby. She says we're running out of time. At twenty-six?"

"It's the biological clock thing. I'm twenty-eight. If I had a fiancé, I might push it, too."

Ram stiffened.

"Er … or, I don't know, maybe not." Caught off-guard, Julie focused her attention across Fishermen Colony Lane where a sari-clad woman squatted in front of her threshold, smearing antiseptic cow dung from a bowl onto the concrete slab. This was the first step to creating the intricate, flowered *muruja* designs thought to keep evil from the home.

"Oh God." Ram threw back his head, dread etched across his brow. "I'll have to break it off so she can move—"

Brakes squealed as a yellow taxi swept around the woman and came to a screeching halt at the rump of the cow rooting through garbage near their table.

"Hey jackoff, back up," Ram said to the driver, who hung out of his window and laid on the horn. "Can't you see this road is too narrow for taxis?"

When the driver didn't respond, Ram bolted from the table but hadn't taken more than two steps when a burlap bag of sand hurtled down and burst at his feet. "You stupid bastards." He shook his fist at a row of shirtless workmen who peered from the rooftop next door, as dull-eyed as the cow holding its ground in front of the taxi.

As the vehicle reversed, Ram charged back to his seat, exhaling so hard Julie stifled a giggle.

"I can't take it. Illiterate idiots like them are all over India."

His actions confirmed he was North American. Otherwise, he would have sworn in Hindi for the most impact.

"What kind of stories do you write?" Ram's question, at the end of a diatribe against other stupid types both in and out of India, seemed aimed at calming himself.

Since writers didn't impress Ram, Julie spared him the phony hype about working at *National Geographic*. "I'm an adventurer. I write about my discoveries."

"Really. There's over a billion people here, so I'd say there's not a helluva' lot left to discover."

Had this sarcastic tone come from anyone else, it would have brought out the worst in Julie. "But there is. Out there, offshore. A lost city."

Ram drew a hand over his slow smirk.

"Eyewitnesses saw stone pillars and arches after a tsunami in the eighties." A fervor rose in her gut. "Don't you see? It could be at least two-thousand years old. An undiscovered Babylon. I've been trying to hire someone to take me diving for it, but they scatter when I tell them what I'm looking for. It's weird."

Ram pinched his lips between his fingers and gazed sidelong at the floor.

"It's weird. Right?" she asked.

Between the pursed lips and hunched shoulders Ram cut a striking similarity to the *Speak No Evil* monkey.

"Come on. What's out there that nobody wants to talk about?"

Ram forced out a sigh. "Never mind. Nothing. And if you can't find the underwater city? Then what?"

She sat back and leveled a cool gaze at him. He wasn't nearly as good at hiding the town's secrets as he was his own. Ram didn't have the kind of devious mind needed to keep a lie going. She should know.

"Remind me to skunk you at poker some time," Julie said. "You'd be terrible at it."

"What?"

"If I can't find the underwater ruins, then I'm screwed," she finally said, "because I won't have the money to go after the Big Kahuna."

Ram shrugged.

"The lost manuscript. About Jesus in India. I already told you, didn't I?"

"Nope."

"Okay then." She jabbed a finger in his direction. "Tomorrow. Be here for a reading of *The Secret Life of Jesus Christ*."

⚜The next morning, Julie cracked open her volume of Nocolai Notovitch's book. A loose page fluttered to the concrete to soak up a splotch of ketchup.

Ram pointed to multiple layers of tape around the binding. "Doesn't look like much of an artifact."

Julie worked on the ketchup with the diligence of a soldier polishing his boots. "These are just modern reprints of the Russian explorer's writings. It's the original set of manuscripts he found that are missing from a monastery in Ladakh. Those are priceless. They're about Jesus living and studying in India."

Julie opened to a page. "Listen to this, 'When Issa' — that's a Muslim variation for Jesus — 'had attained the age of thirteen, when an Israelite should take a wife' … blah, blah, blah … 'It was then that Issa clandestinely left his father's house, went out of Jerusalem, and, in company with some merchants, traveled toward the Sindh that he might perfect himself in the divine word, and study the laws of the great Buddha.'"

Julie paused for effect, but Ram's eyes were half-closed.

He moaned. "That proves nothing."

"No? Then how about this: 'The earth has trembled, and the heavens have wept because of the great crime just committed in the land of Israel. For they have put to torture and executed the great, just Issa in whom dwelt the spirit of the world.' Sounding familiar?"

"Yaa, but says who?"

"Traveling merchants. The parts about him studying at monasteries are first-hand accounts written by Buddhist monks and historians. Nicolai Notovitch discovered it at a monastery near the border with Tibet. After his brother published the transcript of the original, poof, the real one in Ladakh disappeared."

"Still."

"Whaddya' mean, *still*? They sent Notovitch to a labor camp in Siberia when he tried to publish it, charged with …" Julie flipped through to the opening pages. "'Literary crimes against society.' He died there in 1893, but his brother eventually published it for him."

"Ho-hum. And I suppose you think the Vatican stole it in a cover-up?"

"Of course, I do. Notovitch showed them his notes. A dumb move, if you ask me." Julie flipped through to a different part of the book.

Another page escaped which Ram slapped between his palms, mid-flight.

"Here it is," Julie said. "This is what the cardinal told him. 'Why should you print this? Nobody will attach much importance to it, and you will create numberless enemies thereby.' Then the cardinal offered to buy it off him." Julie's voice rose. "I quote, 'For his trouble!'" She held the book out. "Here, do you want to read it? I can lend you the whole thing."

"Naw, I've got other stuff on the go."

Julie grunted. He was likely talking about his penchant for tapping out "Letters to the Editor."

❖Julie plopped onto the seat opposite Ram at Suni's and craned toward his laptop screen. "Every time I come in here you've got your nose in that thing. What are you writing? An indictment against all of humanity?"

Seeing him slam the screen shut, she arched her eyebrows. "When you act like this, I think you *are* a terrorist planning a horrific attack. Maybe a spy. How sexy would that be?"

He shoveled sugar into his coffee and whipped the spoon around like a whisk. "There might be more to this town than you think."

"Aha. That's it." Her index finger poked at his laptop. "So, which is it?"

They dropped into a stare-down before Ram leaned in, his elbow close to hers. "An indictment. Against the CIA."

"Wha-at?" People turned to look as she cackled. "That's a losing proposition."

"Could you be a touch more subdued for once?" Ram scanned the room. "Someone might be trying to kill my father." With suspicion bordering on neurosis, he pried open his laptop; his index finger hovered over the delete key before he withdrew it. "Here." He spun the screen toward Julie. "Read this."

> *Dear Editor:*
>
> *It's an outrage India has given no security cover to scientists working on important nuclear projects. Between 1998 and this year, 2002, eleven nuclear scientists have had unnatural deaths: blasts, suicide by hanging, drownings at sea, and three described by the Indian Department of Atomic Energy as death by 'mysterious circumstances.' The Indian people should demand that the US Central Intelligence Agency prove they aren't involved.*
>
> *Ram Sepoy, Geologist, Oil & Gas Exploration*

The sudden realization his father worked in nuclear energy sucked the life from her animated grin. At the end of the letter, her head snapped up at something even more troubling. "You work for the oil industry?"

"A Swedish company."

Julie gaped.

"Most of the time, I pour over the sonar mapping at my flat in Stockholm." His sheepish expression betrayed the matter-of-fact tone of his confession. "Last time, my team set up wildcat wells in Western Mongolia. When I get run down, I come to Suni's where cell phone reception is spotty. The office usually can't get through."

"Sounds peachy."

"Well. It's a job. Somebody has to do it."

"And your father's a nuclear scientist?"

"He was in research before he joined the local plant where they store nuclear waste. I—I'm sorry. This isn't the way I imagined this topic playing out."

"Pools. Of. Spent. Fuel. Rods." The words slithered off her tongue, toxic as the waste itself.

"It's five kilometers along the beach. Onshore from that underwater city you're trying to find. The area is off-limits, which is why you won't find anyone to take you there."

Julie shot him a black look. "Jesus, Ram. That plant is a deadly cesspool that shouldn't exist at all, never mind next to a resort."

"Why are you so opposed to nuclear energy? They even built a rail line into the plant to keep the fuel rods off the highways. If you want an Indian middle class, how is the country supposed to power the plants and factories needed for that?"

She glared up and down at him. "It makes sense. Why you didn't want me to know your background. Is poisoning the planet the family business *you* aspire to? I'd think more highly of your father if he pushed that metal cart around town collecting garbage."

Ram winced. "I trust my father to have the highest safety precautions in place."

Even when she rose and loomed over him, his boardroom voice never wavered. It was maddening.

"Yeah. Management said that before the last ten nuclear accidents, too. Take a look at those."

"Don't be stupid. Of course, I've seen them."

"Whoopee. I've made your hit list of stupid people."

"Why are we doing this here? Now?" Ram cupped her elbow and steered her out to the street, but she yanked away.

"Where else? In your hostel? Not my place, either. Right? Who wants to be seen with the foreign slut on the beach?"

"Come on." Ram reached for Julie once more. "It's not that way at all."

But she had already strode onto Fishermen Colony Lane. How in the world did he end up in such a predatory industry? No doubt pressured into it by his father—a greedy, corporate yes-man with nothing but profits in mind.

Maybe it's for the best, she thought, not even halfway home. *Stop wasting time with Ram and get to those ruins—even if it means rowing myself there in a rubber dingy.*

Paula called to say her beloved, aged mother had died. "I'm an orphan again with no other family to speak of."

A rare moment of self-indulgent pity, it made Julie's decision so much harder. "Oh, honey, the two of us will always be a family. I'm going to miss her so much and you know I'd fly back for the funeral if I wasn't so close to finding the underwater ruins here in Vakkali."

"That's okay."

"Why not fly here? The Christmas holidays are coming up," Julie said. "The school district can find a replacement aide for the deaf and it's not like you don't have the money now from your inheritance."

"You know my work in the classroom was never about money. The beach sounds like a good idea though."

Julie set Paula's Vakkali arrival in a month as a self-imposed deadline to complete the exploratory dive.

She headed to the surf shop, thinking they might not be as hostile as the fishermen, and tripled the offered payment to three-hundred dollars. It was more than one fisherman made in a month. Julie was now officially broke—but it worked. Within an hour, the owner discovered someone willing to take her inside the restricted area of the plant's breakwaters.

She agreed to meet the man at closing time inside the whitewashed, windowless cubicle. With the surfboards lined up, there was barely enough space to move around, but within minutes the silhouette of a bow-legged figure in shorts appeared against the setting sun.

The owner left, and as her new prospect pulled down the metal shutters hand-over-hand, the same dried-out complexion of the fisherman with the tooth-patterned skiff came into focus.

"Ah." He grunted. "You never forgot me, after all."

Julie's glee at finding a boat, any boat, dissolved into uneasiness at his superior tone, stripped of its former friendliness.

However, after she slipped him an advance of five-thousand rupees, this man named Jathia warmed to her. "Nobody is allowed to surf or fish around there," he said. "We must get inside the breakwater. Probably, that is where your city is."

"Why do you think that?"

"I was hired as a grunt worker to build the place. Almost everybody was. More money than fishing. I liked to shoot the shit with the American guys, practice English. One day, I heard the Indian divers talking about something like old houses under the water."

"I wondered why you spoke such westernized English."

"I asked the Americans about it. They told me to shut up or I could get fired. So many secrets in that plant."

"Don't I know that. I belonged to an anti-nuke movement. Long time ago. Pretty tame. We scrawled protest slogans inside the plants. My favorite job was sneaking into a sea base where missiles for warships were stockpiled. Thousands of them."

"Really. *You* did that?"

"Sometimes we posed as contract painters or delivery people. That time we walked in as vending machine maintenance with our phony identification to get as close to the missiles as possible. U.S. Nuclear Safety totally freaked out."

"Did you get caught?"

"Every time. That was the idea. We waited for security to arrest us, so the press would cover it. What a joke. Sister Mary was the oldest at eighty-three, Father James was sixty-nine, and I think his brother Peter was sixty-seven. I was nineteen."

"Catholics?"

"Strong clergy. They called themselves the Plowshares Three." Julie shook her head. "Our last job, we had this new guy and the idiot goes over and pours blood into something electrical. Peter had worked in a nuclear plant but didn't have a clue what it was. We were likely facing jail time. Still, he pulled the fire alarm to get security in there. Those three cared about people, even if it meant they were going to spend the rest of their lives behind bars."

"Did they?"

"Father James ended up serving six years. He'd get out on probation and go right back to it. When our trial came up, people were still pissed off about the Greenpeace ship blown up by the French government. That judge had to let the rest of us walk." She paused, lost in a moment of longing. "It was the last time we were together. Three of the finest people I will ever know. Peter, James, and Mary."

❄Julie arrived before sunrise for her second meeting with Jathia. He herded her inside the surf shop and yanked down the metal shutter. When her eyes adjusted to the candlelight, she saw the outlines of three other men.

"Some other fishermen want to meet you."

She panicked and ran her hand along the wall for the shutter's cord.

Jathia grabbed it. "It's okay. You are safe."

The men were crouched around a large schematic spread out on the concrete floor. The whites of their eyes flashed in the flickering light. No one moved except Jathia; a hollow *flip-flop* of plastic on concrete echoed in his wake.

When one of the men stood and sidestepped around the map, Julie stole a glance at him. Under his slacks he wore street shoes and socks. All the men did—except Jathia.

"It is the storage buildings and dykes." Jathia kneeled beside the others. "We have questions about how the plant is working."

Astonished, she asked, "Where did you get this? It's so detailed."

"We are a local group angry with the plant so close to Vakkali," Jathia said. "I am the only English speaker, so I will translate. From the drawings," he asked her, "is an accident possible?"

"Of course." she said. "An earthquake might crack the cladding around the pools which cool the waste rods. Or a tsunami could flood the systems. Once that water's gone and a fire starts, the containment building could explode and give everyone in town a lethal dose of radiation. Didn't you tell me waste has been stockpiled since the plant opened?"

After Jathia translated this, one of the men spoke up.

"Arjun is asking if terrorists can attack."

Julie nodded. "That too. The 9-11 terrorists thought about crashing a passenger jet into a reactor instead of the Twin Towers. The spent fuel pools are particularly vulnerable at this site because they're above ground."

Jathia looked to Arjun who responded with an emphatic nod.

"I told the guys about the blood messages. They want to do the same thing. Embarrass the bosses. Maybe close it down."

"I doubt they'd close it. Only a catastrophic accident would—"

Arjun snarled something at Jathia and waved his arms.

"Arjun says you only help us set up. He trained in diving with coast guard. We are going on a different night from you."

"I don't know if I want to get involved. It's India. He'll probably end up in jail for the rest of his life. Tell him that."

But instead of translating her warning, Jathia asked, "Those friends, the protestors. They would be afraid to help?"

No. If still alive, they would gladly help, Julie thought.

*C*onditions were ideal for the night of the dive. Julie relaxed to the purr of the motor as soon as they pushed off. She could barely make out where the fifteen-foot skiff stopped and the water began. The faint light of a new moon, an overcast sky, and low-lying fog provided the cover she, Jathia, and Arjun needed.

At the bow, jumpy as a squirrel, Arjun peered into the dense white-out. Another piss-poor local and one of the most ill-tempered men she'd ever met, he harped at both her and Jathia until they allowed him along to scout a beachhead for later.

In addition to the fee, she had paid for all the gear and tank rentals. If she didn't sell something quick, she'd join their destitute ranks.

As a faint outline of the plant loomed ahead, the queasiness in her stomach returned while she recalled everything which could go wrong. If caught in the restricted zone, at best, she might be kicked out of the country. At worst—she didn't allow her mind to go there. What if *National Geographic* found out they'd been dragged into an illegal act? Most importantly, could her friendship with Ram survive if anything went wrong? As manager responsible for plant security, fall-out for Ram's father was assured.

With the engine cut, the skiff glided through the breakwater opening.

Jathia dropped the anchor. No backing out now. The yard lights, twinkling through the mist, and the hypnotic hum of the cooling systems lent a deceptively tranquil mood to the deadly site.

They donned their scuba gear. Arjun went in first.

She had enough oxygen for a one-hour dive and assumed that the seafloor couldn't be any more than thirty feet down, being so close to shore. If not, she would have to allow extra time to prevent decompression sickness and the rest stops would eat into exploration time.

After falling backward into the water, she swam straight down under the skiff. At twenty feet on the depth gauge, the floodlight picked up nothing. Twenty-five—blackness all around. Julie worried she might be in a deep offshore trough, but within minutes, faint outlines appeared in the distance.

At forty feet, the beams passed over a shiny surface. As soon as she touched it, she knew it was man-made. Julie's palm rested on pristine marble textiles. The first person to do so, perhaps, in two millennia.

She swept her beam in a circle, her heart thumping. Just two stories high, the semi-circle of concrete seats seemed ready for spectators to the next play. Behind her, the light passed over what was left of a bronze statue of Apollo, ancient God of the arts. Could it be possible she hovered over the main stage of a Roman theatre?

At the top of the watery stairs, she saw her hunch was right. A murky outline of pillars might be the city's forum, still standing beside a domed temple.

Her camera whirred as she floated down cobbled streets, past eroded obelisks and blue-tiled villa courtyards with marble fountains. At the public baths, sardines darted between columns overlaid with pink and white seashells and, at the pool's bottom, a glass mosaic of Neptune riding a seahorse-drawn chariot. All but free from algae from having been buried for centuries, the entire city was an incomparable treasure.

At the temple entrance within the forum, she captured the goddess, Venus, on one side and the god, Mars, on the other. Inside a low stone structure—the straw roof long gone—her light skipped across an expansive stone countertop. Terracotta jars still rested inside cutouts. Likely a shop. Her next magical discovery left no doubt. A piece of it would remain with her the rest of her life.

She lifted the heavy granite lid on one of the jars scattered behind the counter to find it filled with gold coins. They sparkled in her translucent beam as if they'd been deposited minutes before. It proved the city's occupants had come to a sudden, deadly end. A tsunami? Or her nemesis—disease?

The Roman profile and words *Caesar Augustus* on the coins meant at least one corner of India had been part of the Roman Empire. Yet, the Romans never carved out an overland bridge to India. Had they come from the sea instead?

With hundreds of photos banked, she checked her pressure gauge, then her watch. Not only was she running out of air, but the cover of darkness at the skiff. She found her way back to the amphitheater stage for her ascent.

As soon as Julie broke the surface, she yanked out her mouthpiece. "It's Roman. A Roman city."

Jathia's scowl reminded her to tamp down her excitement. He scanned the dark waters along both sides of the boat. "Goddamn Arjun isn't up. It will be light soon."

Out at sea a slim band of light was spreading along the eastern horizon. More than an hour had passed, and only the odd puff of fog swirled above the waves as cover. She handed her camera and gear over the gunwhale and climbed in with Jathia's help. Inside the spotless, dry pail Julie packed along to rinse the saltwater off her beloved camera, what does she find stored there but Arjun's putrid red socks? *Jackass.*

Finally, the boat rocked and Arjun appeared. They hauled him over the side, tanks and all.

"Stupid bastard." Jathia jerked the motor to life and with the skiff rocking through the waves, it took Arjun the entire return trip to doff his gear and find his socks in the backwash around their feet.

Back at Vakkali's beach, Jathia told her Arjun had found a shoreline access into the plant. Julie gave the two what she stressed would be her last advice to them—ever. "There'll be cameras everywhere. Choose a foggy night. Paint the protest on any wall and leave."

Arjun's ill temper and long absence from the boat were unsettling. The socks didn't help. As hard up for money as Julie was, to be rid of them she told Jathia to return the gear to the Kolkata dive shop and keep the deposit. When he refused, it all ended up on her balcony.

—❋—Back in her suite, Julie popped the photo card from her camera into her laptop and downloaded the images. Operating on adrenaline alone, she kept at it until the best photos were safe at *National Geographic*'s desk.

This was Vakkali's discovery, too. How sad she couldn't share it with a single local. Not even Ram. Especially not him.

To the single gold coin on the table in front of her she gave a sly spin. Like pirate booty, it was. Although the emperor's face wouldn't reveal *why* the city died, it would tell archeologists *when* the end came.

She fell into an exhausted sleep filled with endless ringing. Roused to consciousness, she grabbed her cell phone from the side table.

"Yeah?" Her voice cracked.

"Who is this?" a husky voice boomed.

"Me. It's Julie."

"I thought I'd reached a rubbie in a park. It's Jack in Washington. The photo editor at NG. We got your photos."

"What, was I asleep for ten hours? What time is it?"

"Well, it's five in the morning here on the East Coast."

"You're working at five?"

"The overnight guy called me at home because we're thinking of this for the cover. I should be able to get you at least six with an advance payment of five-hundred through Western Union. But you're gonna' have to resend them at a higher resolution. They're grainy."

Holy shit. The cover? "Jack, I'm sorry, I completely forgot what you told me. Maybe I was tired after the dive. I'll resend them."

"What about the copy?"

"I can describe what I experienced, but you'll have to get someone else to examine the photos. I don't have a single expert source. Nobody but me knows or cares this is here."

Well, other than those few thousand nobodies in Vakkali of which plenty would care about the jar of gold coins, restricted zone be damned.

"Nobody knows? Sounds odd. I'll see what I can do from here. Send the photos at the proper res. I'll be waiting."

She hung up but sat motionless a long time, content to inhabit the air around her—knowing her place in it had changed forever. Six? He meant six-*thousand*. Didn't he?

Aweek after his argument with Julie, Ram decided to blink first and call.

Not only had Julie cooled down, but her voice was annoyingly shrill, as if she'd fallen in love. He was smart enough not to give himself credit. If her newfound joy had anything to do with a dive near the nuclear waste plant, the topic was a minefield best avoided for now.

Locals swarmed the streets in celebration of Kali Puja. The fireworks version of Christmas without all the boozing was how he described it to Julie. After climbing hand-in-hand along a rocky trail in the dark, they halted near a hunched figure dozing next to a gate. Ram handed him a wad of rupee notes and pointed at the soaring white outline of the lighthouse.

Julie squeezed his hand and stepped back. "Whoa. I hear snakes go for the heat radiating off those stairs at night."

"That's what this is for." From his backpack, Ram pulled out a high-powered flashlight used in the oilfields and they started the steep, circular climb. "Stick close behind."

At the top, gemlike clusters glimmered near the dark edge of the ocean. Lights flashed at sea like solitary fireflies.

"If you look over there," Ram said, nudging her elbow with a pair of binoculars, "you can see the Andromeda Galaxy."

"When I was a teenager, I set up telescopes in the orchards with other astronomy geeks." Julie looped the binoculars' strap around her neck.

As a fountain of trailing embers exploded overhead, Ram slid his arm along her back to turn her and caught a whiff of tea tree oil in her hair. Perspiration shone along her bosom.

"Suni's wife told me about this lighthouse," Julie said. "In colonial times their guesthouse used to be the residence of a Lieutenant Governor. He had a wife and family back in England but fell in love with a low-caste woman. When the British found out, they ordered her taken to the top of this tower and thrown off to make it look like she jumped. Are you in any particular caste?"

Ram knew she asked it in innocence, but shame arose in him. "How can I think of myself as Indian anymore? I was schooled abroad. I'm not interested in living here. I have, I should say, had, a fiancée that's Swedish. My father is so desperate to get me married, the only criteria left on his list is that the person be a female of childbearing age."

"No other siblings?"

"None worth mentioning. Alana probably phoned my father and he's pissed I've ended it. He met her in Boston during my convocation."

"It's over for good?"

Ram pursed his lips and nodded. "I guess we're still friends."

When the fireworks petered out, Julie arched back, lowered the lens, and closed her eyes. "Oh, I could stay out here *all* night." Her voice soared, the fatigue and constant worry drained away. In its place was a sublime energy he'd never seen in her before.

"What about *your* family?" he said. "Tell me something."

Julie stared at him and her buoyancy faded.

"It's not a trick question. I promise." He chuckled to hide his confusion at this strange reaction to such a routine query.

"My father died of a massive heart attack in his sixties."

"Your mother?"

She raised the binoculars to her eyes and swept the stars.

He could wait, give her the time she needed — or settle for silence.

"She let herself go after my father died," Julie said, still sweeping the sky.

"And?"

She lowered the binoculars, a surly curl on her lips. "Last I heard she was giving hand jobs at pullouts on Highway 5 for small change."

Ram stepped back and regarded her with pained empathy. "No. Really?"

"Just kidding." Julie shrugged. "But we should go." She dropped her chin to her chest, her fingers digging to free the binocular straps from her wild hair.

She didn't trust him with what pursued her, yet he ached to comfort her. He pressed the tips of his fingers together, mesmerized by her wind-lashed locks. Beside her at the beach, or alone in bed—always this same fantasy of threading his fingers through that field of tight curls.

Trembling, he moved in and yanked the straps and Julie into his chest. At the same moment, he lifted the wisps of hair at the nape of her neck and pressed his lips to hers. She edged away, but in the dark was a gleaming smile.

"Listen," Ram said, taking the binoculars from her, "I should go in front on the way down in case you trip, but you hold the flashlight." He dug it out of his backpack and waited for her to tug it from his hands. "Julie?"

"He was supposed to protect us." She stared through him as if into an endless night. "Not attack us."

"Who? Your father?"

"The dog. It used to rest its head on my mother's feet while she chopped vegetables in the kitchen and snarl if we got too close.

"From day one it was hers. We couldn't believe it when she flopped onto the lawn and let it climb on her dress and lick her face. She laughed so hard tears ran down her face. And she went right on crying for the rest of the day in her bedroom."

Julie stepped to the edge of the parapet. "Before I met my friend, Paula, I thought all mothers were that sad." Seconds passed over the crashing of distant waves. "And angry. One time she choked me until I passed out. I'd be dead now if my aunt hadn't walked in on it."

Told in a steady, neutral voice, he had scant experience responding to memories which must be so excruciatingly painful. "Have you talked to anyone about this?"

"Paula. And now you. Not the police, if that's what you mean."

"I'm talking about therapists. This is huge. Since you mention it, why didn't your aunt go to the police?"

"I've never asked her, but at the time I guess I wasn't the only one who thought this was normal for a mother."

The minute Julie walked through her door from the lighthouse date, pebbles peppered her balcony.

On the beach below, Jathia beckoned to her.

She swore under her breath but joined him to walk beside the surf.

"About draining the storage pools. Arjun thinks that is more powerful for the group."

Julie halted and grabbed Jathia's arm. "Are you crazy? You'll kill everyone in town. That can't be what you want."

He shrugged and continued to plod along the shore.

"The guards will shoot him before he makes it into the containment building," Julie said, a high-pitched hysteria taking hold. "Not only that, he's wasting his time. Any bomb compact enough to carry won't have the power to damage the pool's cladding. It's reinforced concrete and steel."

"He will not go near the building."

His casual tone drove a chill into her.

"He wants to ask the Kolkata cell for anti-tank, rocket-launchers. They will hijack a coast guard boat and take the rockets close enough to strike."

Julie rolled her head. "Nooo—You're a bunch of fucking idiots. Jathia. I'm serious. Get the others to stop. It's insane." She slogged along the beach, seething, then cut him off. "Security will see that coast guard ship the minute it rounds the breakwater. Have you thought of that?"

"Arjun went to the pools that night. No guards. Everybody knows the guy that patrols the shore is always drunk or sleeping in his car."

Julie gaped. "Bastards. You put me at risk along with yourselves. They planned this from the start. You lied and used me, didn't you?"

"No. I did not know about this until last night. I am not with their Kolkata cell. But you are right. They wanted to attack and, in this way, I too was fooled. I'm sorry."

Sorry? A nightmarish dread crept into her bones. She slapped her palms against her upper arms to try waking herself. She wanted to slap this Jathia guy. Infuriatingly jaunty most of the time, now docile as an ox.

Like a captive at the end of a muzzle, Jathia hoisted his arms overhead. "But I ... I am a real fisherman. It is my boat. The other fishermen must not know I help you. They hate when you tell them what to do on their beach."

"*Their* beach? It's no more theirs than the tourists or the sick dogs."

"For hundreds of years they feed their families with fishing. When dogs steal the fish, less for them."

"Oh, for God's sake, as if a few sandy fish taken by a starving dog will matter."

"Sometimes, dogs rip the nets. Cool it, okay? Those card guys are violent. Sometimes, their wives go to hospital. Now, they talking to teach you a lesson."

"Just let them try and I'll go to the police. And if they keep hurting the dogs, I'll report them to the town *panchayat*. Maybe the Indian branch of the SPCA."

"Here is not like your country. If simple like that, we would not need you to help close this plant."

Close it? A minute ago, they wanted to blow it up.

"I don't get why you pulled me into this violence. I wanted a ride, you needed money. Why didn't we stick with that? In fact, why did I pay you and rent your gear, too?"

"It was not your money we wanted. I can refund it. We needed your name on the scuba gear and tanks you rented in the city. That's all. Not even I am safe anymore from the special forces hunting us."

Nausea set in. The rental receipt could have been used to prove her connection to Arjun, had he been caught. *I need to get as far away as possible from Jathia and his stinking friends.*

Neither did she know whether to resend the photos. If Jathia's group attacked the plant, these could be evidence against her. She came up with one excuse after another to stall *National Geographic*. The magazine wired her advance payment and said they had contacted the Archaeological Survey of India to start the research. *Send the photos ASAP*.

Had she not been so distracted with an impending nuclear accident, the bit about contacting the Indian government would have registered as a red flag.

For the next few nights, Julie couldn't sleep. She kept rising and going to the balcony to see if Jathia's boat was out. She was certain the Kolkata cell wouldn't try to hijack a coast guard vessel until the night sky darkened or clouded over.

What was the real story on this guy Jathia, anyway? Julie headed out to find Kabitha.

This Nepalese woman's pixie face and inclination to coddle the vulnerable around her, whether intentional or not, was the perfect foil for her opinionated personality. Suni constantly joked about who he had to answer to.

Kabitha's information didn't surprise her. "Stay away from him. There's talk he's helping terrorists, the Maoists in the jungles."

Who were these communist insurgents operating in India? At first, Kabitha said she didn't know what they wanted. "They bomb government offices and train tracks. Terrorize and kill villagers who won't cooperate with them." When pressed, she said, "They want what we all want—an end to corruption and poverty." Her last bit of information devastated Julie. "You know he's Ram's older brother, don't you?"

Julie recalled Ram's response to her question about a sibling. *No one worth mentioning.* She'd been helping a group of terrorists, not harmless and tractable fishermen wanting to stage an act of peaceful civil disobedience.

Julie's years with the Plowshares Three were a thing of pride for her. At least she got that right. But her legacy wouldn't matter unless she could stop this attack.

She paced her balcony hoping Jathia would turn up at his skiff so she could explain the dire fall-out from setting the waste rods on fire. Not likely he could understand the horrors of out-of-control nuclear fission. Arjun might get it, but she sensed him to be the true madman of the bunch.

When Jathia didn't appear, she asked around and ended up inside a one-room, mud brick dwelling on the outskirts of town. Surprisingly well kept for a terrorist, a typical rural hut in every other way.

The furniture consisted of little more than a low table with an outdated television, a wooden wardrobe bursting with everything a household needed, and a squeaky iron bed shoved against a wall. Occupants cooked and washed outside with water from a common well. Toilet business took place in a field or on nearby train tracks. But she noticed he had an indoor squat toilet in a closet-sized room at the back. Quite presentable.

He sat on what seemed a freshly laundered bedspread and motioned to the threadbare couch for her. "Sorry I kept you waiting outside. Just tidying a bit."

"Jathia, I'm worried sick the town could be attacked any minute. Do you understand how dangerous this plan is?"

"Yup."

"Did you talk to Arjun. Have you convinced him, too?"

"Yup."

"And the others?"

"Yup."

Why am I so worried? He's completely taken care of it. Embarrassed to have needlessly invaded his private space, she stared at the concrete floor between them. A red object the size of a toe stuck out from under his bed. She rose, crept forward, then jumped back. "Jesus. Are those Arjun's socks?"

Jathia pursed his lips and peered over the side of the bed. "Actually, it is all of him." He grabbed an ankle and in one forceful tug, pulled most of the stiff corpse into view.

There were no signs of violence other than a strange, twisted facial grimace.

"What the hell? Now you've pulled me into a murder. How much more fucked up is this going to get? I'm outta' here."

She headed for the door but Jathia grabbed her arm. "I thought you might be happy. I fixed things." He looked as crestfallen as the boy who tried to bake mama a surprise birthday cake but dropped the batter on the floor. "No more Arjun. No more attack."

"This is *not* what I meant when I told you to convince the group." She yanked away from Jathia. "Christ, he looks tortured. What did you do to him?"

"Tied him up. Poured pesticide down his throat. Like the farmers use to suicide if they cannot pay their debt."

"That's horrible."

"Yes. This bastard was trying to die for two hours. I could not even fish. Just sitting and waiting."

Julie paced with clenched fists but had to agree: her immediate concerns were solved. She collapsed in a heap beside him on the bed. "What now?"

Jathia rose and perked up like he'd been formulating an answer for weeks. "We splash whiskey on his shirt. People will think he is sozzled. *Then* ..." Jathia blinked in earnest at her slumped form at the foot of the bed. "We drag him out, in the dark, when nobody sees us, and drop the croaker in the boot."

Julie rolled her eyes. "Um, intoxicated people don't need to be in the trunk. They're usually okay in the back seat."

Jathia jabbed his finger at her. "Good point. Find a rubbish field and discard him. Like a suicide farmer. Or a drunk hobo.

No one is giving a shit. And if the police recognize him, they can boast to the newspapers they killed a rowdy sheeter."

In Jathia's search for the perfect place to dump Arjun's body, Julie figured they must have passed through at least six villages, each one more deserted than the last. The only sign of life was the flicker of television screens in open doorways.

Within minutes of ejecting it into a ditch, their headlights picked up a woman wailing in the middle of the road near a dwelling.

When Jathia tried to speed up around her Julie ordered him to stop. She spotted a man carrying a child of about four or five years in his arms.

The woman ran to the vehicle.

"Don't get out," Jathia said. "It could be a trap for a robbery." But after the woman shouted at him through his closed window, he said, "The child is dying. They want us to take her to a hospital. I'll say no. We might get sick too."

Julie burst out of the car to the child's side.

The man held up one of the girl's arms then pinched his own in an exaggerated movement. She burned with fever.

Julie motioned for Jathia to circle his car back. "I think it's malaria. It's not contagious. We can put the father and daughter in the back seat if you're worried."

They argued back and forth until the man slouched to the ground with his unconscious child in his lap, and the woman collapsed beside him, wailing.

"What if it was your child?" Julie asked.

Jathia hung his head and waved the father over.

Less than ten minutes later, they arrived at a roadblock with another drama in progress. Police in khaki uniforms, armed with pistols and semi-automatic rifles, milled around what appeared to be six corpses under sheets.

As Jathia's car idled behind the barricade, two women and an old man pulled up in a bullock cart. When a policeman flung the cloth back from one particular corpse, the women shrieked and fell on their knees.

Julie bolted from the car and stood her ground, hands on hips, while one of the policemen pointed his rifle at her. "This child is dying," she said. "We need to get her to a hospital."

A man in a crisp white uniform with matching cap stepped forward and peered into the back of the vehicle. He motioned, the barricades parted, and they continued.

When Julie's breathing slowed to normal, she said, "What the hell was that?"

Jathia glanced at her, nonplussed, but questioned the sick girl's father. "He says they're local farmers. The police shot them for hiding revolutionaries and giving them food. The one they uncovered was the man who was going to take his daughter to hospital yesterday."

"Do you mean they were executed?"

"Probably. Low-caste farmers don't have weapons for a gun battle. Might be for the station blown up. Exactly six police killed."

"Why would villagers risk their lives for revolutionaries? Doesn't make any sense."

"It does if the Maoists bring in teachers and doctors. This girl should have seen one a week ago." Jathia squared his jaw. "Now, she'll die right here in this car."

Julie stared at the child's drawn, gray face in the rearview mirror.

Only fifteen minutes later, a wave of chills shook through the girl's withered body. Her pained panting slowed and dimmed.

Then stopped.

The man rocked the limp corpse against his chest without a pause in his low, rhythmic chanting. His blank expression never changed, but he leaned forward and said something in a raspy voice.

"He wants out. His daughter is dead. He can get a ride back."

"Doesn't he want to know what she died of?"

"He has no money for that. He will need it for the funeral wood if he can't find anything dry himself."

"I have the money. Tell him. Continue to the hospital and I'll pay his way back to his village."

"My friend, you must be a wealthy person in Canada."

"No, just a bleeding heart."

Jathia's eyes widened. This was one expression not in his lexicon.

After that night, Julie avoided Jathia. If he'd split from the violent wing of the Naxals, she figured some good came out of a potential catastrophe. But her fear of an attack on the nuclear waste plant, mere kilometers away, never left, especially if she heard a train rumble by.

She remembered what Jathia told her about Arjun. "He wanted to be a martyr, anyway. Join the guys in Kolkata for the big attack."

"Such as?" she said.

"Blowing up one of those trains carrying the waste rods."

Arjun was no longer a threat. Still, *the guys in Kolkata* didn't need him for that heinous act.

This place looks interesting." Paula stopped and peered into the dim interior of Suni's ground floor as Julie put pressure on her elbow to keep them moving. "And lovely cool. That arrow says there's a rooftop café with an ocean view. I'm just about to faint from all this sightseeing. You *know* how I am in heat." Her ivory complexion and upper chest blazed with a heat rash, her long-sleeve cotton tunic limp with sweat.

"I never go in here. The food is supposed to be terrible." Julie glanced around, frantic to find somewhere she wouldn't run into Ram's newly arrived friend.

Goran creeped her out with his roaming eyes and misogynistic remarks that Suni's young, female guests were like "ripe tomatoes." According to Ram, wealthy intellectuals, especially ladies, sought his friend's grotesque-themed paintings. No doubt misled, Julie thought, by his boyish physique and halo of shoulder-length auburn ringlets.

"I nicknamed him Drac because of his wild eyes," Ram told her. "Lucky bastard gets away with unwashed jeans flecked with paint and those tacky gypsy vests. You're going to love the guy."

Well, she didn't, even before she found out his family were rich, Bohemian aristocrats. He used Ram's Stockholm penthouse as a mailing address, but to Julie the guy was an outright stray, always looking for a warm bed and a bowl of food.

She steered clear of their surfing whenever she attended to her beach dogs. Ram would contact her once Goran left.

She did a quick scan. No Ram, no friend. "Okay, let's sit over there." Julie maneuvered around the packed tables.

"Julie." Suni almost crashed into them with an armful of dirty dishes. "No coming. Long time."

At this warm, welcome Paula eyed the two of them while Julie yanked out the menus sandwiched between his fingers. "So busy. Hey, Suni? Good, good." She patted his arm and turned on her heels toward the table.

Paula flipped back and forth through her menu and Julie pretended to do likewise until she spotted Goran using the wooden railing to vault down the stone steps from the upper floors.

At the bottom, slamming to the concrete, he jerked his head up. His beady eyes met Julie's before he darted into the toilet cubicle.

"What in the world's going on with you, sweetie?" Paula laid down her menu. "You've got a vice grip on that thing."

Julie flicked her menu to the table.

"Even at the airport, I could see you're not yourself. You've always been intense about one thing or another, but you'd snap out of it. I don't see any joy at all. What's happened?"

Julie chewed her thumbnail. Where to start? The terrorists? Or maybe the dying dogs and threats from the fishermen? Her anger at the nuclear dump near town? Or the recklessness of trespassing into it and then trying to pass off illegal photos to *National Geographic*? She opened her mouth to confess the dive when she sensed someone at her back.

"What is it again? Julie …? Julie …?" Goran snapped his fingers near her face while his attention flitted between her and Paula.

"Julie Paglia." She rolled her eyes—just an excuse to meet Paula.

"I'm Paula." She offered Goran her hand.

He pressed it to his lips and pecked at it, gazing into her eyes. "Well, aren't you an oasis of beauty for this little hellhole of a town."

Paula's demure smile rarely left her face. At Goran's attentions, she vibrated with nervous energy, flung her head back and let fly with her jackhammer laugh.

Diners skimmed over her ethereal beauty as the unlikely source.

Goran's eyes flew open, then narrowed, shining with lusty fascination.

Unaware of the heady effect she now had on men, the awkward duckling had stopped shouting long ago thanks to her cochlear implant. While Paula's slim hips sailed from side-to-side, so too did the stares of hypnotized admirers. She looked sexy in a long, denim skirt and desert boots, which was what she usually wore. The husky voice only added to her mystique.

"Okay then. Let's get together sometime, ladies." Goran nodded to each one in turn. "Paula, and Julie … Paglia." He punctuated her last name with a jab of his finger. She watched him bound back up the steps and frowned at the thought of her contemplative friend, Ram, with this flighty maniac.

Paula yanked her shoulders around. "Is that your friend Ram?"

Julie snorted.

"Good gosh. Those eyes. I felt like …" Paula's eyebrows knit together in concentration.

"You were being raped?"

"No. Something good. Really good. Why are you so negative about men, sometimes?" She scowled at Julie. "So, they look at my big boobs. Who cares? It's just human nature. I bet your friend Ram would too."

"He certainly would not. He's a gentleman and a real sweetheart." Julie decided to save the confession for a private setting.

Y ou're sure of the name on the photos?" Ram had asked Goran so many times his friend was clearly annoyed.

"*You* know my memory is photographic, but if you don't trust me then go to your father's house yourself."

Another surf day over, the men strolled along the beach with their boards.

"Come on. How many photographers named Julie do you think this town has? I'm telling you, she's in deep shit. Your father's ready to lay charges once the police find her. That won't take long."

"But how did *he* get them?"

"Bro', listen. Time to go home and get the story straight from your father."

"My God. It's such a stupid thing to do," Ram said. "Maybe she didn't see the Restricted Area signs or the flashing ambers." He wanted so badly to give Julie the benefit of the doubt.

Goran scrunched up his face and guffawed at Ram's portrayal of a guileless Julie. "If you don't want her in jail, tell her to destroy all traces of those photos and leave India right away."

A few days later, from Suni's rooftop, Ram saw Goran in the surf with a woman and three puppies. This must be Paula. Goran hadn't stopped talking about her since the meeting at Suni's and Ram saw why. By the looks of their intimate body language, they'd probably spent the night together. He headed down to ask about Julie.

"Excuse me. Hi. I'm Ram. A friend of Goran?"

Paula jumped up, entangling her feet in one of the puppies. "Yes … oh, you're … hello … I'm Paula. Of course, you know I'm Julie's friend."

"That's why I'm here. I keep phoning her cell, but her mailbox is full."

"She's in Bangkok renewing her Indian visa. Took advantage of my arrival. I'm looking after the puppies."

"You should see them bro'. They ran around all night. I laughed so much I hardly slept." Goran clambered up from the sand and turned to Paula. "Sorry. That wasn't very respectful to you, was it?"

"Don't worry about it. But I don't think the puppies were the reason you couldn't sleep."

Ram chewed at the inside of his cheek while his friend's wild eyes kept him cornered. It usually meant *trouble ahead*.

"Sit down, we all need to talk." Goran's officious tone was so out-of-character. Once seated on the beach, Goran pulled two items from the pocket of his cut-offs: a photo card from a camera, and a floppy disc used to store files. "Every photo of that underwater city is here. From her camera and the computer. I made sure there's no way to retrieve them from the hard drive."

Ram stared. This wasn't like Goran.

"After he told me about the illegal photos," Paula said, squeezing Goran's thigh, "I gave him permission to erase them. That girl has done some stupid things, but this time I'm scared for her. This is India. I don't want her arrested."

Ram took in the ocean waves. "We throw those into the water and Julie's problem is over?"

The other two nodded.

"If I keep them, I'll cave in and give them back," Paula said. "She's so obsessed with *National Geographic* she'd risk jail time."

Goran shook his head dramatically. "If she finds out I have them, I could end up losing my gonads during the night. But look, my friend, I think your father should see them first. It's wild what's down there. A Roman city, here?"

He could easily destroy the photos, but Ram didn't see a happy ending for anyone. At best, the authorities would kick her out of India. Or, they might throw her in jail. Either way, she would never speak to him again.

"Okay." He held out his hand. "Give them to me and I'll deal with this. No one needs to know who took them from her place."

That night, Ram figured out a way for Julie to publish the photos without being arrested. He had a powerful bargaining chip against his father. One he'd never pulled out.

On Mr. Musahar's day off, the two men sat inside the Musahar den and viewed Julie's underwater images.

"Are these not unbelievable?" was all Baba said after Ram's dreaded confession about Julie. "A little grainy, but look … one of those arenas where the gladiators fought. I am thinking your friend is most definitely talented. To do this underwater, at night."

This was Baba's version of 'she's got balls.' His admiration for Julie boded well for the outcome Ram wanted.

Mayawati, his stepmother, peeked into the den, her eyes misty. He hadn't set foot in his childhood home for almost three years, which was likely why the woman insisted on taking over from their chef and, an hour later, appeared with enough food to feed six.

She sat beside Ram, her gaze fixed on him, rather than the photos.

One Indian appetizer after another disappeared into Ram's mouth, starting with his favorites: the spicy deep fried *pakoras* and sweet *malpua* flat cakes. The faster he chewed, the more Mayawati swelled with delight. Finally, he sat back, the feeding frenzy halted.

She dabbed one well-manicured hand at a crumb of cake stuck to the corner of his mouth, then licked her finger, and grasped one of Ram's hands firmly between her own.

He eked out a smile for such an oddly intimate moment between him and his stepmother.

"The fact is," Mr. Musahar said after Mayawati left. "Your friend took these photos for financial gain, but if they get out, it puts the plant at risk." He pursed his lips across the sad cherub face he did so well.

"Who gave you the photos?" Ram asked.

Mr. Musahar arched his eyebrows. "The *National Geographic* magazine had no idea what they were dealing with until they sent the photos to the Archaeological Survey of India. When one of the archaeologists and the mayor arrived at the plant yesterday, I knew I was in trouble."

"Why?"

"One photo shows our water inlets in the distance. At the time the plant was proposed, I was remiss in reporting this ancient site to the Atomic Safety Commission." His father paused and tucked in his chin.

Ram thought: *another case of political graft.*

"We finally had the approval after all that opposition—and money spent. The archeologists could have easily closed us down. There were the families I already promised jobs to."

"So, what are you thinking?"

"Your friend could be charged with trespassing—or worse. Because I've dealt a generous donation to the archeological survey, knowledge of these photos will go no further than local police. No harm has been done. I am willing to forget everything if you assure me her photos will be destroyed."

Ram hated how he pouted and lapsed into the Indian head waggle. Never had he been so torn between two people he cared about.

Mr. Musahar brushed his fingertips over the back of Ram's hand. "If it was up to me ... Well, this is not my decision. I am not owning the place. I would lose my job if the safety commission finds out I not only allowed a security breach but failed to report the ruins during construction."

Ram hadn't thought of that. With his father already at risk, how could he follow through with his threat to break off all contact with him? Ram nodded and tried to forget about the impending destruction of Julie's photos.

The arrival of an ice bucket of strong Bengal Black Label lager helped. His father's efforts to be a renaissance man of the people stopped short of his crotchety, colonial-era beer brand.

After dinner, they moved to the living room where a wall of windows caught glints off the ocean. Five kilometers from the town's center and in the opposite direction to that of the nuclear storage plant, the Musahar mansion perched at the pinnacle of a seaside rock face.

The red and black Kashmiri carpet, spread from one teak-paneled wall to another, lent a formal mood to the room. Today, the scene was anything but staid. The two pulled out the chess board for a 'grudge match,' remembering who lost the last one three years prior. 'Best out of three' took them long into the night.

The bucket was dry by the time they brought out the dusty photo album from Ram's university graduation in Boston; the only time they were together in America.

"Baba." Ram pointed to one of the photos of Mr. Musahar line-dancing in a honky-tonk bar, his head sandwiched between the breasts of two towering, buxom blondes in cowboy hats. "This may be the closest you ever get to a threesome."

"I am only guessing at what this expression means," Mr. Musahar said, peering at the photo. "But I will venture that you are wrong."

"That's just the beer talking."

While they exchanged grins, it occurred to Ram, with his baba's guard down, there might never be a better time to ask for the truth about his mother's apparent death during childbirth.

At the door, Ram faced him. *Did you get rid of Mama?* He cleared his throat to ask but gasped when his baba's arms, like plump loaves of warm bread, enclosed him in a bear hug. He blinked back tears of affection for this man who had given him the best education any child could want.

"Why do you never talk about Mama?" Ram broke from their embrace and rested his palms on his father's shoulders. "Did you not have any respect for her. Is that it?"

His father grasped Ram's arms in turn. "I dwell on the future. You are the future. India depends on you."

Ram searched his face for an answer but drew a blank once more.

"We will talk about all this again someday, heh?" Mr. Musahar said. "Drive safely."

Ram mounted the scooter. In the rearview mirror, his baba slouched against the jamb of the open door, looking defeated and aged by what Ram imagined were the secrets he held.

The black night enclosed the taillights of the scooter. It would be up to Mr. Musahar to uphold his title at the next grudge match, but that event would never take place. Neither would the conversation about why he didn't talk about Ram's mother.

Julie circled the ramshackle room at Suni's with a wary curl on her lips; at the ceiling an obligatory bare bulb swayed from its electrical cord. "So, this is your cozy love nest."

After fetching her from the airport in Kolkata by private taxi, Paula and Goran insisted she stop by their room before going home. No reason given.

Something seemed off—and not just the sour odor of rotten eggs inside the discarded take-out cartons, which lay atop a fire-engine red plastic side table. She poked her head into a washroom mottled with rust and mold stains; the cracked enamel sink hung precariously from its mounts, a pipe and shut-off valve serving for faucet and taps.

Julie's gaze drifted from a sagging mattress and springs to a rickety-looking wooden chair. "Uh ... I won't be staying. I should check the dogs."

Goran's clothes hung off every surface, looking like the carnage from a volatile rummage sale.

"I'd open a window for some air. It stinks like B.O. in here." She yanked the surviving shreds of a red-checkered curtain aside and slid the pane up for a view of stained bricks. Immediately, a blast of fine gray dust blew in, carried on the din of hammers and chisels from below. "Oh, shit." In tandem, she slammed the window shut with one hand and doubled over in a fit of coughing.

"We don't spend much time in here," Paula said. "Just showering and sleeping and ... you know. This is Suni's most isolated room. We don't want to disturb anyone because Goran's so noisy during ... you know."

Julie's grimace faded to fear. "Don't tell me you two did it in *my* bed while I was away?"

"Oh, for Pete's sake. Of course, we did. Goran was over every day helping me with the puppies. I washed the sheets. You should be thankful, not treating him like he has bubonic plague."

The next stop on this mystery tour of la Boulangerie was Ram's room. Despite the lighthouse kiss three weeks earlier, and lofty intentions, on her side, at least—their sex life was stalled. She wasn't about to inaugurate the erotic side of their relationship in a dumpy hostel room.

Oh, how he struggled to change the topic now if she goaded him into continuing his tales of sexploitations. He was antsy, all right.

Julie stopped and turned to him in Fishermen Colony Lane one evening. "Are you thinking of coming over, or what?" He'd never walked as far as her door but tonight he trundled along further than ever.

"What?" Ram jerked his head up like a sleepwalker roused from a jaunt. "Uh … no. I want to stop at the surf shop."

"We passed it way back there. It's closed, isn't it?"

Ram glanced at his watch. "Yeah. I guess I'll head back then."

As if he didn't know when the surf shop was or wasn't open. Under an unfettered grin, Julie watched the slouched figure of Ram Musahar recede from a guaranteed lay at her place. Impressive as his white-knuckled celibacy was, she guessed Ram's reluctance to enter her suite had more to do with Indian morals and being in his hometown, than her.

In the meantime, he kept Julie satisfied enough helping her with the beach dogs every sunset. It was here where he made his case in favor of finding oil deposits across the globe.

"What's the difference?" he said. "I'm doing work every bit as worthwhile as yours with the dogs. Without my tests, there wouldn't be any fuel for industrial plants. *And*, I get paid to travel the world."

Damn if he didn't know the right carrot to dangle in front of her.

They crossed in and out of each other's spheres, never needing to orchestrate anything. If they met by chance, they shared a meal or an intimacy about a mutual friend.

Ram answered the door of his room at Suni's and Julie stepped into a gleaming space with an ocean view, a bar fridge, a glass coffee table, and a rattan couch for lounging.

"Hmmf. Not bad, at all."

"Suni's best," Ram said, his grin and slobbered kiss too forced for comfort.

"This is all very nice," she said, wiggling from his embrace, "but I've missed the puppies so I'd best—"

"I've got a Kingfisher and a Corona." He flung open the bar fridge's door and grasped the neck of a bottle. "Both cold."

She eyed the couch. *Ram insists on frosted, half-pint glasses.* Anticipating the cool liquid in her parched mouth, she decided her canine friends could wait a few more minutes. She let her bag slide off her arm and curled up on the couch in a ray of sunshine.

He sat on the edge of the bamboo lounger directly across from her, so close the knees of his long legs bumped up against hers.

Is he seducing me? Think again, buddy. Sex in the middle of the day? She glanced at him and his shit-face smile was gone. *What in hell do you want?* She almost said it out loud. *Something was wrong with the dogs.* Her hand trembled. She bounded to her feet. "It's the dogs, isn't it? That's why you don't want me to go home."

"They're fine." He motioned her to sit.

His index finger tapped triple-time against the armrest. He rose. "I'll just get to it. The police know you dove in the restricted zone of the nuclear storage plant. They're looking for you."

She raised her eyebrows in mock surprise and drained the beer mug with one graceful flick of her wrist. Nothing but silliness. First thing tomorrow, she would lock the photos in a safe deposit box in Kolkata. If the police had the grainy ones, they wouldn't hold up in court. That particular screw-up worked in her favor.

"The police asked Suni if he knew a Julie Paglia," Ram said. "He doesn't know your family name so, of course, he said no." His sentences dribbled out flat, hardly the tone of someone warning a friend of their imminent arrest. "The police are threatening to lay charges of trespassing into the buffer zone under the Prevention of Terrorism Act. This is serious trouble you're in."

"Ooo, I'm soooo scared. So, somebody told you I took photos in a restricted area. Big deal. It's what I do, and I won't apologize for it. I'm tired and I'm going home. I'll see you in the morning."

She grabbed her backpack and headed for the door, but Ram slammed his palm against it as she reached for the handle. It was a big palm attached to a big arm. Julie wasn't going anywhere until he removed it. She spun around. The odor of garlic seeping from his pores hit her nose.

"What is it you want from me? I'm not buying this crap about the police because they don't have a bit of evidence. The photos are safe on my hard drive. Someone's trying to stir up trouble for me. That's all it is. Maybe the fishermen, or your own father."

Ram didn't budge. "I've seen the photos on your laptop. For your own good I erased all of them. I broke into your place when Paula wasn't there."

"Oh, really?" She forced out a sigh and her eyelids fluttered. "Exactly how?"

"She always left her handbag with me whenever she went to the beach with Goran. I took the keys and found your laptop and camera."

"Okay, then." Julie sidled from the door. "Here's a skill-testing question for you. Did you find my camera and laptop in the desk or on my table?"

"Inside your desk." He straightened.

Unfortunately for him, she didn't have a desk. She reached for the doorknob, but Ram pushed his body against the door.

"This is all that's left of the photos," he said, reaching in his pocket and opening his palm to reveal a photo card, barely larger than his thumb. "Believe me, everything else is wiped from your hard drive."

She gazed at the card, and he curled his fingers inwards as if protecting it. Julie's throat tightened. The storage disc looked identical to the one she'd used during the dive. If these *were* her photos, it didn't matter how he got them, only that she retrieve them. She grabbed at his hand. "That's private property. You have no right to it."

He flipped his wrist over, dropping the disc to the floor. His eyes flared. Then he slammed the heel of his sandal down, shattering the fragile disk into a dozen pieces.

Julie gawked at his act of vandalism. "You mean fucker." In shock, she pushed Ram aside, wrenched the door open, and pounded down the stairs two at a time, not slowing until she burst through her own door at the other end of the beach.

While she waited for her computer to boot up, she looked for the photo card. It was gone. She paced and cuddled each puppy in turn to calm herself. If he thought this funny, then she had a thing or two to say. Ram wouldn't stoop to violate her property. That was more like Goran. Paula and Goran. In here.

Her hands shook as she searched all her files and backups. She collapsed into her rattan chair. It was true. Everything was gone. And with it the closest she'd come to being taken seriously at *National Geographic*.

Even worse, without money, her search for the Jesus manuscript also lay in ruins.

Julie lay in bed with Caesar Augustus in the palm of her hand and listened to the howling and barking along the dark beach. Bow-wow-wow-wow-wow. A scattershot of betrayal to the gut, then a yipping whine trailing away into the distance. And nothing more.

She'd never amount to anything. Isolated and depressed long enough, a fear more devastating than career failure always surfaced—she might be as rotten as her mother.

She let her cell ring—had to be Paula at this hour. It went to message as had an earlier one from an in-flight magazine. The only call she wanted—wouldn't come. Julie imagined her photo on a cover that would never be. A watery temple dome, Venus on one side, Mars on the other.

Mounted in place with a fridge magnet, of Machu Picchu, no less, was the Western Union receipt—the only indication she had ever contributed to the famous magazine. The sunken city had proven every bit as difficult to uncover, after all.

Pay to the order of Juliette Paglia the sum of Five-Hundred US Dollars for Services Rendered. Editorial Advance. National Geographic Society. Not bad for an advance but nowhere near what she might get for her gold coin of antiquity. She circled her finger around the Roman profile on the coin and realized this was her only surviving evidence of the sunken city and her time there.

━❀━"Thank you for waiting. May I come in?" Paula stood outside the open doorway of Julie's Vakkali suite.

Two weeks into her isolation Julie took a call, ready for a story. Instead of a magazine editor at the end of the line, Paula's husky voice jumped out, asking to come over.

Julie glanced up from where she sat on the floor before continuing to scrub the puppies' sleeping cage. Behind her, the door clicked shut.

"Are you still letting him screw you?" Julie said. Hearing nothing but a long exhale, Julie stood and spun around to see Paula standing motionless, her lids half-closed.

"I'm here to tell you what an ass you're being." Paula's affectionate plea was lost on Julie.

"I don't need any more flak, especially from you. Just when I felt my career falling into place, I get stabbed in the back." Julie shoved her Western Union receipt and gold coin across the table. "Look. It's all I've got to show for six months of work."

Paula fingered the coin. "What's this?"

"Caesar Augustus. Arrogant little shit that he was."

"Oh, all right." She shoved the coin aside. "You're upset. I would be too, if someone destroyed my property. But blame *me*. I'm the one who pushed it. Because I was afraid for you, not because I'm trying to sabotage your career. Geez, you're doing enough of that already."

When Julie shot Paula a dirty look, her friend sighed. "Sweetie, I want you to be successful, but sometimes you try to do too much. Dangerous things. How can you expect anything but trouble from that?"

"To hell with you all. I'll be fine. Awesome." Julie dropped to her knees at the cage and dug the rag into a corner, batting Jimi out of the way so hard, the puppy yelped.

Sweeping it into her arms, when Paula tucked Jimi into her friend's lap, it covered Julie's fingers with apologetic licks.

"I miss my friend," Paula said, turning up her palms in a supplicatory plea.

Julie snuggled Jimi to her cheek to hide her tears and said, "I miss you, too."

Before leaving, Paula pecked Julie's cheek and uttered her signature goodbye, "Sweet dreams, my friend."

Alone once more, Julie slumped over the table, her head in her hands. After everything she'd planned, lost sleep over, searched for, and fantasized about—Was one gold coin and a single pay stub the sum total of her career? Of her entire friggin' life?

She opened her laptop and pounded out a letter addressed to Mrs. Sara Paglia. The first correspondence she ever wrote to her mother amounted to another one of Julie's half-baked inventions — this time, from one liar to another.

> *Dear Mum,*
>
> *I'm finally working for National Geographic and the pay is fantastic. They're going to use one of my photographs of an underwater Roman city for the cover. The publication date hasn't been set, but when it is, I'll send you a copy of the magazine. In the meantime, here's one of the souvenir coins I kept from the dive. It's valuable, so don't lose it or throw it away. And don't tell anyone about it because I'm not supposed to have them.*
>
> *Julie*

The next day, she caught the bus into Kolkata and couriered the coin, the Western Union receipt, and letter to her mother.

It didn't take long to regret it.

Before she even stepped off the bus in Vakkali, Julie felt sick to her stomach. What kind of pathetic person mails a copy of their paycheck to their mother? The same kind that gives a precious stolen coin to a lunatic felon.

Taking a detour home to avoid friends, she skulked and gagged through the foul evening fish market, then cut through the unlit cemetery. Had she lost her effing senses? This stupid stunt to get her mother's attention would no doubt end badly.

Julie first met the dog and old woman under the government awning where a cranky clerk sold price-controlled fruit and vegetables. She assumed the old woman picked through the moldy remains dumped outside before the dogs, cows, and goats got at them.

Yogi—the name Julie gave the dog—with its long, downy-soft, white fur and floppy ears, was a step up from the typical street mutt which could be found from one coast of India to the other.

For weeks, the toothless woman trailed her fingers through the daily bowl of rice Julie set down and dabbed at her mouth but always left the vegetables. Softer sweet cream puffs became an easier option and soon, with whipped cream smeared to the top of her nose, she made eye contact with Julie for the first time, her dull eyes sparkling ever so slightly.

Julie arrived with the parchment wrapper of pastry one day to find the woman lying in blood, her skull smashed in and the dog gone. *Why?* She had nothing of value except for the silken-haired dog.

This morning, the dog was back, wet and shaking, curled on top of the blood stain in the beating rain. Now wasn't the time to take in another puppy, but with the dog's labored breathing, it wouldn't survive the night outside.

Jimi, Rocky, and Yogi thrived on an abundance of food and love. What would become of them when the time came to go?

✽Days later, while the dogs ran free on the beach, she waved to Jathia, who was hauling his skiff onshore. Since her split from Ram, she'd been friendlier toward his brother.

However flawed his terrorist methods, at least Jathia had the magnanimity to think of the less fortunate around him.

Helping Jathia was the teenager who spread his canine terror wherever he went, and today was no different. He nailed Jimi with a stone and the puppy dashed to Julie's side. Julie had found the beige puppy in the abandoned building next door just weeks after she'd arrived. After a night of high-pitched yips she ventured in to find a bony leg visible from behind a pile of oily rags. As she bent down, the terrified puppy rocked side-to-side through the trash in a pathetic attempt at escape, one of its legs bowed out and broken.

Although female, Jimi was named after a young boy who met the puppy outside Julie's door and sometimes walked her to his family's home and back.

Julie marched to Jathia's boat and pointed. "Did you see this boy throw a stone at the puppy?"

Jathia scanned the beach in both directions.

Not her first run-in with the disturbed teen; his eyes flashed with hostility.

"What is the use of saying anything? He is dumb," Jathia said.

"What's he doing with you?"

"I take him on the water. Keeps him out of trouble and calms him down."

"Didn't look like it to me. Why is he allowed to run amok? Someone should supervise him or … I don't know … find him a home for the disabled."

Jathia's bare belly rolled with laughter. "That is what I *am* doing. Giving his poor parents a break. The whole village is his home. We look out for him. And if he goes too far, we give him a good smack. Like when he killed the old woman with the dog."

"What?" Julie gaped. "That was him?"

Jathia swept his affectionate gaze over Rohan, who grinned and rocked on his heels. "The fishing families keep him around to remind the Brahmin priest." An injustice far beyond a smack simmered in Jathia's eyes.

She hesitated. *How much do I want to know this?* "What did he do?"

"Rohan was five-years old when he saw the priest giving sweets to children outside the temple. He wanted one, so he followed him inside. The priest saw him there and smashed his head against a stone pillar."

Jathia motioned for Rohan. He pulled the teen's head forward, parted his hair, and traced a scar from his forehead to his crown. "Doctors did not expect him to live."

"Why in God's name would the priest do that?"

"Rohan's family are Untouchables. If they enter the temple, it has to be cleaned in a ceremony. Police often ignore this kind of violence against the lower castes."

Beaming at the attention, Rohan peeked up at Julie.

"I wish Akuti's dog, Geeta, was still around," Jathia said.

"Akuti? Wha—?" *Of course, this old woman had a name, a family, and a husband who had cared for her.* At some point, disaster placed her under a street awning on her four-square feet of the earth.

Jathia cocked his head at Julie's reaction. "Her name was Akuti. She named her dog after her daughter."

"The old lady … er … Akuti. Her dog is at my place. Come by some day. I've got three now."

Jathia howled. "We thought Rohan killed the dog, too. I must tell Mo. He loves Geeta. He's the dhal vendor."

Julie recalled shopping at this man's stall. It always had a hodgepodge of ailing beggars cupping steaming bowls of rice in their hands. They crouched amid the overflowing bins of green, yellow, and red lentils.

It wasn't until Julie heard a phone ringing within the innards of a desk one day that she realized Mo also helped tourists. He shoved aside an avalanche of brochures, manila folders and full ashtrays. "Mo's Travel and Ticketing." The vendor squeezed the receiver against a well-oiled cheek with one hand while weighing handfuls of dhal with the other.

The iron-ballasted scales could have been plucked from the era of Marco Polo. A broad grin of nicotine-stained teeth and laughing eyes invited customers in as co-conspirators in his one-stop shopping enterprise.

"Old Mo. His heart is wide like the sky." Jathia's own heart seemed to bloom as he spoke. "Always feeds street dwellers who cannot get a rice ration card. He kept Akuti alive for ten years. For the glory of Allah, he says."

At the sound of the other fishermen's boats, Jathia hurried to gather up what he needed. "I must go. Never had a dog. Just a floppy-eared goat. Loved that thing. There is a good story for you."

Julie replied with a cutting parody of the Indian head waggle. This nationwide nervous tick mystified her until she learned how to use it. Today it meant, *Sure, why not?* Under other circumstances it could mean, *I don't give a rat's ass.*

Jathia observed Julie off the tip of his nose. He didn't crack a smile, but the slow-motion shake of his head meant he delighted in her defiant streak in a way Ram never could.

In the following days, what was flat now pulsed with a world of personalities and social order. The greasy-haired guy selling the dhal was a saint. The toothless, old woman with whipped cream all over her face had once been a radiant bride.

Vakkali had its dark side, too. A respected member of the community had attacked an innocent boy, smashing his skull until the cerebrospinal fluid dribbled down, staining a sacred pillar of the Hindu faith.

At sunrise, a month after the argument, Julie pounded on Ram's door. "Ram. Open up. I have to talk to you." There was a metallic squeal, a pop, and the creak of a hinge. Two red-rimmed eyes appeared in the gap. She shoved through. "Come see what those bastards have done."

Heedless of his frantic hopping from one foot to another, she paced while he tried to pull his jeans up and over his bare ass. Shirtless and shoeless, he stumbled after her onto the beach.

"Look." She swept her arm in an agony-filled arc. Dozens of dark mounds dotted the sandy expanse.

Squinting against the rising sun, Ram took tentative steps toward the closest mound.

Julie screamed in frustration. "They're my dogs. Strangled with ropes. And poor Yogi too." She pounded to the beachfront doorway of Suni's café and fell to her knees beside the lifeless body. A length of rope cut deep into the dog's neck, stretching the mouth and bulging eyes into a ghoulish grimace.

Just weeks before, Suni recruited the dog into service behind his pastry counter. Her sole task: bark at would-be thieves entering late at night after the restaurant closed. The downy-haired dog accomplished this through unapologetic racism.

She sorted the creepers from the guests through skin color. Except for those Yogi knew well, such as Ram, she barked at any person of Indian descent. So acute was the dog's racial profiling she didn't bark at African Americans. The occasional noisy kerfuffle with benign visitors was collateral damage Suni was willing to live with if it meant he didn't have to hire a "night boy," the likes of which could be the worst rascal of all.

Julie sat on the sand and caressed the dead dog's back. "Probably mooching around the beach and the fishermen chased her to the back door. If only she could have made it to the front entrance." She glared at Ram through sobs. "They strangled her right under your balcony. Didn't you hear the barking?"

"I guess not. I went to bed loaded last night. It's been most nights." He slumped with the bruised theatrics of a child.

Julie ignored him.

"You should go home and rest," he said. "I'll get Goran to help me check if any of them are still breathing. There's a chance."

"No. I don't want that guy involved. It should be me."

They started from the far end of the beach and worked their way back. When they were within yards of finishing outside Suni's, there was the telltale whir of a fishing boat motor.

She churned through the sand toward it. "You fucking dog killers. I'll beat the shit out of all of you."

Ram overtook her with the ease of a pouncing lioness. He pinned her thrashing arms to her sides as one would a toddler having a tantrum and tucked her under his arm until they were inside Suni's. "Let it go," he said, steering her upstairs to his room.

He sat her on his couch, locked his door from inside, and slipped the key into his pocket. "You're going to stay here until you calm down." He pointed an accusing finger at her. "You start attacking people, you'll end up in jail."

Julie glared at him and yanked her top and pants back into place. *Looks like not much has changed. I'm a hostage in Ram's room and headed to jail.*

He opened his bar fridge. "Beer? It's icy cold." He dangled the words, acting like that's what she came for.

"Are you kidding me? It's seven in the morning."

"Well, it helps me relax." He popped the cap and threw the opener on the table. "I'll order herbal tea if you like. I heard Suni opening downstairs. I'll bet he saw Yogi when he unlocked the back door. I should dig a grave for it in the side lot."

She grasped Ram's wrist as he lifted his beer to his lips. "Please bury the young cemetery dogs. They're beside each other at the far end. You know them, right?" No doubt he would do it, if only to keep her happy. "I don't want to see Yogi buried. It's too much for me. I need to go home and hold Rocky and Jimi. I promise not to do anything."

He hesitated. "Fine. I better get out there before the town panchayat sends someone to pile the bodies into trucks."

Rage swept over her at the thought of it. She grabbed a nearby broom handle and beat the couch with it.

"Good, good." He took a swig of his beer and retreated to a safe distance.

By the time Julie got back to her suite, a monsoon-like downpour had begun, releasing one final flood of tears over the dead dogs.

❀The next morning, from her balcony she watched Ram's back muscles tense under his wet shirt as he dug the shovel into the mud. Her neighbors thought dogs were dirty vermin which should be disposed of in a dump. They would have stopped him if not for the curtain of rain.

Before filling in the grave, he crouched on his haunches and stared into the hole.

She wanted to believe he was studying the dead dogs' frantic expressions, frozen in time, that a part of him ached for any innocent being forced to endure a violent end.

Likely intending to take Fishermen Colony Lane back to his room, Ram shuffled up her street from the beach, shovel in hand.

"Thank you," she murmured, stepping from the cover of her stairwell, fists knotted against the dampness.

He looked up, his eyes wide. "Julie. I didn't know this building was yours."

Had he forgotten his lie about breaking into her apartment? Or was he too spent to keep it going?

"You're tired and wet. Come and dry off and have a hot chai."

He scanned the beach behind him, then the balconies across the street.

"It's okay. Not a soul will see you entering a proper ladies' residence in this rain." She arched one eyebrow to entice him in but came to regret it.

Every garment she owned dripped from her balcony line. Tending the street dogs every day, especially with the dirt and diseases they carried, meant she ran out of clean clothes quickly. What she had left to give him while his own clothes hung in the wind was the rose-colored Thai lunghi she wore herself. She took down the mosquito netting from over the bed and wound it around her body like a thick trailing sari.

She'd never seen him in anything remotely traditional, but his tall frame and frizzy mane of blue-black curls gave him the appearance of a warrior-king from tales of the Bhagavad Gita. His chest had only the slightest hint of dark hair. Most had migrated to his long thick legs, so different from the archetypical sticks wading into the waters of Mother Ganges on postcards.

The pink stood out against the mocha of his broad back. Her own skin tone only hinted at olive. Despite centuries of the Sicilian sun, somewhere along the way blond Nordic marauders entered Julie's family tree. She had an aversion to 'anemic Norsemen' who flicked their tresses in her eyes after climaxing, then dodged out the nearest exit.

He sat on the bamboo lounger, his arms clasped tight to his chilled body while Julie shut the door on the watery static outside. A lull enveloped the room, akin to a concert hall before the first sweet pull from the violin.

She frisked his upper arms until she felt the heat rise, then moved to a stool and lifted his foot into her lap. Entranced by the deep curve of his instep, she hardly noticed when he began to stroke hers.

For an instant, they shared a ragged smile, their faces tight with fatigue.

Her gaze followed his fingers circling along her inner thigh with such delicacy, it didn't match the ardor building in his eyes.

To this masculine touch moving across her body, she surrendered. The euphoria terrified her.

In one fluid motion Ram extracted his hand from the netting. The puppies yanked on the trailing bits clinging to her ankles as he steered Julie into the bedroom.

"Hey. That's my job," he said, and shut the door on their yelps. Beginning at her chest, he plucked at the sheer strands, hand over hand, as if bringing in a catch.

The netting peeled away, revealing, layer by layer, her pale torso floating and spinning in the muted light.

Steam, thick with a white aura, rose from their flesh. Ram brushed a clump of auburn hair aside at the nape of her neck and in that moment a breeze from the open window wrapped them in her heady female musk. In one frenzied move he released his lunghi and tore the rest of the netting from her hips.

With a slight nudge of his knee she fell backward across the bed. He straddled her, burying his face in her neck and inhaling every inch of it before circling her shoulder in affectionate pecks. With the touch of his lips sliding down her breast, she succumbed and let her arms fall from his hips to rest at her sides.

In one swoop he pinned both her wrists above her head and brought his mouth down around one nipple. He was a predator, devouring her breasts.

Julie's body shook. She tried to writhe out from under him, but his hands and thighs bound her firmly to the bed. "Let go of me. Get off. I can't breathe."

Ram shot off her with such force he smacked backward into the wall.

She struggled to her feet and lunged through the doorway into the kitchen, flicking her fingers as if shaking off a putrid liquid. On the balcony, she crumpled in on herself in one corner, her chest heaving.

When Ram wordlessly tried to wrap a sheet around her naked body, she backhanded it, inadvertently hitting him in the face. Not until she was overcome with wild shivers from the rain-soaked wind on her bare skin, did she pick up the sheet from where it lay tucked beside her and hug it around her shoulders.

As soon as she heard a rustling at the clothesline, Julie raised her head and glanced sidelong at Ram.

With his back to her, he yanked his damp jeans over his bare buttocks as though he were pissed off.

But so was she. What a mess.

"I'm going now."

Julie dared not look him in the face in case he became aggressive again.

At the sound of the door opening, she whispered, "See you later," but she wasn't so sure.

❈ With the relationship blockade in place, Paula showed up once again to tell Julie to *snap out of* her excessive self-pity. Paula's overwrought indignation had Ram written all over it, as if he'd prepped her.

For fifteen minutes, Paula pumped her for the story. Still: *Nothing happened.* "Ram is worried about you. He won't even tell Goran, so I can't ask him."

Julie gaped at her friend, cross-legged on the floor with Rocky in her lap. "I should hope not."

Paula's eyes narrowed. If pressed, her friend could be shrewd.

"You've been intimate with him," Paula said. "You can't simply push him away without an explanation."

"Is that what he's saying? That we had sex? We were naked, but we didn't do it. Did. Not."

"Now we're getting somewhere. I just made that stuff up."

Julie was incredulous. Goran's cunning had tainted Paula. To hell with trying to bury the nasty truth. "He held me down and forced me. Why, when I trusted him the most?"

"Oh, my goodness." Paula stood and drew a trembling Julie into her. She eased her friend into one of the straight-backed chairs.

"It's your panic attacks, not him. Anyone can see what a good guy he is. Tell him. He'll understand." She propped up Julie's drooping chin with the back of her fingers. "He cares about you. Don't do this again … not like the others."

Julie bolted up and backed away. She raised her hands as if seeking deliverance from a long-running ordeal. "What, exactly, is the point in bringing up those pricks?"

"You make out like you're such a victim, and yet you've had good guys like Ram come into your life. You always chase them away."

"No, you're wrong." Julie's index finger jabbed the air. "I seem to have this talent for attracting all the assholes in the world."

Paula bit her bottom lip, a cloud passing over her expression. "Has it ever occurred to you that you might be the one that's the asshole?"

Stone-faced, Julie marched to the door and opened it. "Don't come here again."

Goran was at her door within the hour, but Julie left the chain on. "You've got a lot of gall coming here after ransacking my place for those photos."

Goran squared his jaw. "I don't know what you said to her, but Paula is utterly distraught. I have no idea why she defends you. If you don't come and talk to her, I'll make her see what a poisonous influence you are on her life."

In the course of their friendship, men had come and gone. Goran was different, and Julie knew it.

❧ The first thing she did to set her romance with Ram right was load up on clothesline. One could never have too much of that in India. In addition to drying items, it could be used to drape off private areas in confined spaces.

But its real utility came with tying things down.

Julie was too embarrassed to tell Ram it was a panic attack. She'd had them before during casual sex with men she'd never see again. She always told herself it was their fault.

"I'll do anything," Ram said, as they stood inside his room at Suni's.

"It's usually better if I'm on top. I need to know you're not going to overpower me again."

"Okay. If you tie my arms down, would that make you feel safe enough?"

"Maybe."

Ram grinned.

So, this wasn't a new idea for him.

❀ At her place that evening, Julie pulled reams of clothesline from a drawer and cut lengths from it. Ram lay on the bed with the arms above his head.

She looped a piece of rope around each wrist and tied them to the bedpost with the taut-line knot he taught her while they sat with the beach dogs one afternoon. The knots secured tarps at the oil projects and could be tightened or loosened simply by pulling on the knot. His arm would be the tarp fluttering in the wind. The bedpost would serve as the stake.

She worked with methodical intensity, giving the knots an extra yank. When she went to his feet, he balked.

"Is that necessary? I'll be sort of vulnerable having my legs spread like that."

"I thought that was the idea, so I could feel safe with you. You said you'd do anything."

"I did say that, didn't I?" He cursed under his breath.

Tied down, Ram was completely at her mercy. She'd never tried this before but it appealed to her more than she wanted to admit. Ram's part was easy. She even put the condom on.

She rolled her hips around and around. Up and down. 'Round and 'round.

"Sweet mother," he whispered and at the moment he closed his eyes—Julie's cell rang in the kitchen.

She knew of only two people who would phone her in India at this hour. One of them was tied up at the moment. The other, Paula, knew better than to call this particular night. *Was it National Geographic? Or Aunt Dot?*

"I should get that." She jumped from the mattress.

"What the hell?" Ram said.

By the time she answered, the ringing stopped and she didn't recognize the number.

Cell phone in hand, she turned toward the bedroom. Reflected in the mirror on the door was Ram scrutinizing his withered penis.

"Not again," he moaned. The condom hung limp.

With the bedroom door open, in trotted Rocky to the off-limits zone, the adventurous one of the bunch. He thumped his paws against the floor and wagged his back end like a noodle.

Ram craned his neck to the extent the ties would allow, not looking nearly as amused as Julie. His frantic twisting didn't seem to be accomplishing much more than snugging up the knots.

Sidling next through the doorway, Jimi peered around, hyper-cautious, while Rocky bounded forward, sliding, taking the beige puppy's legs out from under her. They tore around and leapt onto the bed, landing heavily between Ram's legs, gnashing at each other's bottoms.

"Ow, ow—OW."

Back and forth, their pointy nails dug into his legs and torso. Jimi bit into the dangling condom and shook his head menacingly but Rocky tried to grab it away. While they stretched it to the limit, Rocky let go, sending Jimi backward off the bed and yelping in pain.

Julie moved to the open doorway.

"Thank God," said Ram. "Get these dogs off me before I lose a nut."

She scooped Jimi up and pulled the condom from his mouth. "Baaad puppy. You too, Rocky," she said, lavishing kisses on them.

Julie and Ram's sex life eventually settled into a more typical rhythm: for the first time Julie had a constant partner and said she felt some safety in that. Still, whenever he tried to dip into her well of childhood pain, she revealed little more.

"It's rare for a mother to be so abusive. Why did she do it?" he asked her.

Why, indeed? Julie had been searching for an answer since she was twelve.

"No shit, Sam," she said, the night her sixteen-year-old brother phoned from the detention centre where he was serving time for auto theft. "It's a real thing. 'Filicide' — killing your own children."

Tramping through encyclopedias of medicine at the library, Julie had found sanitized accounts of spouse revenge, acute breaks by neurotransmitters, and something called *altruistic filicide*. How could those two words even sit beside each other? It was like saying, *soggy desert syndrome*.

"Have you figured out why she did it?"

"Not really," Julie said. "Must be soggy desert syndrome."

❀ A month later, Paula and Goran traipsed into breakfast on Suni's rooftop, fresh from their stay at the Sri-Something-Or-Other ashram in the south. All but naked and covered in ash, Goran had a loincloth wedged between his butt cheeks. He fancied himself a Holy Man. His matted dreadlocks looked so dirty Ram wondered out loud whether they might be sheltering homeless mice.

Cleaner, Paula wore the white robes of a disciple with her hair reduced to a brush cut.

Between chuckles, Ram tried to reprimand her, but his attention settled on Julie, stuck in the disinterested funk that defined most of her days since the start of their sex life.

He didn't assume he knew what ailed her. He went to Paula once again.

"She probably can't handle her first true intimacy with a man," Paula said. "No doubt she's depressed about the dead dogs. But there's more. We took away her dream when we destroyed her photos."

Ram winced at that memory.

"She's broke," Paula said. "I've tried to give her money to go north after that manuscript, but she doesn't understand generosity. She'll only take it if I go with her. No way am I leaving Goran. She needs to grow up."

"Would she go to Thailand if I offer? It's romantic. Lots of story possibilities, too. It's time I got back to work, anyway."

"Heavens, no. She'll think you're trying to control her." Paula's shoulders sank. "Maybe fate's going to solve this. She won't be able to get another visa without returning to Canada. I'll probably find her hanging out at my place when I'm finished here. So typical."

Although Julie's life had been anything but 'typical' for some time, fate did resolve his lover's lethargy. Unfortunately, not by anything as innocent as *hanging out at Paula's place.*

※ The laneway of carving stalls served as an ideal spot for Julie's vaccinations. Dogs milled around, knowing a few of the carvers would toss them scraps of food. Today, also at work were a few of the Italian carvers who spent the winters studying the forms of the Hindu deities.

While she rooted around in her medicine bag, a young dog lifted its leg to one of the finished sandstone carvings lined up outside to lure in potential buyers. Most of the artists took it in stride as part of the risk of placing their work on the street.

The puppy yelped.

Julie looked up and her heart sank.

One of the Italians held it down with one arm. Above it, a clunky iron and wood hammer wavered, poised to strike.

Instinctively, she grabbed another hammer three times the size of his. "You hurt that dog, I hurt your sculpture." She spit into the dirt. "*Pezzo de merda.*"

She hoisted the hammer directly over the elephant tusk of Lord Ganesha and hoped he didn't notice her hand straining to keep the behemoth airborne. Whether it was the hammer, her Italian curse, or the spittle she deposited next to his work of art, the guy gasped. He knew she was serious.

Julie refused to contain her lunatic grin and felt a bit guilty later because the slight upward tug of his hammer may have been nothing more than a nervous tic. She let gravity pull her arm down and Ganesha's tusk shattered like crystal.

How appropriate she whacked the God of New Beginnings and Remover of Obstacles. At the time, Julie had a lot of obstacles in her way. Her next destination created a whole lot more.

Julie sat on a splintered and worn wooden bench across from two teenaged Indian women. One stared apathetically out of two black eyes. The other, possibly an older sister, held her hand.

Why did Indian police stations have to look so depressing? Grimy, gray, metal desks lined concrete walls whitewashed at one time but now streaked with mold. The bent drawers screeched open and closed, jarring her already frayed nerves.

An officer in one corner, barely visible behind a tower of manila folders and take-out food cartons, alternated between picking his teeth with a matchstick and belching loudly. Conversations in progress sounded more like shouting matches. An officer who hadn't joined the card game had a half-cheek planted on a desk while he hit on one of the prettier female officers.

Someone poked their head out of an office and barked an order at Casanova. He peeled his butt from the desk and headed in Julie's direction.

Here we go. A quick signed confession and payout to the Italian glaring at her from across the room.

Out of courtesy to Ram she would wait for him to show up. Why not let him think he was rescuing her?

❖ In her sleep-deprived haze Julie stamped her feet in glee like an imbecile. After fifteen minutes of cavorting with it, she concluded the mouse-sized cockroach was surprisingly light on its feet. *Like hell I'm going to muck up my shoes.*

"This arthropod will live to fight another day," she said to an imaginary audience. "Just do it in someone else's cell." She herded it under the iron bars into the dark hallway.

Ram's shoes came into focus.

"Oh, no. Look at you," he said.

She raised blood-shot eyes to him, a third restless night in Vakkali's local jail over. "Did you bring the clothes and rubber boots? Pleeease say you did. I'd rather piss myself than cover my runners in the shit around that toilet again."

She scratched at a constellation of red dots edging the sleeves of her linen kaftan top. "Bed bugs and fleas. I'm used to the fleas from the dogs, but these bed bugs are so itchy." The edges of her eyes watered.

Ram's mouth sagged. "They're probably inside that mattress on the floor. Not much you can do. Here, I'll hold up the blanket so you can change."

Julie poked the stained flannel through the bars and grabbed the change of clothes with the other hand. She sent a breathless snivel into the flimsy partition and yanked at her clothing. "I love you. I really do." A pathetic princess plea. The kind of manipulation she never let other women get away with. "Did you talk to that guy?" The last time Julie saw Ram he was headed to the local *thakur*. A well-connected landowner, Ram said, with a wallet almost as big as his multi-tiered belly. "You know … about getting me out of here?"

"Yeah. Just … get dressed and we'll talk."

That sounded like a *no*. Dread choked off her words. Why were they still holding her? The illegal dive and trespass at the nuclear plant had to be back on the table. She ripped the blanket from his hands, her pants around her ankles.

"Try to look decent, sweetheart." He pointed, as patient as a parent potty training a toddler. "Okay. Good. Bring that chair over here and relax. I have a plan. I told him they were holding you without bail and he said he could talk to someone in Justice if it was only a misdemeanor, but he didn't want anything to do with terrorism. That was way above him."

Julie scowled and stomped her foot.

"He suggested I go to my father. He may not be as influential as the thakur but he's just as respected."

"No, no, NO."

Ram slipped his hands through the bars and grasped hers.

"He's the one who put me in here." Gasping and doubled over, she tried to extricate her hands, but Ram clung to them. "It's still that damn, stupid dive. Didn't you say they couldn't charge me without evidence?"

She rose. One final tug set her free and tipped the chair. She paced the cell. "Your father obviously has a copy of the photos. I'll bet that bastard Goran gave them to him. And *now* you think your father's going to help me?

Ram's hands flew to his head. "Of course. I haven't told you, yet. I'm so tired I'm not thinking straight. It's not the trespassing they're holding you for. That just made them dig deeper in their database. They've uncovered a picture of you blowing up an oil pipeline outside of Mumbai. I haven't seen it yet."

She turned the statement over in her mind: *Blew up a pipeline?* Nope, no recollection of that whatsoever.

"I'm going to my father, whether you like it or not. I need to see this photo and the only way I can do that is through some big-time lawyer he knows."

His hands through the bars, he encircled Julie's waist. "I know you wouldn't do something like this. I'll find out what this is about. Don't worry."

But she *did* worry. A memory poked its head up—an anti-pipeline demonstration near Mumbai during her first trip to India. She was covering a minor dance festival when she tagged along with an Indian freelancer heading to a pipeline demonstration in the hopes something big might happen. It sounded like fun—until something big *did* happen.

Ram returned so late Julie worried she wouldn't see him until the next day. He trudged down the half-lit corridor, the bare bulbs playing on his sallow face like a flickering newsreel.

"It's you all right," he said. "Younger, but definitely you." Ram looked at his feet.

Bracing himself against his rage, or too weary to get angry?

"And you're throwing a Molotov cocktail at the pipeline." He looked at her and shook his head. "Jesus. Two people were trampled to death when the police released tear gas." He ran his hands through his hair. "And by the way, this one is a subsidiary of my company."

"Wh—"

Ram slapped his palm against the bars near her face.

"Will you let me explain?" Julie said. "Yes, I was there. I remember now. But I didn't throw anything. I was an observer. That's it."

Ram held up the photocopy he carried. In it, a man was caught at the moment of throwing a flaming missile at the pipeline. Beside him, Julie's arm was also in the air.

She'd seen the photo before and her explanation was the same now as then. Stepping backward from the violence, she slipped on a rock and her arm flew upward, making it look like she was throwing something. Unfortunately, she couldn't prove she had nothing in her hand because a figure in the foreground blocked it out.

Yes, she'd been arrested and had skipped bail and left India. Yes, it was a stupid thing to do. She was only twenty years old at the time.

"This photo changes everything." Ram closed his eyes. "There still might be something my father can do to get you out of here. I'll be back in the morning." He handed her another change of clothing, some take-out, and drinks. "They're from Paula. She's at the flat looking after the dogs. She said to tell you she's sorry she can't face coming in here, but she loves you."

She still loves me and, unlike you, still believes me, too. Just as she did years ago when she wired the bail money knowing I was going to skip.

You're sure it's her?" Ram's father was known to be a cautious man who tackled problems methodically and sensibly. This morning, seated at the desk in his study, his face sagged like the wax from a spent candle.

Ram nodded from the leather easy chair, well-aware of the gravity of what he wanted from his father. "If you could use some of your influence to arrange bail, I could pay it. I don't know about the bribes we'd need. Those would probably be beyond what I have."

"And then what?" his father asked. "Even if she's released, you know this friend of yours will still have to face a biased justice system."

Ram had prepared himself for this question. It was the reason he hadn't slept all night. "Obviously, she needs to be smuggled out of the country and we both know who can help with a fake passport."

"No. Absolutely not. You are entering dangerous territory. This, I can't abide by." He rose to close the study's door, then frowned at Ram. "Why put our family in jeopardy for a stranger?"

Ram squared his shoulders. "I plan to marry Julie."

His father hung his head and sighed. "Still, I am not willing to do this simply because you are having relations with a certain woman."

"Stop right there. How dare you insult her."

"I am merely being realistic. You might think differently in a few years. Time has a way of working things out."

"If you don't do this for me," Ram blurted out. "This will be the last time you ever see me in this town. Or in your presence." In the fog of last night, it occurred to Ram he might have to throw down this bluff. Since he no longer knew his baba's mind, it was risky.

✤ Ram trudged down the corridor to Julie's cell late the next morning. From the looks of his bloodshot eyes, he was likely getting even less sleep than her.

"Come closer," he said.

Julie wondered if he had a confidence to share or was too drained to speak any louder.

"We're getting you out of here tomorrow morning. You can't go back to your apartment."

Julie opened her mouth to protest but Ram jumped in. "No. You'll listen until I'm finished. Paula and Goran are packing your things as we speak."

Tears spilled from the corners of Julie's eyes. "Why? Please don't do this. What about the dogs?"

His upper lip quivered. "Don't fight me on this. I know it's hard, my love. Jimi is going to the Gupta boy. The family loves her."

He was right. She let Ram's managerial tone wash over her fear.

"My stepmother will take Rocky. When you get out of here, you're leaving town and I'm going with you."

"I won't see the dogs to say goodbye? Noooo ..." Her voice trailed off into a mournful wail. The thing she feared most was happening.

"Please keep it together, sweetheart, so we can get you out of here. Look, I don't know what happened at that pipeline. I've decided I don't care. But this is serious shit you're in. You skipped out. It won't go well if you stay to defend yourself." Ram's voice shook with emotion. "But I love you and that's good enough for my father. He's arranged your bail."

"Why would he do that?" Julie gasped between sobs.

"Because you're family and that's what families do in India. They help each other no matter what. If you're going to be my wife, you'll have to accept Baba the way he is. He's not so bad, you know."

She jerked her head up. "Your *wife*?"

Ram's cheeks blazed with color at his gaffe.

"Are you proposing to me inside an Indian jail?"

He nodded with a boyish charm she'd never seen before.

"That's about the lamest thing I've ever heard." She smiled and slid a backhand across her wet cheeks.

"Will you?" he asked.

Surely, he knew her answer. Julie entwined her fingers around Ram's through the bars and kissed them. "Oh, my God. Yes." Their foreheads touched, and tears streaked down both of their cheeks.

Julie left the jail early in the morning, recognizing the family's white limo and driver, Ganesh, from the night she first noticed Ram inside Suni's. No doubt Ram's father was the same Mr. Musahar his son accused of killing women and children. With no alternative than accept help from this rough character, she deloused herself at the family's home and slept for twelve hours.

That evening, while perched on the edge of the Musahar's seaside balcony, Julie swung her legs to an internal manic metronome. On her behalf, Ram's father had used the very thing she opposed — graft and bribery. Ram put up bail of five-thousand US dollars while his father covered the bribes, a behemoth sum her lover refused to reveal.

The enormity of what Ram was giving up also left her numb. He could end up on a terrorist watch list, too, for helping her escape and jump bail. He might never visit his father in India again—not that she would be able to return, either. That her precious manuscript was last seen in a province of India was too painful to contemplate.

Under the distant waves lay the Roman ruins. "Stay safe, be patient," she said under her breath, as if they were an animate object disappointed with having to remain hidden.

In the growing gloom of twilight, she slid the terrace's glass doors aside, stepped in, and froze. A peppered head of thinning hair poked above the easy chair; a newspaper stretched to each side of it. No doubt, this was Ram's father. She must acknowledge him. "Sir, I want to thank you for everything you've done to clean up my … uh … messes."

He craned around at the sound of her voice, then grunted slightly.

Taken aback, she searched for some veiled importance to this sound, but none came to mind.

"I am imagining you mean the bribes I paid to ensure your release?"

Julie nodded.

He grunted again, motioned to the easy chair opposite, and waited for her to sit. "Unfortunately, this is the reality in India, and it is at the root of much which is wrong here. I did it because Ram made it clear you were family." Mr. Musahar smiled broadly. "Well, to be blunt, he said he would never see me again unless I helped you get out of jail.

"I have another son. Estranged from the family."

Julie glanced away. *Don't tell me he knows I used Jathia for the illegal dive.* But his open face showed no change. This balding, squat man with pudgy cheeks was nothing like the ogre she imagined. It was only when a hint of mischievousness rose in his eyes that Julie realized who he reminded her of. *Sneezy. Or was it Sleepy?*

"I fear he is lost to me, so how could I bear to lose Ram too?"

She imagined his reserved wife as Snow White.

"I suppose I acted as a willing hostage. Can I speak to you as I would a daughter?"

At this confidential turn, Julie shifted her gaze from his cheeks.

"I was born into a simple, rural family." He folded his paper and motioned around the room. "All this here … Some argue I should not be entitled to it. Others say it is a miracle." He winked. "There was some luck involved.

"When I worked as a young laborer in the fields, I accepted the black and white of my fate. I was poor and illiterate. But prosperity brings more options and then those lines become fuzzy. Everyone working at my soap factory and goat farm are Dalits from the lowest castes. So, too, are many at the nuclear waste plant."

"It's called reverse discrimination," Julie managed to squeeze in but Mr. Musahar barely noticed.

"I have much to be grateful for. And now I am having to pay a bribe to keep my son close to my heart." He shifted to face her. "I am willing to live with that. It does not mean I am suddenly a bad person. Our goodness seeps out one drop at a time. I watched it happen to my other son."

Mr. Musahar leaned forward, palms on knees. "There is no miracle to my prosperity but the gratitude I felt the day I got Ram back from the orphanage. It is with me still." He laid his hand over his left breast. "Here."

Julie straightened to stare at him.

"Oh, did you not know? As my son's future wife, you should know Ram's character has been informed by his time as an orphan. My actions put him there."

She swallowed hard. "*You* put Ram in the orphanage?"

Briefly, he looked through her to something only he could see. "There were no relatives to take him after his mother died in childbirth. I returned for him five years later when I had the money to raise him. Such an odd little man he was with no idea of the world outside the gate. He begged me, 'Uncle, stop. We have to take my bowl or I will not be able to eat without it.'"

A smile passed over Mr. Musahar's face but there was little humor in it.

"I remember the soccer ball filled with water. The children used it for their bowling game. Oh my, but didn't they cherish it. A tiny boy came to push it through the taxi's open window as a parting gift. Ram was pulling, the boy was pushing, and both were crying.

"It is unbelievable to me to think how cruel I could be. When it finally cleared the window, I threw it out and it split open. Ram was so shocked he immediately stopped crying.

"The injustices to me as a lowly laborer. I felt that same hatred at one time. How, then, could I expect others to change when *I* myself wasn't willing to do so?"

As he reached forward to pick up a thin paperback from the coffee table, Julie noticed a red scar running the length of his forearm.

"I read from this book every day, especially when I'm confused or depressed. These are the Dhammapada verses of wisdom by Gautama Buddha. Ram told me you are interested in Buddhism."

"Not really. I'm looking for an artifact at a monastery in Ladakh."

"Please." He rose and offered it to her. "Take this as my gift."

"Oh, I don't—"

"Cherish it. I wish it to be given to my friend, eventually. His name and the temple he works at are written inside in Hindi. By great fortune, he lives in the direction of the monastery you're looking for. He may be able to help you in some way."

❋It hadn't been much of a two-way conversation, but he had a way of putting people at ease, Julie thought later as she lay in bed, surrounded by the vast silence of the home. He managed to defend himself on actions that were, at the very least, unscrupulous. He opposed bribes yet used them. He called himself a simple, humble man, yet held a half-stake in a multinational soap enterprise and worked in management at a nuclear waste dump, one of the most catastrophic sources of pollution ever created.

If he knew her history of railing against corporate greed, was he mocking her when she could least defend herself? *Men like him didn't allow anyone to control them—not even their children.* She turned the gift over in her hands as if she could see the trap laid out.

Someone rapped at her door. Ram poked his head in, the sultry masculinity she'd missed since before Cedarwood shining in his eyes.

"Raaam, you know you can't sleep with me in your parent's house until we're married."

"There's someone else here who wants to sleep with you even more than I do." He opened the door a touch wider and in bounded Rocky.

With Rocky at her feet she fell into a bittersweet restfulness born of letting go of the old. There were other beings to think about now—human beings.

❦The delightfulness of winter on the Bay of Bengal was over. For Ram's intimate parting from his childhood sanctuary, a curtain of dry heat and lethargy descended on Vakkali and the Musahar home the next morning. Mr. Musahar engulfed his son in a wordless embrace before turning into the house, every line of his face etched in sadness.

Ram's stepmother walked beside the family limo as it backed out and refused to unclasp her hand from his until the last second. From what little Julie had seen of this distant woman, it was a startling display of emotion.

On the highway, Julie waited until a comfortable silence lay between them. "Your father told me you were an orphan. Is it true?"

Ram nodded and sank further into the plush leather.

Julie couldn't imagine this gregarious man as a lonely orphan. Ram loved meeting people and making his coworkers feel appreciated.

"Was it terrible?"

"Not at all. I was better off there than in a foreign boarding school. The ayyas looked after us like their own children. We were all in the same predicament, so it felt like I had hundreds of brothers and sisters. Even when I was home during school breaks, I never felt as loved as I'd been at the orphanage."

Convinced there must be more he wanted her to know, she caught Ram's eye and held on.

"I was already in my teens when I found out he was my biological father and not a distant relative." Ram wore the same hurt expression she imagined from that day. "He told me my mother died giving birth to me and he was too busy starting the dairy to be bothered with me. Something about an investment from a foreign soap conglomerate. It gave him and my uncle the profits to build their own factory. As if that would matter to a teenager."

"But Ram, it's incredible. A dream come true for any Indian company."

Ram scowled at her. "So what? He lied to me. He doesn't have a single photo of my mother. I've always wanted to know what she looks like." Ram gazed out his window. "He's *still* lying. I think he killed her."

Whoa. What happened to: My father isn't so bad — ya' know? Ram was either in denial most of the time about this dark side of his father, or delusional.

He continued to stare out his window. "Maybe my mother had an affair. Wives are killed for far less here. I might not be his biological son, after all. Mayawati might figure into it, too. He won't even utter my mother's name."

She had an urge to ask if Ram had anything other than a hunch but could hear Paula already. *This man who wants to marry you, has gone to hell and back for you, and all you can do is belittle his beliefs?*

Julie caressed Ram's shoulder and gently turned his face to hers. In his tortured confusion she saw a piece of herself.

"I've never felt comfortable around my stepmother either," Ram said. "She can be strange. I was ten when I caught her in the garden chopping the head off a puppy. When she saw me, she ran off with a sack in her hands and left the headless body behind."

"What the hell. She has Rocky."

"She's kind enough. I don't dislike her. My father said it was already dead, but I was sure scared of her afterward."

Julie slipped her shaking hand into Ram's.

"When I was older, he told me she practiced Black Magic at the local cemetery. Took animal heads there for her spells. He thought it was funny. Said he didn't mind since it was her only flaw." Ram sighed. "It happens. The police find a headless body in some backward community and suspect rituals. Of course, those people aren't already dead."

"You mean people are murdered and their heads chopped off for Black Magic? That's medieval."

"The police don't care," Ram said, "because it's always the lower castes doing this stuff to each other."

All the way to the airport Julie thought of heads rolling around in cemeteries. And fathers who abandoned their children at orphanages. Ram's family was not what she thought, after all.

III

Kathmandu, 2005

Julie couldn't understand why Ram chose to hitch himself to a controversial and dirty energy source when he knew full well the future lay in anything but petroleum.

"There's so many choices besides oil. You could build wind turbines. No lack of wind on these mountains." She motioned out the window of their brick bungalow at the Himalayan range enclosing Kathmandu.

"Hmf." All he offered was a glance over the top of his newspaper.

He was doing it again. Or rather, not doing it. Ram no longer wanted to debate how to save humanity. At some point during their first year together their political banter stopped being a prelude to sex and began having the opposite effect.

She didn't blame him. The thrill of discovering oil deposits had lost its charge. He arrived home with an inertia so contrary to the man she knew it sometimes scared her.

At the slightest glimmer of the old playfulness, Julie tried to entice him into the dance once more. "What about solar? These new lithium batteries are able to store more energy all the time."

"Uh, huh. Lithium."

"Ram? Ram."

He dropped his newspaper into his lap, accordion-style. "I am a geologist in the oil industry. I dig things up or pump things out. That's it."

Julie pouted. "You're wasting your talents. You could do so much good in the environmental protection field."

"Hey." His face brightened into a goofy grin. "Uranium comes out of the ground. I can switch to nuclear energy. It's one of my favorites."

"Errr."

"Come on. I'm just trying to get you going. Lighten up."

Those who knew him best thought his life within Big Oil reeked of an irony. As one friend said: "It's not you. It makes me think of fat fuckers in toupees who hang out in strip clubs with glasses of whiskey, neat."

Far removed from that stereotype, Ram thrived among the details of his scientific journals and gazed into the ethers of deep space at eleven-dimensional planes of possibilities. He had his utopian dream of how the nuclear age would bring electrical-powered prosperity to every dark, impoverished corner of India. How it could single-handedly put back together everything broken since the British left.

Yet each morning at the wildcat wells, he awoke to the past. Lumbered along the powdery rims of dust bowls on high mountain steppes which some cost-benefit analysis had underlined. Past camel trains bobbing heavy with Bedouin wares.

He returned at dusk in the open Rover, a gloomy wind already biting into his face, to the clapboard trailer, devoid of amenities, with the stinking chemical toilets out back and sonorous gas generators that never abated.

Every day, no matter how trivial, he tapped out emails to her: *Going out to the site tomorrow. This is the most desolate place I've ever seen. And it's fucking cold here. Love you, Ram.*

The Great Rift Valley, alive with giraffes and lions, pyramid-dotted deserts of Egypt, or blue and green jungles of Brazil. To Julie, each one was as precious as a feathered dreamcatcher spinning in the sun.

To him—just another Roadside Hellhole.

Still, in the early days of Kathmandu, they lived the grand romance. He flew in from the field, chilled and oil-stained, longing for sweet-smelling skin, soft to the touch. She filled their chipped claw-foot tub up to the brim with steaming-hot water heated on the gas burners in aluminum buckets. They eased in up to their chins, drifting, being reborn in this watery womb.

He pounded out his reports during the first week, then ordered the office not to call unless it was an emergency. There was an urgency to his lovemaking, the interludes lasting about a month until he began to pace and was gone, off to a new desolation.

Their Kathmandu bungalow stood jammed against a hillside with the other crumbling dwellings thrown up after the earthquake of 1934. Most days, Julie rode her scooter into the core to write at her favorite cafés, clustered amongst the patchwork of winding side-streets surrounding one of the city's soaring bell-shaped stupas.

She never tired of this backdrop of gilded-gold and bone-white peaks, where Tibetan refugee women in long multi-colored aprons and ochre-robed monks spun prayer wheels past black granite Buddhas and griffins.

The steep stone stairways which ran in parallel lines down to their neighborhood square were the only routes in and out. The two-hundred-seventy-five stairs to their door was an inconvenience Julie was willing to put up with to be above the thumping festival music and megaphones during raucous political protests. Ram withheld judgement as he only had to climb them every second month.

❀Ram flew in from the Brazil field project at the start of their third winter in Kathmandu and Julie greeted him with the news that Rocky had collapsed and died suddenly. Julie thought back to the stone thrown by the fisherman and wondered if it was a blood clot which had formed.

The next morning, unable to sleep, she crept out to their stone terrace and curled up under a blanket beside the trickling terrazzo fountain. She smelled snow in the air.

The engagement ring on her finger sparkled as she lifted the coffee cup. Ram had insisted on buying the diamond in India to get more for his money, but she guessed his real motivation was that his family accept her through a ring all would honor.

The white wedding hadn't materialized. Julie didn't need it—she had Ram. Now in management, Ram, unfortunately, had his job. Even in Kathmandu, he stationed himself in front of his laptop from early morning until long after dark to coincide with Stockholm's workday. Julie couldn't understand this steadfast dedication in the face of his growing distaste for tedious boardroom meetings.

Neither was Julie any more fulfilled by her writing. Her desire to find the Jesus manuscript was still alive, but the only remnant of that dream was a fridge-top coffee can marked *Ladakh Fund.* Every few months, she dusted it off, opened it to look at the meagre amount inside, and returned it to its lonely corner.

With Kathmandu's English newspaper in hand, Julie shuffled to where Ram sat hunched over his laptop. "Winter's coming. Look. This is the last outdoor concert at the Reggae Beat tonight."

Ram groaned but didn't look up from his screen.

"Come on. We should go."

"You see all this work?" He waved a hefty report at her but kept his attention on the screen. "Go find a story to write. If you're bored, why not fly over to Hong Kong or Thailand."

"Because you might be gone when I get back."

"You're being silly."

No. She wasn't. Ram had become like a visiting lover. One time, when he came and went from his field project before she arrived back from her story, they were apart for four months.

He removed his hands from the keyboard and looked at her. "You were much happier looking for that manuscript thing."

"And how in hell am I supposed to cross the border into India?" The question overflowed with the frustration she felt every time she lifted the lid on the coffee can.

Ram swiveled his office chair so abruptly she jumped back. "Then find another way in."

He had a point, so that's exactly what she did. She discovered another way into India. Buoyed by her new scheme, she soon replaced the coffee can with a bank account.

Unfortunately, in the banal activity of Julie's hillside crow's nest she'd lost the sensibility the world continued to convulse itself inside-out with violence, and it wasn't long before Ram brought the residue home with him.

The door slammed. Ram was home, this time from the Nigerian oil project. She heard his briefcase hit the floor, then light flooded both the kitchen and living room before the fridge door snapped shut. Beer in hand, he plodded into the living room where Julie backhanded tears from her cheeks while one of Andrea Bocelli's classical hits reached a fever pitch from the corner CD player.

Without so much as glancing at her, he flicked off the volume and dropped into his overstuffed man-chair, shaking out the newspaper in his hands. "How long are you going to let that Italian make you cry?" Ram said, as if expecting an answer from the stories in front of him.

"I know." She swung her body in a dramatic arc onto the armrest of his chair and pecked his cheek. "But it makes me so deliciously sad."

He didn't move an iota. A pair of dark crescents underlined bloodshot eyes.

"What is it?" Julie sat and rubbed the back of his head.

"You don't want to know." He rattled his pages.

She waited.

"Another bombing. Not at the pipeline though." Ram folded up the paper and shifted to face her. "They destroyed part of the Niger Delta refinery. Two of my guys are dead. Both foreign nationals. Remember that young Canadian engineer from Calgary I liked so much? I had to phone his parents yesterday and tell them his body would arrive by private jet. Anyway, what's left of it."

They were the Ogoniland Front for Freedom from Oil Bondage. Julie admired their mandate to stop oil spills on tribal lands, and halt government seizure of those lands for distribution to the Western-based oil corporations.

Frustrated with the glacial pace of political lobbying, a Robin Hood inspired offshoot had sprung up to siphon oil from the pipelines and sell it on the black market. How quickly the media had lost sight of how the rebel money was helping destitute local tribes, choosing instead to focus on the fighting between guerrilla rebels and the oil corporations' soldiers.

"Such a violent episode for you to deal with," she said. "I hate to see anyone suffer whether it's a fellow Canadian, or tribal children dying of malnutrition."

The whites of Ram's eyes flashed at her.

Why in hell did I say such an insensitive thing? "Do you need a drinking buddy?" she asked. "I promise to keep my foot out of my mouth. Or, even better, why don't I fill the tub, get out that djembe drum you brought back, and do my striptease again?"

Ram's scowl turned to disgust. He rose and pulled a dusty bottle of whisky from the cabinet and took a long swig.

He's right. Alarmed, she saw herself as if from far away. *While a country tears itself apart over oil, we fill our homes with endless crap we don't need, and I sit in my paradise making flippant comments about musical striptease. Have I really become so complacent in my comfort?*

'Shame on you' is what anti-nuke Mary would say. There was no voice more vociferous against the rampant greed of the oil corporations than the matriarch of the Ploughshares Three. "Such a godless line of work to be in," she once said.

God vs. Big Oil. That would finally even the playing field.

Julie sipped her beer in silence, trying to sort through this while Ram read his documents and downed a third of the whiskey.

He rose to his feet and read aloud from the paper in his hand: "'We seek to repatriate the Niger Delta's oil revenues for the impoverished people of this region. We will not stop until we have destroyed the capacity of the Nigerian government to export oil. You must surely realize the

Nigerian government cannot protect your workers or your assets. Leave our land while you still can — or die in it.'"

He threw it on the coffee table as if releasing something sticky. "That's from the Ogoniland Front, addressed to me personally, *Ramprasad Musahar, Niger Delta Chief Well-site Geologist, PetroCarbonSwede*. So. What's for supper?" His sarcasm meant the whiskey had done its job.

❧It took a week for Ram to emerge from his bender, and when he did, he had put the deaths behind him. Back to the cheeky irreverence she loved.

Julie tugged a paper from the printer and waved it around. "With the money from this assignment I can finally buy my tickets."

"You're leaving me?" Ram said in a monotone from inside the kitchen.

She walked in, planted a hard kiss on his forehead, and stepped back from where he circled a ladle inside a pot of chili.

"The point is, I could if I wanted to. I will now be within striking distance of having the money for …?" She arched her eyebrows.

He winced at first. "You're still on that scroll thingy about Jesus in India?"

"I will *never* let it go. Not until I find it."

Ram dried his hands on his pants to embrace her tightly, all but burying her words: "I'll be famous and probably rich, too."

"Sweetheart," he said over her head, "if you didn't insist on paying half the rent, you would've had enough for this trip a long time ago. I'll write you a blank check right now."

He released Julie and stepped away, but she pulled him back. "I don't need your money."

He groaned. "Not this again."

The first time Julie's thirst for financial independence drove a wedge between them was when they visited Stockholm together. Stunned at the prices on a menu, she told Ram she couldn't see herself living there. She insisted on paying her own way with everything. When Ram whined that he felt emasculated, Julie quipped, "Then go get yourself a gold digger on the side and we'll all be happy."

Tonight was Ram's turn to joke. "You're sure I can't interest you in the life of a concubine?" As he tried to snag Julie by the waist again, she arched an eyebrow. "You should have stuck with that Swedish girl of yours."

Ram looked away — but not nearly quick enough.

Julie clung to the panic in his eyes. "How long have you been screwing her?" Getting no immediate response, she kicked his foot and raised her voice. "Huh?"

"It was only the once. After the fight about the photo card I flew to New York, but you and I weren't really together yet."

She snorted and shook her head. "Your face says *fresh fuck*."

Ram clutched his stomach as though he might throw up.

It struck her how high his pedestal had become. *Stay with it. Give him time to count them up.*

"Since we got together I've been with Alana four times. That is the absolute truth. I tell her not to contact me, but when I'm in Stockholm her friend at head office tips her off."

He stopped and stared. She would not rescue him from the uncomfortable silence.

"The last time was after the bombing. I was loaded and …" Ram pressed his hands to his head. "Before that it was more than a year. It is completely over."

"You stood at the top of a lighthouse four years ago and told me it was over, too. Bastard. I trusted you." Julie picked up her purse and jacket. Before walking out, she said, "I was kidding when I told you to find yourself a fucking gold digger."

When she allowed Ram into her bed two weeks later, a chilly divide remained down the middle. At times in the past she doubted his love, but it was always short-lived. Since discovering his infidelity, she found herself deep in that dread every waking moment.

➶She waited for him to climb into bed, impatient to get on with the conversation she'd rehearsed all day, convinced it would get them back on track to happier times.

"Ram?"

"Mmm …" He didn't stir.

"Why don't you ask your company for conference calls from here? That way we could spend more time together."

"I can't do that."

"Can't or won't?" She shifted to shake off her climbing anxiety.

"I can't. That's what I said. Why is my travel such a problem after all these years?" He switched on the bedside light. "I said I'm sorry. What more can I say?" A shrill, unrecognizable voice came at her. "I'M SORRY. I can say it until I turn blue and pass out. Would that make you happy?"

"I want to have a baby. It's time. I'm almost thirty-four." She was on autopilot, still going with her script.

"Oh, Jesus. Where did this come from? I'm so goddamn tired. I can't go fight with the world and come back and fight with you, too. I need down time and a baby sure as shit isn't going to give me that."

His tone moderated as his head hit the pillow. "Honey, please, you're driving me crazy. Let's just sleep." Ram flicked off the light and when she thought he had fallen asleep, he turned away on his side and mumbled, "Why are women so needy?"

Julie lay immobile, off-track and confused. She didn't sleep at all. She thought about what he'd said and of another time she'd heard it. *She's driving me crazy. Why do women want so badly to have babies?*

At the time, she felt sorry for the woman he was talking about. Julie was now that woman and she knew what came next—Ram would leave her.

➶As the end of his month-long break from field work approached, she expected the call any day.

"I'm leaving on Sunday for work." Ram leaned against the kitchen counter with a beer in his hand while Julie washed up the dinner dishes. His infidelity had injected a new tension into every corner of their bungalow that no amount of casual posturing would ease.

"They've got a conference in the Stockholm office around mapping data from the Brazil fields. I tried to send my ideas through the network but they're adamant that I be there."

Julie knew about these conferences during which the staff disappeared down a rabbit hole for days to bounce theories off one another. While Ram hated the stuffy sessions, he also despised being in the field most of the time. Therein lay Ram's disaffection with his life.

"Come with me, Jul." The forced perkiness did tug at her heart a touch. "It's been so long since you've seen the place. I'll be in meetings until late every day, but you might find a story there. It'll be fun."

Julie lifted her head and smiled half-heartedly while circling the rim of a glass with her dishrag. *I do love him still,* she thought.

What of my own secrets? Funding terrorism. Helping his brother dispose of a body. How do those compare with his infidelity? Equal? No, probably worse.

"Sounds good," Julie said. "But I've got to shoot a Thangka display in Bhaktapur and, of course, I can't miss the Shivaratri for the in-flight. You know. The one you call the hashish festival."

Ram rolled his eyes; he didn't do drugs. He slipped his arm around her waist and kissed her.

While still entwined, Julie whispered, "I don't think I could stand to be alone in that penthouse where you were with her. Sorry sweetie."

Using his broad arms, Ram drew her into him as if he wanted to absorb her into his very being. Still, her tape kept looping back on itself: *Why are you so needy, Julie? You're driving me crazy. You're driving me away. It's obvious — he's not coming back.*

As usual, she stayed until his flight took off from Kathmandu's airport then caught a taxi home. As she hung her jacket on the hook by the door, her hands trembled. A jolt of electricity spliced the air and shattered into particles around her, stinging her skin and pounding in her eardrums. The walls sagged and slid in on her.

She staggered outside to draw fresh air into her aching lungs and screamed at the precipice of stairs.

Her landlord ran from her house next door and steered Julie into the family's garden until the panic passed.

She hadn't had a panic attack since her first intimacy with Ram.

The next day she biked to the Bagmati River for the Shiva festival. Near sunset the place filled with near-naked holy men toting hash-pipes.

That evening, after sending the story off — more panic. The next week she hopped on the bus for the Bhaktapur exhibition but had another one halfway there. That piece never got done.

❈ "I want to go home. Can you come and take me back?"

Waves crashed at Paula's end of the call. "What do you mean?"

"I want to go back to Cedarwood. To your house. *Our* home."

"What's going on? Is Ram there?"

"He left me. He went to Stockholm."

"What in blazes?"

At Paula's end she called to Goran and whispered for him to phone Ram.

"No," Julie said. "Please don't call him. I'd go myself but I'm having panic attacks all over the place."

❈ "You didn't phone him, right?" Julie asked Paula a few days later at the Kathmandu bungalow.

"Not me," Paula said, and glanced at Goran who was stretched out on Julie's sofa. "I had more than enough matchmaking during the Vakkali days. Goran?"

Goran reared up from his supine posture. "Nope. Me neither."

"Good," Julie said.

"You're sure it's just the two bags?" Paula hoisted a duffle bag onto her shoulder.

Julie nodded.

"Your laptop is in the backpack Goran's going to carry, then?" Paula asked.

"Nope. It's over there under those magazines on the coffee table."

Goran extracted a twisted lump of gray metal from the pile. "*This* is a laptop?"

"Not anymore, I guess. I had an altercation with it last night. I don't see myself writing anytime soon. I like the idea of spending time with that naturopath of yours," she said to Paula.

Goran slapped a staccato beat against the tiles with one foot and cracked up before launching himself through the front door with Julie's backpack dangling from his shoulder. Already halfway down the first flight, he bellowed, "Don't forget to lock the door."

"Tsk." Paula frowned and stood in front of Julie. "Are you okay to go, honey?"

It was a viable question considering Julie's waning energy.

The end of her second month in Cedarwood, Julie sat at Paula's kitchen table, recapping her latest session with the holistic counselor. "She's asking about my family background now. There's so much I still don't know about Doni's death. Do you ..." Julie halted mid-sentence.

"Sorry, sweetie. What was that?"

Something much deeper than packing for her upcoming meditation retreat was on Paula's mind.

"I'm biking to Aunt Dot's to ask why she's been protecting my mother."

Paula's face dropped, still as a stone.

"I should have done this a long time ago." Under the table, Julie stamped her foot. "What's wrong with me? She's just an old woman."

In an instant, Paula's raspy voice turned deep and fierce. "She wasn't always old." She leaned across the table to Julie. "You've done well, my friend."

"No, I haven't. I didn't help Doni, did I?"

"It wasn't up to you to save him."

"But I could have."

"No. You couldn't. You were five years old."

Julie pushed herself from the table and shuffled to the window with the mechanical weariness of someone much older. Out there was the Kettle River — and Doni's trembling, blue lips. During that summer of 1979, whenever a spackled steely light filtered through the birch leaves outside her childhood window and rippled along the ceiling like a stream, it reminded her of the car's interior, an echo of real waves against the dash.

❀The night of the murder Mrs. Sara Paglia drove to the edge of the riverside park's deserted lot and got out. Julie sat with Doni in the front. Sam stayed in the backseat with their baby sister.

The Paglia kids often ran wild in playgrounds while Sara Paglia smoked and paced beside the station wagon. Never after dark, though. Never beside the Kettle River after a record-breaking snowmelt washed away the shoreline's lawn.

Outside, a match sizzled. The end of her cigarette glowed in the rearview mirror.

Behind Julie, Sam flung open his door. At nine years old, he no longer feared the dark.

Thump.

"Stay in the goddamn car," his mother told him.

Julie stood on the front seat, beside Doni, and stared at her mother through the back window. She blew smoke rings through the fish lips she sometimes made, but it wasn't funny this time. Her eyes bugged out and her hands were flat, pushing against the glass.

"Sam. There she is. Is Mummy trying to get in?"

Sam twisted. "Oh, no. Take off Doni's seatbelt. Hurry." He yanked at the baby's straps.

Something bad must be after them. Julie waved her arms. "Mummy. Here we are." She started to cry. "Use the door."

The station wagon jolted forward.

It tumbled over a ledge and slammed her to the floor. "Muuummmy!"

She rolled with the car, further and further away. "Sam." Tears and snot flowed together. "Where are you?" For the first time in her life—she was alone.

She remembered her mother's hands pushing against the window. That was Julie's last thought before something smashed into her nose. Everything went quiet and dark.

When she woke on her side, bits of dinner peas and corn kernels floated before her eyes in the icy water.

A screeching stray cat blasted her ears.

Doni?

She climbed on the seat and against the rising water and Doni's flailing arms, tugged at the metal clasp holding him. "Stop hitting me!" River water the colour of blood dribbled down her chin.

He fell loose.

She tried to lift him into the back seat where the door still hung open, but his legs wobbled like noodles.

"Crawl over, Doni. You can do it."

His teeth chattered above the water gurgling around their armpits. "I can't. Ju—lie." He whimpered for the one person she knew wouldn't save them, then fell silent, his arms cold and slippery like a salmon she once saw on a dock, no longer moving except for the mouth.

Opening. Closing. Opening. Closing.

"I'm going over," she croaked. "You can float to me."

It made no sense, but in a child's world, all things are possible.

His blue lips quivered. Tiny fingers, stiff with terror, slipped away from hers. Doni sank from view.

Someone yanked Julie from the car onto the pebbled beach and when she raised her head, the black current was swallowing the station wagon in great gulps.

Aunt Dot's usually flawless make-up hung like melted wax on her wrecked face. She held Sam's hand and in Aunt Dot's arms the baby cried.

Julie clung to her hips and felt her aunt's body spasm. *Where was Doni and what was her mother doing below them?*

At the water's edge, her mother squatted, and splashed water down her dress like a preening duck. She turned to them. "Is it enough?"

As if forcing her head through sludge, Aunt Dot nodded. Through tears, she pried at Julie's fingers and pointed to her truck down the street. "Oh, sweetie. I promise not to drive away until I see the police arrive. Be a brave girl, now."

Julie didn't want to let go of Doni—then or now. Perhaps Paula was right. She had to.

—❀—While Julie hauled Paula's bike from the shed, she heard the back porch's screen door slam and felt something rubbery placed in her hand.

"Sam asked me to return this to its owner," Paula said, uncupping her hand from her friend's palm.

With barely a glance, Julie shoved the rubber duck into Paula's chest as if it were on fire. "Nope. No. I can't go there."

"You *can*. He wanted *me* to do it. It should be you." She unzipped Julie's jacket, slipped the duck into the inside pocket and whispered in Julie's ear. "You can."

—❀—As soon as the yellow dot disappeared from view on the Kettle River, Julie pedaled the rest of the way across the railway bridge and headed out of town, following the rock-strewn road which once served as a railbed.

Near the end of her aunt's narrow lane she shuddered at the sight of the house.

"Julie," Aunt Dot said, emerging. "Well, isn't this a wonderful surprise. Sara told me you were back in town."

Julie managed a wan smile, wanting to start the business at hand on a proper tone. She glanced sidelong at the front window where Uncle Hank peeked from behind the curtain. Not overly friendly the last time she saw him, Julie had no reason to think he'd changed.

"Can we chat by the lake?" Julie asked.

If Cedarwood had a paradise, this wisp of a lake, shared with one neighbor, was it. One mile long by half-a-mile wide, a jeweled hush skimmed its surface and cradled a reflection of peaks and craggy grottos.

As a child, Julie floated with her brother, sister, and cousin within its twinkling subterranean pools. They bounced their voices into secluded caverns where they imagined pearly water nymphs and elves dwelled.

Where Aunt Dot and Julie stood shoulder to shoulder at the shore, she crouched, and swept a branch from the overhead pine in a wide arc over the water, sending ripples in every direction. "I hear they're building a new wing at the hospital," Julie said. "Naming it after that doctor who delivered Doni." Her dead brother's name hit the water and the weight of it sucked the sun from the sky.

Julie rose. Rather than the shame she expected, her aunt's face was a mask of exhaustion.

"I couldn't understand why you took her side. We needed you on ours."

"Her side?" said Aunt Dot. "If anything, I was on my own side. I decided a long time ago not to let Doni's drowning ruin my life, too."

"You didn't give a shit?"

Her aunt pressed her palms to her forehead. "Nooo … I'm not explaining myself. I wouldn't allow Hank to ruin my life. That what I meant."

"What does he have to do with any of this?"

"Have you never wondered why we happened to arrive at the river in time to pull you from the car? They were having an affair. Him and your mother. For years. Over there." Her aunt pointed at the wooden boathouse.

Julie walked and stood with her hands on her hips as if the old shack was to blame for everything.

"That's how they hid it for so long," her aunt said, coming alongside. "On Sundays, when I took Bobby to sports games and you kids went to mass with your father. They even used it in winter with a kerosene heater." Her aunt shook her head and grimaced. "Sara thought she was in love, but Hank told me he used her for sex. Can you imagine, doing that to my own sister?"

Julie pulled her gaze from the shack. "She tried to drown us kids because he left her. Is that it?" Unravelling her rancor at each new twist, she added, "I don't care how old she is. It's time she's held accountable for what she did. That's what I've come to tell you."

Aunt Dot touched Julie's arm. "When so much time has passed some secrets should never come to light."

Julie didn't believe that crap. Not then, or ever. And told her aunt as much just before Hank's voice drifted to them.

"Listen, we've got an appointment to sign over the garage to Bobby. There's something else I should tell you."

Julie agreed not to contact the police until after the family dinner at her sister's house in a week's time. Ram would be in Cedarwood by then, too, for support.

At the end of a handful of phone calls Julie accepted from Ram during her treatment, she told him she was at a crossroads. After the last one, she realized that was likely where they were at in their relationship, too.

Ram had so readily revealed the darkness in his heart around his father, yet she still could not trust him with the most defining event of her life. She didn't need anyone to tell her, unless she did, unless she stopped holding back the most intimate part of herself, Ram's love for her would never survive.

When Julie phoned Ram in the field to say she'd been seeing a psychiatrist in Okanagan Valley, he asked if it would help their sex life. Riding on the vast range in the shadow of hump-alone-mountain, he seemed ever hopeful her libido would improve—but the anti-anxiety medication made it non-existent.

"Sure, we can have sex," she said. But if he wanted intimacy, that was something else.

Their first night in bed at the well-worn gold rush era hotel, Ram brought her hand to his crotch out of a comfortable habit, but when he shifted to face her, she flashed a nervous smile and turned her back to him.

The trust which he had laboriously watered and tended since they became a couple, died when Julie found out about Alana. Given the slightest opening, she also knew Ram would claim it was her fear of intimacy which caused him to stray in the first place.

❦Because Aunt Dot insisted everyone meet Ram, after six nights at the hotel, they made the hour-long drive to the upscale Okanagan Valley home of Julie's younger sister, called Little Sara. On the way, Julie filled Ram in on Uncle Hank's affair with her mother but stopped short of revealing Doni's murder. Her mother was called Big Sara, Julie said, and when Ram asked if she was an imposing figure, Julie guffawed. "Only in her own mind. Her lung disease has whittled her down to ninety-five pounds."

As they pulled up, Julie spotted her uncle entering the house and her head sank to the dashboard. Dot had assured her he wasn't coming.

"We don't have to go in if it upsets you," Ram said.

"Julie. Oh, my god. They said you might be here." Her sister-in-law, Carol, stuck her round, rosy cheeks in through the open passenger window and gave Julie a hug. A coy grin tugged at the sides of her mouth as she leveled an inquisitive gaze at Ram. "Thank you for taking care of our Julie."

They were caught. If they ran into anyone else, they could beat a retreat, but Carol was someone Julie truly missed. It would be the next best thing to having the brother she loved with her today.

As Julie emerged from the vehicle, Carol, a perky, albeit naive, girl, who had no concept of the world beyond Cedarwood, grasped Julie's elbow. "They say Sam killed that man. You don't think he killed him, do you? *I* don't think he did."

Julie's aunt had updated her on Sam's latest incarceration—this time for life on aggravated assault and second-degree murder. *Yes*, Julie thought, *I do think Sam killed that man and probably a few more nobody knows about.* Jail was a good place for her brother, where he couldn't hurt his children, or wife, or anybody else, while he still seethed with resentment.

They'd release him when he was old and feeble. Until then, he was better off as a prisoner—as he'd been his entire life.

Once inside, Julie nudged Ram to where her mother sat, pressed down into an overstuffed chair and looking like a corpse being fed with oxygen. Her phlegmy lips vibrated between each drag on her cigarette.

"Mum."

Her mother looked up and frowned.

"This is Ram, my partner."

The old woman hesitated, then said in a rasping drone: "What kind of business?"

"No. I mean we've been living together for over four years."

One lifeless eyeball, barely visible at the bottom of its veined tunnel, rolled around in an attempt to size up Ram, before turning away with disinterest.

Uncle Hank, watching baseball on television, twitched in recognition as the couple passed by. Aunt Dot already lavished hugs on Ram at the entrance.

Julie tucked Ram in behind the bar in the games room where he could drink and serve his only "customer," cousin Bobby, already listing on his stool.

Little Sara insisted she show Julie her new house. The rambling rancher was awash in dreary variations of creamy white. Objects, including her three-year-old twins, playing in the basement games room, appeared to have ordained stations.

Little Sara rattled on outside the upstairs sauna. "We put in an indoor hot tub, but let me tell you, they *do* cause mold, so we ripped that out and put in a steam room, but Bill's blood pressure is so high I'm afraid I might find his parboiled butt tit's up in there some weekend after shopping."

Still turning her brother-in-law's flushed buttocks over on the rotisserie of her mind's eye, Julie jumped at a sharp yelp behind her.

"Here it is! I've been looking everywhere for this." Her sister yanked at something jammed inside a laundry hamper. "I thought you could use this." She almost fell over as the knotted blob came loose. "It has a little wine stain and the threads caught and puckered along this side, but otherwise you probably have something that would go with lime polka-dots."

Mesmerized, Julie peered down and scrunched her face as she imagined a surgeon might upon discovering a malignant pustule in the testicles of a ninety-year-old.

"Oh. It's a scarf." Grasping it gingerly, she dropped the green pustule into a side pocket of her handbag.

❧Stifled, girlish giggles burst from the hallway behind where Julie and Ram sat at the dining table.

"Hey," Little Sara bellowed.

"Don't tell me you gave the nanny the day off," her husband said.

"We haven't had a nanny for a week, Bill. I fired her. She was stealing."

"Oh no. What did she steal?" Carol's brow wrinkled with a childlike gullibility.

"I don't know yet. But she gave me the creeps. Always sneaking around."

"What the hell kind of a mother would abandon her children in the Philippines, anyway?" Bill said.

"The kind that needs the money, I would think," Julie said.

"Well, Jesus, she can collect welfare for that," Bill said.

"Maybe there isn't any welfare in the Philippines, or not enough to live on." She folded one arm into another across her chest and Bill's eyes bored into hers.

"That's what taxes are for. Are you telling me they don't have taxes in the Philippines?"

Bill was hardly the informed debating opponent Julie enjoyed. She glanced at her watch and groaned, a mere twenty minutes since the canapés and wine arrived.

"What the hell is holding up the caterers?" As their host barged through the French door leading to the kitchen the corners of Little Sara's mouth twitched upward.

"Do you spin yarns for a living like Julie, Ram?" Aunt Dot sat across from the couple.

"No, the only things I write are Letters to the Editor."

Even after Little Sara jumped in with a smug, "Ha … ha. Very funny," Aunt Dot pushed on with her congenial attempt at uniting everyone. "There were some great yarns told at the farm around that wood stove when we were growing up, weren't there, Sara?"

From the head of the table Big Sara wheezed.

Sullen, Uncle Hank sat in his own world directly across from Ram, who looked increasingly uncomfortable—and not only because Bobby had passed out against his right shoulder.

With Aunt Dot losing her battle, Julie reached for what was left of the wine.

"*This* is a special cheesecake from Cheesecake Heaven." Little Sara set it in front of Julie with flourish. "'*Our CHEESE … cakes never stop smiling*' is their motto. Get it? Cheeeese."

Who gives a shit? Julie thought.

"Don't you ever get more than you bargained for gallivanting around?" Uncle Hank curled his lip at Julie.

"No, never." She felt Ram's gaze burning into her.

"How did you guys meet?" Carol's dreamy voice asked.

Bless her heart, Julie thought. *Always looking for the romance in everything since it's so lacking in her own life.*

"I met Ram on the beach, I guess. Didn't I?" It tickled her that Ram's smile meant he also thought of the night of the rabid dog as their first meeting.

"Was he homeless?" Everyone turned in time to see Uncle Hank glance down at what was obviously Aunt Dot kicking him under the table.

Ram's eyes narrowed and Julie cringed.

"How romantic." Carol cupped her chin and gazed at Ram, but Little Sara used the information for a splenetic quip. "Nobody could keep Julie away from the bad boys with ponytails. Hell, by the time she finished high school she'd jumped into bed with every one of them. There's something you probably didn't know, eh Ram?"

Julie said nothing, determined to keep peace with Ram present.

"That. Is. E … nough." The wheezing matriarch slammed a veined fist down, sending the empty gravy boat dancing to the table's edge, and Sara bounding forward. "Jesus, mum, this is limited edition Royal Doulton Baroness." She turned the china over in her hands.

"Royal Doulton Ba … ro … ness," her mother mocked, a violent coughing fit cutting the performance short.

Julie slumped. *Time to head out.*

Before she and Ram could do that, Uncle Hank threw himself into the ring once more. "Sounds like India was a

Julie stood outside the Paglia family home on Willow Street.

So her aunt's claims were true. Julie's mother had jacked up the condemned house and poured a new foundation. She had returned to it after almost twenty years in the same Spanish colonial vineyard home which the Paglia's moved to in Okanagan Valley when Julie was fourteen.

Those who didn't know Mrs. Sara Paglia likely thought she was hard up for money. Nobody knew, nor would she say, how much was in a bank account from the sale of their prime vineyard land to a developer. But it was likely in the millions of dollars.

Once again, Julie pulled the loose brick from the porch to find the house key.

Inside, she spotted a figure lying on a couch in the same alcove as years earlier, and, as then, wearing her papa's clothes. Bolder than before, she side-stepped toward the man, leaned over and whipped the cap off his head. Two fixed eyeballs stared back.

"I suppose you came for your money."

Julie wheeled in the direction of the voice. "What the hell is this?" She threw the mannequin's cap at her mother's feet.

"Scares away the thieving little shits." She hobbled toward the kitchen, a cigarette in one hand; in the other was a cane she used to thrash at the tangled mess of oxygen tubing on the floor in front of her. It looked like a slick umbilical cord running from her nose to an unseen hissing monster.

"That greedy Bill can go bugger himself. Nobody's getting anything until I'm dead," her mother said, slumping onto a cot beside the fridge.

If that wasn't an invitation … Julie watched her off the tip of her nose, surprised her sister and Bill hadn't pushed the woman down the basement stairs to expedite that scenario.

"I'll probably go there for dinner and they'll put arsenic in my food."

"I didn't come for the money."

Her mother's bloodshot eyes pierced to the center of her own with suspicion.

"Aunt Dot told me the story about you and Uncle Hank. Why you tried to drown us. Why you killed Doni." It felt good to finally say it. *You killed Doni.* She didn't expect remorse; she knew better. But the contempt coming off her mother as Julie spoke drove a chill into her bones.

"You're always causing trouble wherever you go," her mother croaked. "We were fine before you showed up with that … *thing.* Go away and leave us."

"You bitter old bitch. I'm not leaving until you admit it— you murdered Doni. He was just a baby and you pushed him into the river and drowned him. Say it." Julie hovered over her mother but jumped back as the woman propped herself onto an elbow and swung her cane.

Her mother's chest heaved despite the extra oxygen.

Good. Die. You deserve it. Julie didn't need the confession. She had a better idea. She marched down the hall to the back door. There, plugged into a socket, the oxygen tank hissed. The plastic tubing snaked along the hallway with her mother's life force.

She wrapped her fingers around the electrical cord. *Go on. Unplug it. Nobody will know. When she's dead, plug it back in.*

She imagined her mother's face, rigid with agony, as hers had been in the same spot on the kitchen floor at six years old. As Doni's had been while he slipped beneath the surface of the Kettle River.

Her hand trembled. She closed her eyes and inhaled, long and deep. The machine's hypnotic pulsing rose and fell in rhythm with her own breath.

When she opened her eyes, it was to a dream she never dared create. Was she hallucinating? Julie crept forward to peer at the wall above the oxygen tank. Here they hung, side by side, mounted on black velvet in matching gold frames; her Roman gold coin and *National Geographic* payment receipt never looked more glorious.

The few seconds she stood there, slack-jawed, ticked by like an hour, then she bolted, slamming the back door on her way out.

At the same moment she passed the kitchen window, her mother picked up a wooden cutting board and swung it against her own skull in a sickening *crack*. Julie cringed and looked away. *Crack.* She could hear it outside. *Crack.*

Stop it. Stop hurting yourself. Something inside her shifted. *That's your mother. Do the right thing and go stop her.*

Old grudges die slowly. However right it was, Mrs. Sara Paglia's daughter kept walking.

J ulie and her aunt stood in front of the satellite police portable which had come to Cedarwood.

"What's *he* doing here?" Julie nodded in the direction of her aunt's truck across the street where her mother and uncle sat in the cab.

Aunt Dot hesitated then pointed to a bench on a grassy patch beside the detachment. "Let's sit. There's something that might stop you from turning your mother over to the police."

This moment had been so long in coming Julie doubted anything could trump it, but she still respected her aunt's opinion.

"You remember the drowning was a week after they let her out of the psychiatric ward with baby Sara?" Aunt Dot began when they'd settled in. "Hank told me about the affair, then he phoned Sara to say it was over. That night, before your father got home from his shift, she turned up at our house with you kids in the car and the newborn in her arms."

Julie nodded. "I remember waiting in the car."

"Your mother screamed the baby was Hank's. He could look after it. She didn't want it. I was so shocked I ran into the bedroom and shut the door." Tears formed in the pockets of her aunt's eyes and her lips trembled. "Oh Lord. Why didn't I take the baby from her arms?"

Rather than comfort her aunt, Julie stepped back, numb.

"Sara was in such a state, I told Hank we should go after her. That's when we found her pushing the vehicle into the river under the railway bridge."

Her aunt's chest heaved, her face ragged, as Julie remembered her the night she plunged into the rushing river with Hank. "I stayed while Hank phoned the police anonymously from the hotel but you might remember we took off when the sirens were close."

Their eyes met. "That still doesn't explain why you've protected her."

"It wasn't about protecting *anyone* but myself. What would people think of me? My husband sleeping with my own sister." Her chin trembled. "I asked her one day why she tried to drown you kids. It was supposed to be her and the baby, but she realized what a burden the rest of you would be on your father."

"You've got to be kidding." Julie said this as if it were a surprisingly good joke. "I wish she'd stuck with Plan A to be rid of two bitches at once—her *and* Little Sara."

"You know that's not fair. She's had your mother on her hands all these years. We eventually confirmed it with paternity tests but Little Sara still doesn't know she's her uncle's child."

"Did Papa find out?"

"The three of us thought we were hiding it, but ... He was the one who wanted the paternity test."

"Oh, God. Poor papa." Julie arched back as if to separate herself from the intensity of her aunt's words.

"Your mother pushed the vehicle into the river. But we all played our part. We should have reported it at the time. Christ, I knew she was beating you kids, I should have reported *that*. But in those days people thought children should stay with their mother, no matter what."

"You think *you're* to blame for Doni's death. I thought *I* was because I let go of his hand. Why is it the two people who *are* to blame couldn't care less? Has Uncle Hank ever shown one bit of remorse? I don't know how you've stayed with him."

"I didn't think I could, either," her aunt whispered. "At some point I realized the easiest way to deal with my own despair was to help him with his. It doesn't make what they did right. But we repeat our stories over and over until we come to the end of our life. Then we wonder why we've never had the happiness we deserve.

"It didn't matter to me whether I stayed with him or not, as long as I didn't hold onto the anger and shame. I wanted to love myself. If I stayed with him, I would have to love *him*, too."

Julie slumped and for an instant caught her mother's exhausted expression across the street before it retreated into a mushroom of cigarette smoke.

Dammit. Why muck up a perfectly evil crime with all these other people?

Aunt Dot squeezed Julie's fingers. "Can I tell you something about your mother?"

On the bench, Julie closed her eyes.

"Sara and I were close as kids and I could see she'd been given something terrible through no fault of her own," her aunt said. "She'd drop into those depressions and it was so hard for her to get out of bed. Pa didn't stand for that on the farm. She was so distracted and clumsy. He stopped using her name and called her, 'stupid and lazy.' Stupid and lazy, go collect the eggs. I could have cried along with her each night, it made me so sad."

Thinking the story was over, Julie looked up to see her aunt shaking her head in disbelief.

"I saw him haul off one day in the fields. He hit her so hard she almost fell into the blades of the combine. She was fifteen and I would have been twelve. Early the next morning, I watched her go downstairs into the kitchen and tip all the change inside the cookie jar into a bag. Couldn't have been much more than twenty dollars. For months I noticed whenever Pa gave us change for a sweet in town, she never used hers. She'd been thinking about taking off for a long time.

"I put my coat over my nightie and caught up with her where our driveway met the road into town. Our Chocolate Lab … well, really, old Chico was her dog since he never left her side. When they got to the main road, Sara sat on the ground and Chico put his head in her lap. She was crying so hard I thought she was going to faint.

"Then she got up and marched toward town clutching her suitcase like it was her only friend. She kept turning and yelling at Chico to go home. She finally threw a stone. He yelped and stopped. I imagine she met up with the early Greyhound to Vancouver. She came back three years later but by then Chico had died. She never once went to the farm or saw the old man again. For me, your mother will always be that sad girl stumbling down the road."

Aunt Dot focused her plea on Julie. "Doni's drowning was her cry for help. One that was never answered."

Julie bolted up. "Her cry for help? Is that how you live with it? What about Doni's goddamn cry for help? Or mine? I want to hear her admit to the police she did those things. Like she should have thirty years ago."

At this, her aunt stiffened then let herself fall against the seat. "I'll get them now. Is that what you want?"

"Them? Why's Hank coming in?"

"He thinks everything should come out. We'll be found guilty of obstruction. We deserve it. But think what it will do to Little Sara to realize her mother is a murderer and her uncle is her biological father."

Julie hated that she had not a drop of sympathy for her sister. It came as a shock what little she could muster was for the other Sara—her mother. She remembered a breadboard slamming against a skull. How could she have so callously walked away from that? She clenched her jaw against the tears, but they came anyway. Hot tears for herself, and another sadness entirely unfelt until now.

When she raised her head, her face glistened, red and puffy. "I still hate her."

"Of course, you do, sweetheart. I'm not saying you don't."

"Then you know about the gold coin?"

"Did you say 'coin'?"

"The coin in the frame at her house. You must have seen it by now."

"I still refuse to go in there. I pick her up outside."

"And she never told you about it?"

"What in the world are you talking about?"

Julie twisted in the direction of Aunt Dot's car. There sat a cagey woman who had even honored Julie's request for secrecy. *Oh, my.* A startled grin spread across her tear-streaked face before she doubled over into guffaws. "How many decades have I waited for a bit of respect from her? Well … That woman has a diabolical sense of game play." Julie gasped for air. "She certainly knows how to keep a secret."

Aunt Dot pulled Julie into her. "Sweetheart. Are you okay? You aren't making sense."

Oh. But I am.

❀On Paula's porch, the screen door slammed, and Julie turned from her stargazing to see Ram peeling his cashmere turtleneck over his head.

"Pfft. If it's this warm now, what's it like in July?" He draped the sweater over the railing, snuggled alongside Julie, and tilted his face to the night sky.

"The month of May can be weird," she said, at the exact moment Ram pointed to the stars.

"Mars rising." He flashed a self-satisfied grin. "Thinking what I am?"

"Probably. It's not often a girl gets put in bondage with binocular straps. You made my toes curl with that kiss."

"I'd like to do that all the time."

"You will. I just need time." Her words trailed off as she slid her arms around Ram's waist.

"I've been thinking." Ram's face lit up. "About our baby."

"Oh." Julie unfurled her arms and took a step back to gape at him.

"What? You don't want to have a baby anymore?"

"I still do, but … there's something else I want first." She rubbed her upper arms. "Can we have a honeymoon? I don't need the wedding. Just the trip."

He crinkled his brow. "O—kay. You name the place."

"How about northern India, Ladakh?"

"Yup. Coulda' put money on that answer."

It was no laughing matter for Julie, hardly daring to breathe in anticipation of what he might say.

"It's only been four years since you skipped bail. How will you get around that?"

"Give me your phone and I'll show you."

Ram was never without his phone on his hip.

"First we go home to Kathmandu. From there we go to this remote crossing into India." Julie's fingers danced around the screen. "Just listen to what someone said on TripAdvisor. 'This is the most godforsaken border crossing in the world. When you leave the Nepal side, look back fondly on efficiency, cleanliness and kindness, and prepare for a two-kilometer walk through a no-man's-land of refuse and human feces, ending with a long rickety bridge from which vehicles are barred.'" She paused. "You laugh, but it gets better."

Her voice skipped with excitement. "'Leave a half-day to get through because on the Indian side nobody seems to know what they're doing. And if they do, then it will take forever for someone to pull the forms from under a rotting pile of leftovers. If you get that far, you'll have to put up with verbal abuse.'" Julie glanced up at Ram. "Maybe this is where they wanted their bribe."

She resumed reading. "'You can get the horse-drawn carriage to taxi you across the river, but I wouldn't because you'll soil yourself when the whole freaking bridge sags halfway. If you're on bike like I was, then you're fortunate. I checked into the best hotel in town—a filthy hole infested with fleas and mosquitos—so take your pick.'"

Julie jumped up and down while scrolling through the screens. "Look. One after the other. They all say the same thing. It's perfect. Let's go and you can bribe them with a bottle of whiskey."

Ram plucked at his chin, his expression one of utter confusion. It seemed like hours before he spoke. "Oh, all right. But we better leave soon if we're going to make it to Ladakh by summer."

When Julie shrieked, Paula flung open the door. "What's happening?"

"I'm going on my honeymoon."

IV

Bihar, India, 2006

A few days before they were due to strike out for Nepal's isolated western border with India, Julie emerged from their Kathmandu bungalow's shower as Ram said goodbye on his cell phone.

"That better not be your work or I'll hire thugs to tie you up and stuff you into the trunk of our rental," Julie said, rubbing a towel through her wet hair.

"It was Paula."

"Why didn't she want to talk to me? What's going on?"

"It's Goran. He's missing."

"From where? The last time I saw him, he said goodbye to Paula and me at Kathmandu's airport. Three months ago."

"Vakkali. Probably went to Baba's house to lick his wounds. Paddled out into the surf a few days ago. Never came back." Ram sat and rubbed his temples.

"Lick what wounds?"

Ram hesitated. "I wasn't going to tell you until after our trip to Ladakh." He cupped his palm over his mouth and removed it slowly. "Paula told him it was over about a week after you guys arrived in Cedarwood."

Julie gaped.

"You were going through a lot, so she didn't say anything. Paula phoned me almost every day before I flew in." He raked his hands over his eyes and through his hair as if trying to uproot a throbbing pain.

"She even phoned beforehand to let me know Goran would need support. I'm sure he did, but he never let on. Classic Goran." Ram sank into an easy chair and squinted at the far wall. "They loved each other so much. Did you know that?"

Julie crouched beside him and took his hand between her own. She knew so little of Goran's private world, yet, his bawdy legacy of protest would surely survive long after her own. "I don't know what to say. Paula never mentioned Goran around me because she knew I didn't like the guy."

Ram's eyes finally met hers and flashed hot. "This isn't about you. It's about Paula. It's about me. He was like a brother. But mostly it's about Goran."

He fell silent again and a slow smirk soon wiped the frown from his face. A memory. Like the tedious stories the neighbors had …

Whether Ram realized it or not this wasn't about Goran, after all. Not his serial philandering with dull-eyed society wives nor how he decimated the tenuous good character of an idea through the slashes and swirls of his creations.

Ram was dying to lay bare the most tender parts of himself, the ones he shared over and over with Goran in childhood. She piped up for a recitation of Goran's failings. Better that than the yawn pulling at her lips. "What do you think happened? I mean … between them."

"If I had to guess, she got sick of the cokeheads at the beach. For sure, she hated those New York phonies he rubbed up against to sell his art. But worst of all, he never once visited her log home in Canada. That would have signified commitment on his part because that's where Paula was in her groove. Goran never learned to share the spotlight." Ram stared at the floor. "He was manic-depressive. I doubt Paula found it any easier to deal with than I did.

"Couldn't take it anymore. Got on that board. Started paddling and never stopped. Into the sunset. That's so Goran."

Julie had never seen Ram cry before. The way he sat, slumped sideways on his chair like a broken statue while a single tear trickled over his cheek, was heartbreaking. Was she satisfied? When had she become so hard, manipulating a grieving man into focusing on his dead friend's faults and disclosing mental illness?

How easily she could have confided in Goran about her panic attacks. They had this sadness in common. He would have understood in a way few could. She chewed on her lip, trying to push down the heaviness of how she'd treated him. In the only personal exchange she'd ever had with Goran he accused her of being *a poisonous influence* on Paula.

Was it possible Paula thought this, too? On the news of Goran's possible suicide, her best friend had entrusted her heart to Ram, not Julie. That stung.

❧The next morning, a steady June rain sloshed from the downspout outside the kitchen window while Julie emptied the fridge contents onto the counter.

Ram walked in, cell phone in hand. "I'm sorry. I just talked to Baba. I need to go to Vakkali in case Goran's body turns up."

Julie slammed the fridge door closed so hard Ram winced.

"Goran was like a son to Baba and Mayawati. I should be there for them. You can go ahead and look for your manuscript. I'll catch up with you when I can."

"You know I can't do that. Not without you."

"Why not? What's happened to you? I thought you were serious about finding this thing."

"Don't be mean." She pulled the garbage can over and chucked packages of vegetables into it.

"You certainly can't come with me." Ram pointed out the kitchen window. "I'm flying into India and the last thing you want is airport security."

"I'll follow you by land through the main checkpoint into Bihar."

Ram let out a weary groan and cocked his head skyward. "You're asking for trouble. They deal with truckloads of goods every day. It won't be a gong show like the other crossing."

Julie shrugged. "You won't be with me at the border."

"That's *not* what I'm worried about." His voice boomed across the room. "I care about you. I don't want you in jail again. Why can't you understand that?" He stopped pacing and guffawed. "Oh, yeah. *I'll* be the one paying a bribe if there's trouble."

Julie brightened. "You'll come overland with me?"

"Christ. Cut my losses, I suppose. Bribes to border guards are cheaper than ones to judges."

She thrust out her chin in victory while Ram retreated into the bathroom off the bedroom and slammed the door.

Ram's jeans. Her beach shifts. Everything was scattered before her on the bed. It would be cold up north but hot in Vakkali. As she reached into one of the dresser drawers behind her to dig out Ram's favorite ribbed sweater a scene reflected in the dresser's mirror took her breath away.

"No, no, no. What have you done?" She dove through the bathroom's doorway and fell to her knees.

"Satisfied? I did it for you," Ram said.

"What the hell are you talking about?" Spider-like hands raked together handfuls of Ram's severed locks where they lay on the floor. She thrust them up to her nostrils as if the curly pieces could be resuscitated.

Pirouetting, he said, "How did I do at the back?" He pulled the trash over to fling bits in. "Woman, it's over." He clucked his tongue at the scene. "I'm going out to find the rest of my new look."

An hour later, Julie heard the lock turn and flung herself at Ram as he entered. "I'm not with you just because of your hair."

"What? Oh shit, that's not why I cut …" He pushed past her with a cryptic grin. "I know. You're with me for my dazzling intelligence, my sharp wit, my *uncompromising* quest for the truth. *And* my vigorous and capable performance in bed." He rose and peeled his white T-shirt off with the grandiosity of a strutting peacock, then slipped on the gaudy, striped-satin dress shirt he bought, parting the buttons to expose what little chest hair he had.

"The border guards will think I'm a sleazy liquor smuggler." He slid a heavy gold-plated chain over his head and flicked a pair of cheap sunglasses around his ears. With the skintight pink slacks on, he admired himself in the mirror, cupping his crotch in a quick, upwards alignment: "Whaddya think? Substantial package?"

Julie grimaced from across the room. So far she hadn't said a word, but as he started to slather the coconut oil onto his hair, she burst out with an accusing finger: "No way are you getting into my bed like that. Take your *substantial package* and sleep somewhere else."

"Hey." He pointed back at her. "Ditch those hippie clothes and find yourself a skirt. The shorter the better, and a low-cut top. Show some cleavage." He regarded her petite breasts with a dour grunt. "Give it your best shot."

The bus bounced and rattled through the night, a chill seeping in through cracks in the windows, doors, and floorboards, but Julie barely noticed, too steamed at being forced to parade around like an "Eastern Bloc hooker" in faux-tiger stilettos and heavy eyeliner. It took an entire night of arguing to convince Ram to let her cross independent of him.

At daybreak, the passengers disgorged and streamed through the ornate arch which marked the entrance into the kilometer-long transition from Nepal into India.

"Just think." Julie steered her and Ram clear of the meandering line of passengers heading to the immigration building. "I got my entry visa easily enough, even though I skipped bail. Maybe the police have dropped the terrorism charges and forgotten all about me."

"Police don't forget about anything unless someone warms their palm with rupees."

"Your father already paid."

Ram stepped aside to let a group pass from behind. "He bought off enough people to allow you out on bail. But *baksheesh* payments are like falling into a bottomless hole. If there's an active arrest warrant for you in their database, the whole thing starts up again."

"Still. It's been a long time." Julie's childhood violence had forced her to learn how to camouflage fear in the face of authority and possible punishment. She had little respect for those unwilling to take risks.

To avoid any unnecessary attention, Ram carried the four boxed bottles of Johnnie Walker whiskey in a cheap plastic sack which could be discreetly opened from the top if a bribe was necessary. He seemed resigned to the one-hundred-fifty-percent import duty on each bottle.

"Listen up." He checked behind them. "Get ahead of me in the non-nationals line. Give them your forms and passport. If things go well, get out fast. I'll watch and if I sense trouble, I'll flash the bottles as a bribe. Wait for me up the road past the Welcome to India sign where you'll be hidden behind the line of transport trucks."

Julie shrugged. "There won't be any trouble."

"Did you hear what I just said? Don't fuck this up."

She sighed, then repeated his words robot-like, noting his brow was wet with perspiration. "Stop sweating or you'll be the one fucking everything up."

"What?" He scowled and ran a finger across his lips for her to *zip it*.

Fellow travelers carried unwieldy bundles on their heads or in their arms. The sudden onslaught of purchased goods would create the perfect storm.

They'd left their backpacks home in favor of a single, pink, hard-shell suitcase which Julie rolled behind her. A scant acquaintance with tight skirts made her stiletto-induced drunken gait even more pronounced.

The squat customs and immigration building didn't look threatening, but beyond the dust-caked windows, three ill-tempered customs officers barked orders at the jostling crowd. Once inside, she hung back until Ram neared the front of his line for nationals. With a discreet squeeze of his hand, she sidled to the wicket for foreign tourists.

As she approached, the young, sleepy-faced officer's gaze dropped, alternating up and down from her exposed thighs to the oscillating flesh within her plunging neckline.

She tried on a seductive sway but grimaced as pain radiated from her instep.

Nevertheless, the officer grinned, exposing a row of rotten black teeth tinged red from chewing on betel nut leaves.

Let's hope he's as dull-witted as his not-so-winning smile.

She leaned in on her elbows, trying to ignore the reeking coconut oil plastered through his hair and untidy mustache.

His eyes took the boob bait.

Over in Ram's line people elbowed each other amid a tangle of roped boxes, cloth sacks, and an occasional suitcase.

Her eyes locked with Ram's. She recognized dread and quickly looked away lest she catch some of it.

Betel Nut Teeth lingered over her papers until an older coworker squeezed in and snatched them away. He glared at Julie, flicked his fingers in a gesture for her to remove her intrusive elbows, then shouted at the young agent while hammering a finger mid-air into one of the pages. He had obviously missed something important. Her name on a terrorist watch list perhaps?

She dared not make eye contact, riveted on that finger tapping out its ominous beat. She swallowed hard, her throat felt like sand.

Bam! Her body recoiled from the sound in time to see the young agent slam his stamp down on another page.

He handed the documents back and waved her away. It was over.

Swiveling the wheels of the pink suitcase around with the nonchalance of a baton-wielding cheerleader, Julie danced it behind her to the rhythm of her clicking stilettos. She passed Ram, who was counting a wad of one-thousand-rupee notes for the whiskey duty.

As planned, she stripped off her heels, threw them in the first trash can she passed, and slogged up the road through a smoggy corridor of blue exhaust from the idling transports. Welcome to India. As dirty and worn as the sign was, the sight of it ahead focused her every cell on bridging the last ten yards to safety.

She heard Ram call and turned to see him striving to reach her.

The young agent she'd been dealing with marched up the road behind him, waving for her to return.

Ram approached; his eyes flashed with alarm.

"Ram?"

"Stay here." He growled under his breath, striding past.

Julie regarded the agent, who had started to jog, then Ram's departing figure. *You bastard*, she wanted to scream.

You said you'd help if there was trouble. You're about to find out what happens when people try to abandon me.

She renewed her dogged course into India. *What can they do? Shoot me?*

When Ram halted and turned, the whites of his eyes grew large as beacons against his dark skin.

She marched on.

Seconds later a shot rang out. Someone screamed. A hand seized Julie's arm. It interrupted her momentum and wrenched her around. She faced an Indian border guard with an automatic rifle in one hand, his menacing eyes just inches from hers. An acrid odor wafted from the gun's barrel.

The guard said nothing but gripped her arm until the agent trotted up, wheezing for air, his scarlet complexion a perfect match for his stained teeth. He snatched the papers from her hand, pulled one out, returned the rest, and staggered in the direction of the customs building.

"Are you fucking nuts, or what?" Ram said, when Julie came within earshot.

"Oh, there you are. You coward. Don't you ever abandon me like that again."

"That border guard fired into the air to get your attention. You could have been shot for ignoring him." He tugged her into him with all the gravitas of a soap opera, attempting to reprimand and embrace her in one-and-the-same action, but she squirmed loose.

"You scared the shit out of me. Why didn't you stay there like I told you?" he asked.

"Because we're a team. If I go down, you go down. That's the plan."

"Well, let's not *go down* any sooner than we have to. That agent was training the other guy. That's all." He shook his head. "By God, you're headstrong."

"I'm a survivor. Survival—it's all that matters."

He blinked. "You can do better than just survive."

He was about to have the last word. Julie squinted at him as though struggling to see through the patterned noise of an optical illusion.

"Let's get the hell away from here and find a room," he said. "I've got four bottles of booze I'm not planning to haul around much longer."

They had until the next afternoon to relax with a few drinks before catching the overnight train south.

The sound of glass scraping across the floor, then a girlish Indian voice followed by a slamming door. Julie didn't know the savage throbbing of body and mind was a whiskey sickness.

She croaked to Ram, "Get a doctor. I've been poisoned." Only able to move her head, she turned it to see Ram's motionless body. *He drank more of the whiskey than me*, she thought. *He's already gone.* She stepped her fingers up the side of his chest. The bed heaved. Her mouth went slack as the corpse vaulted itself through the bathroom door.

She slid under the covers and held a pillow to her ears to block out her lover's repulsive retching, which sounded like his entire insides were sliding with a splash into the toilet. It was over in less than a minute. She peeked out to see Ram steadying himself against the door frame, naked but for a bit of vomit stuck to his still-oily hair.

He swiped the back of his hand across his mouth. "Thank God that's over with." In his dispassion, he could have been announcing the completion of his tax forms. "I'm ready to get out of this dump. C'mon. We both need a shower."

On the way out, Julie convinced Ram to slip the maid one of the unopened bottles. "If she plays it right, she can get three or four months of salary for it. Two down, two to go."

They bumped along in their auto-rickshaw to the station, past sidewalks of needy hands; sun-darkened and faceless, mangled, clammy and pale, tiny and grubby, palsied, blackened with leprosy, claw-like, pleading and tear-streaked.

Julie and Ram dozed as their train rocked through the valley bottoms of the Himalayan foothills, mostly dry, rocky, and denuded for firewood. But here and there towering Bodhi trees and resplendent mango groves flashed by. It was a minute reminder of an India when kingdoms and empires ruled, not the Congress Party with neighborhoods jammed on top of each other.

The clickety-click of the wheels marked their passage.

"I'm headed to the catering car. I can't wait for the evening meal service." Ram was up and ready to explore the train, or, more likely, his fellow passengers.

"Go ahead. I'm okay on my own. Just bring me some curried rice and a pot of milk tea." She said this from the lower bunk of their private cabin. "Ram?"

He turned.

"I thought you said Bihar was the poorest province in India. That I should prepare myself. But it's gorgeous here."

"You'll see." He slid the cabin's door shut behind him.

Train travel spun a meditative spell around Julie every time she climbed aboard. Tilting the steaming chai to her lips, she stared out at mists tumbling above ravines of monsoon run-off. Horizontal sunbeams split the worn hills into multi-layered hues of blue and purple.

At sundown she woke to the muffled gaiety of Ram holding court in the passageway outside their door. The guffaws, his above all others, added to the sense of being tucked-in and safe.

She and Ram might as well be drifting in a boat on the Indian Ocean, so far removed were they from their day-to-day personas. In this space and time, there were no corporate bosses to please, no environmental battles to fight, or important people to impress. Stripped down, they only had each other's agendas and human urges to contend with.

"Mmm …" She woke again, this time to colored neon flashing by on the wall above the bunk.

Already down to his jockey shorts and a T-shirt, Ram snuggled along her fully clothed back for warmth.

She brought her face in close for a whiff. "What? No drinking?"

"Too old for back-to-back benders." He moaned and snugged his arms around her.

"Am I in your bunk or are you in mine?" Julie asked.

"I'm okay sharing."

"I'm not. Not if we want any sleep. They make these for one person."

"Or how about two copulators?"

Julie snorted and a cool hand crept under her layers to cup one breast.

"Yeow. Your hands are freezing." She rubbed them under her bulky sweater, then shifted to lie nose-to-nose with a man she hadn't seen in a long time—an easy contentment in his eyes.

"We're going to be okay, you know." Ram spoke in earnest despite the awkward angle of his mouth.

She grinned. "Are we, now? Do I get a say in this?"

Caught in this bad habit, Ram lit up the cabin with the same boyish smirk and rolling eyes that undid her when they first met.

As then, they couldn't take their eyes off each other. They bathed each other with their gazes as if pouring pitchers of warm milk over each other's hair and shoulders, until their eyelids drooped and closed in tranquility.

In the vast record of her promiscuity, not once had Julie allowed a man to join the most tender part of his face with the most vulnerable place within her body, but that was exactly what she found herself doing a short time later. When he first slid his lips between her legs, she thought about pushing him away in fear and shame as in the past. But in the safety of the cocoon-like train, she gave herself permission to visit these intimate thoughts and feelings as never before.

She lay back, sinking into that space ... a rocking ... a trusting ... a letting go ... of all control ...

When it was over, Ram nuzzled her neck. The ferocity of the orgasm left her unable to speak.

"Nice," Ram mumbled, before climbing into the bunk above her.

Sleepless, her mind tumbled and crashed at this discovery of the limitless sensuality within her.

She woke before light to her lover's rhythmic breaths above her. Julie expected a cool breeze as she propped the window open. Instead, the humid air hit her like a soggy blanket. Faint outlines of a vast checkerboard of fields meant the train had entered the fertile ground of the Gangetic Plains bracketing either side of the holy river.

Out of the gloom, a rural cacophony emanated from tight clusters of thatched huts. Barking dogs, bleating goats, and cows seemed to compete with the rumble of oxen carts and whine of motorcycles on distant highways.

Soon after, what Ram warned of assailed her nostrils. The sun's first rays beat upon a stinking concoction of human feces, animal carcasses, and fetid watering holes, overlain with wallowing sows and smoldering stacks of charred trash. Vultures circled.

She slammed the window shut.

Through her reflection on the pane's purplish glow, an endless parade of shoeless field workers streamed toward the crops. An odd row of ragtag waifs stood motionless as the train chugged by; their tangled bushes of black, matted hair turned them into scarecrows with faces so tormented one would think they'd crawled from the stringy, web-like lair of a nearby Banyan tree.

There wasn't a single image in this miasma of filth and despondency which Julie could attach to this century. That would be left to the pulsing mass of homeless and their warren of sheet-metal and plastic hovels which soon loomed up beside the tracks.

❧ "Are you absolutely sure you don't want to strike out for Ladakh from here?" Ram asked from where he squinted into a shaving mirror. "Bhagalpur Station is a major terminus."

"Here we go again."

"You've been waiting five years for your chance to go after that manuscript. You're safely inside India. Why wouldn't you, now that you're so close?"

"Well, for one, I need a break from trains for a while. Anyway, we've only got one suitcase between us."

He lobbed his shaver into the stainless-steel mini-sink and yanked the suitcase down onto the cabin's bench. Out flew a pair of jeans, two T-shirts, some socks, and underwear. The remaining whiskey got gentler treatment. "There. All yours."

Julie rolled her eyes but froze when she noticed him studying her.

He sank to the bench. "You're convinced, aren't you? You'll never find the manuscript."

Her stomach was doing somersaults.

"It's just a show, making plans, talking it up. And Vakkali— a convenient diversion."

How could he possibly know the Roman ruins discovery was a fluke? And she was a fraud. That it was daft to think the euphoria from the underwater dive would ever come again.

"Sit with me," Ram said, rubbing a spot next to him.

She did so but kept a safe gap between them.

"I'm a geologist and for the most part I couldn't imagine doing anything else. I'm also your lover. You're a big part of my life. But that alone could never complete me." A flicker of a smile from him. "You're a born explorer. When I met you, you had a pristine curiosity for everything around you. Somewhere, you lost the thread."

The minute she wagged her chin across her chest, Ram leaned over and stroked her hand, his voice soft as corn silk. "If going after that manuscript is making you miserable, then it's not worth it. My love for you won't change."

His eyes danced under the glare of the fluorescent lights, inserting shadows between the creases of his brow's first wisdom lines. "Find your passion again, my love, whatever that is."

Julie pinched the bridge of her nose, barely able to meet his gaze. "Why are you doing this?"

He nodded with a gentle sense of finality and returned to his shaving.

She needed air. Now. Julie squeezed past Ram and broke for the far end of the carriage where a breeze from the open doorway buffeted her. Below the railway bridge, the Ganges River's sluggish brown waters undulated. The arms of this river they called The Mother stretched to the horizon, seeming broad enough to comfort the entire nation.

The metal siding felt cool and solid against her cheek while below, a coupling rattled and bobbed, jarring every bone in her body. And with it a memory of sending *National Geographic* useless, blurry dive photos. *Why?* She was on an assignment with the potential to change the course of her career.

Success, her mother snorted. *Never had any, never will.*

With bowed head, her tears dribbled from her chin and fell to The Mother.

As their train slowed to a crawl, at the window of their coach, Julie slipped her arm through Ram's and squeezed his hand, but he barely acknowledged it. His first look at the city of his birth and home of his late mother's family had him in its grasp.

Metal on metal, the train's ear-splitting screech reverberated along deserted ticket counters and into the vaulted ceiling.

Inside, security guards shuffled through the station's tentative light, tapping faceless mounds of rags to life with the gentle diligence of a priest sprinkling holy water. Plastered on the walls above them were mug shots of those wanted for rape, murder, theft, bombings and arson. Cause and effect, in one tidy display.

They found their driver, the wiry proprietor of his one-vehicle taxi fleet—a Maruti Suzuki four-by-four. He had the beady, watery eyes of a street rummy, or the most likely suspect in a lineup—and an ivory smile which could part the heavens.

"He'll do nicely," Ram said, after circling the car with criteria of more relevance than dental charm. "It's immaculate inside and out. That means the mechanics are well-maintained."

Their driver piloted them through a web of arteries which followed the Ganges west, and wouldn't you know it Ram ignored driver-patron convention and climbed in beside him in the front. The poor guy went mute, answering with the Indian head waggle while Ram rattled on in Hindi.

"His parents named him Ashoka," Ram said while stopped at a roadside chai stand, "after a famous emperor." A frugal soul, Ashoka insisted on staying in the vehicle with a bottle of water, turning down an offer of chai.

Amongst a dusty litter of paper cups, an animated crowd of shirtless bullock cart drivers sipped tea. Tiny heads appeared to sprout from the trunk of an expansive Bodhi tree providing shade.

Inside the brazier-blackened kiosk an arm emerged from the smoke and steam to reach for the volume knob on an equally sooty television on a shelf near the ceiling. One by one the circles fell silent to stare at the figure on the screen. He stood within what looked like India's parliament.

"Weak laws have emboldened the terrorists and appeasement has failed to change their intentions."

"Who is it, Ram?"

He held up his hand, engrossed with the speech.

"This warfare is waged by an invisible enemy," the man continued. "For whom the civil society is both a source of sustenance *and* the target."

"It's the leader of the opposition," Ram finally said. "He wants the government to reinstate the Prevention of Terrorism Act. It's gotten bad since we left. Two-hundred people were killed in a single day in Mumbai and almost a thousand were injured." Ram shook his head. "But this Act is turning India into a police state. They're picking up political protestors and jailing them for months without charges."

"What do you think the activists want?"

Ram raised his eyebrows at her question.

"I have my own opinions," she said. "I want to hear what *you* think."

"Depends which ones you're talking about. The Maoists, or Marxists, or whatever the hell they call them—"

"Naxals."

"Oh. Those jerks. Their methods suck." With a wave of his hand and an indulgent smile, he handed her one of the chai just poured.

What do you think of Jathia? Wasn't that what she was getting at? Still, she got her answer.

One bold child made a break from a hiding place behind the gnarled tree. "One rupee, one rupee."

The boy or girl, Julie couldn't tell which under the grime and rags, thrust a dirty hand at her face, prompting a dozen more tiny outstretched hands to push in on all sides with a chorus of "One rupee."

Ashoka bolted from the car, but the children scattered in a cloud of cries and laughter before he reached them.

"*Saheb*." Ashoka spread his palms before Ram. "I am insisting we depart this rank place before we are set upon."

Hmm. Ashoka knew English after all. Sort of.

"Don't call me saheb. I'm not your master," Ram said. "Nobody is." Even so, he flung his paper cup aside and plodded after his driver toward the car.

"Surely he didn't mean it that way," Julie said inside the vehicle as they pulled away.

Ram scowled at the back of Ashoka's head. "He did and that's the problem. Servant and master for two-thousand years. How can we abolish the caste system when it's part of the fabric of Indian society. Even your Gandhi couldn't manage to legislate it away."

"*My* Gandhi?"

"Yeah. The West adopted him as a hero, but he was never that for the Untouchables. Ambedkar did more for them because he was low-caste himself."

"Never heard of him."

"He wrote India's constitution after the British left. You'll see all kinds of things named after him. It will take another Ambedkar to force change."

Julie tucked a stray curl behind Ram's ear. "Sweetheart, we're at your aunt's house."

He jolted awake as the jeep rolled to a dusty stop within a patch of curdled shadows cast by delicate Sal trees. Two women, one early middle-aged, the other, obviously a daughter in her twenties, along with an adolescent boy, emerged from an immaculate two-story white-brick home.

"Namaste." They placed their palms together in *anjali* and bowed as Ram and Julie stepped out of the jeep.

Ram did likewise and embraced them.

In front of Julie, the older woman dabbed her thumb into a saucer of what Julie knew was red turmeric for the mark of the welcoming Bindi between the brows.

When the boy and young woman fell to their knees and kissed Ram's feet, he took the formality in stride and ceremoniously rested his palm on their heads. The significance was obvious to Julie. After many years, Ram had come home — the seat of wisdom in the Hindu faith.

Once inside, everyone except Julie broke into excited chattering. The boy was the only one who spoke any English, and he seemed eager to try it on her, constructing halting questions he'd obviously rehearsed. Before long, he gave up, told her his name was Palesh, he was in sixth standard at school, his mother and father were Ram's cousins, and his father was away working at his shop in the village. His older sister's children squealed and dashed between legs.

The chaos suddenly halted. The older woman led Julie and Ram into a bedroom on the main floor.

There sat an aged woman swaddled in layer-upon-layer of blankets. The veiled end of her sari obscured her face while two waxy-thin hands rested motionless on each side of the wheelchair.

Ram dropped to his knees and brought his lips to her feet.

She lifted her shaking hands to his head, then cupped his chin. Her veil fell away, revealing eyes glistening as bright as gray-blue marbles in a pool of tears.

Before him sat his mother's only sister, the woman who delivered him into the world and nurtured him as her own before relinquishing the newborn to the orphanage. This encounter could be the closest he would ever be to his mother's spirit.

The woman bent forward and whispered into his ear.

Ram's muscles tensed before he dropped his head forward into her lap and wept.

To give Ram and his aunt privacy, Julie left and shut the door behind her. While waiting, she wandered into a room with the family's Hindu altar.

Tucked into alcoves around the room were colorful figurines and pictures of Lord Ganesha, and the manly God of Love, Lord Krishna, on a flowered swing with his spouse Radha. These were the only ones Julie recognized.

She stooped low to peer at photographs along the altar, assuming they were dead relatives. When she raised one of the photos to her face, thinking she recognized some of the people, without a word, someone snatched the frame out of her hands from behind. Julie gaped as the older woman dashed from the room with it.

From there, the visit deteriorated.

As he emerged from his aunt's room, Ram smiled and said to Julie, "Palesh will take us to the old house where I was born."

The boy trotted ahead of them across an abandoned field, then slowed to a march with the determination of a Ten-Countries-In-Ten-Days tour guide.

Ram had to yell. "Palesh, do you know what the farmer used to grow here?"

The boy slowed momentarily but didn't turn. "Yes, sir. Corn, sir."

Ram muttered under his breath, "Why isn't it being farmed?" He called for Palesh to walk beside him. "Who owns this land?"

"You do, sir," the boy said, gazing ahead and goose-stepping his arms and legs forward in a comic exaggeration.

Ram sniggered. "You mean Baba, don't you?"

"Yes, you … *and* your baba."

"*My* father must have given this land to *your* father to build a house." Ram reached over to tickle Palesh. "So, I guess that means *you* own it."

Palesh giggled, pulled away, and straightened. "Yes, I own it." The boy strode forward with renewed aplomb.

The sun glowed red on the mud-brick hut, giving the tattered thatching the eerie effect of being on fire. Three goats scattered as they entered, leaving behind green-colored droppings on every surface.

"This is it? It can't be more than twenty feet by twenty," Julie said. Inside the dank and dark room, two narrow slits near the ceiling let in the only strands of light.

Ram shuffled to the center of the room and stood immobile. Her lover had come looking for his place under the sun. How could he not be crushed by this depressing hut, barely livable at the best of times?

"How many lived here?" she asked.

He gazed into one corner. Perhaps he imagined his mother there, her chest heaving, her arms reaching in ecstasy for the first touch of her newborn's skin against her own.

He looked at Julie. "How many? I guess there would have been … uh …" He counted on his fingers. "Five adults including my mother during her pregnancy and then my aunt's two adolescent children, one of which you just met. And me after the birth so … eight … no, seven. My mother died, of course."

"No wonder they sent you to an orphanage."

"The problem wasn't space. It was who would look after me. Everyone had to work, including grandpa and grandma." He took a broad step backward. "Let's go. It's not what I expected."

⟨❀⟩They arrived back to loud, agitated voices, a male and female's, in a room upstairs. Within minutes a man came down, nodded, gave his name, and shook Ram's hand briefly, but there were none of the grand gestures of earlier and certainly no hugs.

Several servants moved around the expansive house, but there was no invitation to stay the night, nor did their hosts offer food or even a cool drink. Considering the blood ties and the gift of one of the precious bottles of whiskey, it was an inexcusable way for family to act in India.

Ram shifted from foot to foot during a tense silence, then blurted out they were on a tight schedule to see the dairy the next day.

"What do you make of it?" Julie asked him as they got back on the road. She decided not to mention the strange incident in the altar room. If she could recall the face in the photograph, it might answer their questions, but it had been too fleeting.

"That house they sit in was paid for by your father."

Beside her, Ram's chin rested at his chest, humiliation elbowing its way into a heart already overloaded with emotions he rarely allowed himself to show.

"I don't care about the house," he said. "It doesn't make any sense, though. Unless, of course … my father did murder my mother, then it *would*. Those are *her* kin back there, not his."

Their car crept along the remote road; black, indistinguishable shapes loomed on either side.

Inside the curtain of privacy the night provided, Julie put her arms around Ram's neck and swept a tender lip over his mouth before kissing him with a passion both deep and genuine. "You need to decompress," she said, setting her head against his shoulder. "You don't like chaotic family gatherings. That's one thing we have in common."

They drove into the boonies to a truck stop hotel with threadbare, oil-stained towels inside, and roaring engines outside. At Hotel Bugger King, which Julie thought needed a new orthographer, a squadron of matriarchs had reportedly been at culinary maneuvers inside a nearby wedding marquee for well over two days.

At zero hour, the harmonium and tabla drums began to bleat. The hordes rolled in. Ram snored through it all in a somnolent tune. But Julie wasn't a good sleeper. A confluence of strobe lights and thumping Bollywood tunes at one in the morning sealed her wakeful fate.

❧ The heartfelt reception at the Musahar family dairy near the capital city of Patna the next morning buoyed them for many days. While they walked through the open-air goat-milking stables and along the production lines where the milk and soap were packaged, the workers stopped and bowed. Some prostrated themselves and kissed Ram's feet.

"Oh no. Not this." Ram ducked through a side door and headed across the yard.

"Why are they doing that?" Julie trotted to keep up.

"If I was given an easier job at four times the pay, I might do the same."

"Hey. I know this soap." Julie pointed to a flat of packaged bars sitting on a forklift. "Paula's been using it for years."

"It's in health food stores around the world," Ram said.

The vast Musahar dairy and factory complex employed almost every Dalit family within the district and beyond, he told her. They abandoned their fields, public latrines, sewers, and garbage dumps—and even the funeral *ghats* on the Ganges where they had lived and worked amongst the burning corpses.

Inside his uncle's office, Ram stood at the picture window, soaking up its bird's-eye view of the complex. "Baba sent me here at fifteen to toughen me up."

Snugged within a La-Z-Boy recliner, Julie pulled herself from the brink of sleep long enough to let his words register, and respond, "Good for him." The low bleating inside the feeding sheds and fruity whiffs of harvested mulberry fodder lulled her to sleep—until a growl like a mast about to snap jolted her upright.

Across the room one-hundred-ninety pounds of grown man was using his uncle's creaky office chair like a carnival ride, spinning with his knees in the air. Not just once, but several times.

"I did nothing but sleep off hangovers ... make fun of the workers my age ... and pick fights." Ram separated each confession with a sloppy push-off. "After two weeks, I sneaked out of my uncle's house and caught the bus to Calcutta airport. God, I was an arrogant little prick."

"Don't tell me he bought you a ticket to England instead of marching you right back here?"

"Didn't need to." The soles of his shoes hit the worn carpet with a thud. "I had a credit card in my own name." Ram shook his head. "The coddling was never a replacement for Baba. I admired him like a God when I was a kid but got little in return."

Ram leapt to his feet and headed toward a frame on the wall. "He's an elusive man, all right," he said, fixated on the document inside. "I was barely seven when out of the blue he hugs me and says, 'Without you, my son, I never would have discovered my own goodness.' I'm still trying to figure that one. I'm *not* his only son." He tapped the frame. "I didn't know this was here," he said, before rejoining his window station.

On inspection, she saw it was a high school diploma awarded in 1983, the name in Hindi characters. "Your uncle's?"

"Nope. Baba's."

Mr. Musahar would have already been in his thirties. No wonder it was on display.

◆ Inside the departing jeep, Julie peered out the back window, the distant factory in twilight like an ancient colossus standing guard over a sea of green pasture.

"It's quite a step up from a Patna slum, isn't it?" Ram said. "That can be on tomorrow's itinerary."

"It's stunning." She turned to Ram. "Not a single black mark in all the prosperity."

"I wouldn't say that. There are always winners and losers in every profitable venture. In this case a family got wiped out."

"What do you mean?"

"My father should answer to that."

❧Julie decided long ago slums the world over were the same, only delineated by how much degradation they inflicted. But nothing could have prepared her for Patna's.

From the rise she and Ram stood on, Julie saw people streaming in and out of the gloomy dirt passageway running between a patchwork of shacks.

"Best not to go in," Ram said.

Julie understood why. Every passing face projected suspicion.

Below, a sagging plank served as a bridge over a trickling stream choked with raw sewage which originated from a monstrous pile of rotting trash. At times, the bare feet of those laden with heavy bundles dipped into the reeking slime. They seemed unconcerned, but Julie gagged.

She recognized the plaintive cry of a cow collapsed beside the trash pile, probably dying a slow death from plastic bags ingested into its intestinal tract.

Wild-haired children scrambled on their hands and knees through the towering garbage, shoving recyclables into a huge bag they hauled behind them. Any food scraps were deposited directly into their mouths. Whenever a boy came across something sharp he called to the others. They stopped and cheered while he lobbed it at the dying cow.

Two men came and squatted beside the trickling sewage. The buttocks of one faced them; the dead eyes of the other stared directly into Julie's as he defecated.

"I came, I saw. Your parents and brother lived a nightmare. You were conceived in hell," Julie said. "I'd rather hear the story from your father at his house than through *Show and Tell* here. Can we go?"

"You know, I haven't thought about Jathia in years. He might be dead for all I know."

"Oh, really." That was stupid of her to remind him of his brother.

"He was pretty much gone by the time I arrived. I know so little about him as a person."

Julie knew something about Jathia. She twirled a wisp of hair at her temple. Things she wanted to forget and keep hidden.

"I've always thought I was the victim of my father's neglect, but Jathia had it even harder. He worked alongside him during the most difficult years."

With each passing year, the secrets and lies she spun about Jathia felt as insurmountably sticky as flypaper.

"Maybe it's time to reconnect with him when we get to Vakkali," Ram said.

Shit, no.

While Ashoka's taxi idled at a Kolkata rail crossing, Ram dozed, but Julie stayed alert to spot the many buildings which bore Ambedkar's name. Across the street she saw: *Ambedkar Laundromat and* — the rest was obscured by a man on a scooter who pulled up and stared over his shoulder as if waiting for someone.

Hey, I know you, Julie thought, *you're that bumbling wanna-be terrorist from Vakkali. No shit. Here comes his sidekick bumbler.*

They sped away together.

What would those two losers be doing way out here in Kolkata? They should stick to fishing before they blow themselves up.

The image of an explosion hitched itself to the sickening clang of the rail guard and she knew.

There was a bomb on the tracks.

The train's caboose rattled by into the distance. The safety arms began lifting.

She flung open her door and pulled at Ram's limp frame. "Wake up. We need to move. Now."

He grunted and opened his eyes. "What the …?" He yanked his arm away, which sent Julie sprawling out of the car into the oncoming lane.

She sprang up in the roadway and took a few halting steps backward, clutching her head. "Get out of the fucking car."

Ashoka lowered his window to stare at her.

The first cars in line nudged forward. Ram hung his head out of the doorway in the direction of the oncoming traffic about to bear down on Julie. When he jumped from the jeep, she backed away, hoping he would follow. "Get off the road before you're ki—"

A deafening clap drowned out his warning and threw him off his feet. Like gigantic cymbals the glass windows on either side of the street quaked and imploded, and high above, tossed up by the shock wave, a car flipped end over end, its rooftop in an obscenely perfect line with Ashoka and his taxi.

She wasn't so different after all. In the few seconds before impact, Julie watched with morbid curiosity how those watery eyes peered at the broken windows as the only source of trouble.

The two vehicles met with a dull crunch—both reduced to a fraction of their original height.

"Are you okay?" Ram said, staggering back from the metallic sandwich of fire and smoke.

Chunks of twisted metal, unrecognizable as vehicles, littered the roadway. Across the tracks, a blaze in the bed of a truck crackled and roared, muffling the cries of men being beaten back by the intense heat. The air was ripe. Beside the truck lay a single undamaged drum, its crossbones and skull hazard symbol clearly visible.

"We need to get away from here," Ram said.

She wheeled around. "What? We can't leave Ashoka."

"Ashoka is no more. We need to think of ourselves. There's nothing left to link us with the taxi but pretty soon the police will start checking the identification of bystanders."

She slapped his arm. "You heartless bastard."

"This is not the time to be a hero. There could be a second explosion to kill the first responders. I'm going." He grabbed hold of a trailing sleeve, pulling her off balance.

"Go all you want." She folded her arms and dug in until Ram let go and wandered to a boy crying at the side of the road. Julie followed.

"The kid went to buy a soda at the shop," he said, pointing at the blackened, smoking shell of a chassis. "Their vehicle was first in line."

He slipped his arm around Julie's shaking frame, her breath ragged from delayed shock. Ram was like a finely tuned machine, thinking ahead for the both of them.

"There's nothing we can do for this little guy that the emergency responders can't."

She felt like shit. The boy was her, wet and crying, abandoned beside the Kettle River.

Ram stopped her as she rose to go and motioned to their flattened taxi. "Please tell me your documents are not in there."

She patted her waist pouch. "Only my phone. Everything else is here." His only concern was their money and documents? How shallow.

"How did you know?" Ram said as they left the disaster behind them.

"You mean the bomb?" Julie averted her eyes, knowing exactly what he meant. "Uh … I saw some guys on scooters acting suspicious."

Ram rolled his eyes, but fortunately, didn't bring it up again. "I don't care how long we have to search," he said, stomping out the words with each step, "I won't stop until we find ourselves a decent hotel with fluffy bathrobes and a soaker tub."

Julie squeezed her lids shut. Their money gave them options she didn't want to enjoy because that signaled going to the dark side.

"Tomorrow, we'll get another taxi to Vakkali," he said, which prompted Julie to plow her fist into his shoulder.

"What the hell's wrong with you? We should call Ashoka's family."

Ram hung his head. "Of course. Why didn't I think of that?"

"Maybe because you're too concerned with—"

"I'll compensate them for the vehicle, too." Ram picked up the pace again, lost in thought while Julie trudged behind.

Ram's sense of compassion wasn't as innate as hers, she couldn't fault him this time. He was a quick study.

"Goddamn. Poor Ashoka. Hey buddy," he said, scanning the passing clouds. "Wherever you are, I hope you're finally free from anyone trying to be your master. Rest in peace."

Ram caught a flight back to Bihar to break the news to Ashoka's family before the police did. He planned to give them the five-lakh of rupees he estimated was invested in the taxi. Unlikely the railway would ever pay any compensation.

"The money won't be enough for college, but I'll make sure my uncle takes Ashoka's fourteen-year-old son on at the dairy." When Julie protested the boy should stay in school, Ram said, "He's better off at the dairy. My father provides on-site tutors and a college education for anyone wanting it."

It was hard to attach Mr. Musahar to such a socialist-sounding concept.

Julie arrived at the Musahar's alone, unsure what kind of welcome she'd receive. Under Indian law, she and Ram still weren't man and wife.

Mayawati rushed to the taxi first. "Oh, my dear. How are you?" Ram's stepmother squeezed Julie's hands before raising them to her lips.

This isn't the frosty woman I left four years ago. Had Goran's death thawed her heart or was it the thought of losing Ram in the bombing?

She guided Julie by the elbow as if her daughter-in-law were as fragile as a porcelain doll.

"I can't force you to stay here," Mr. Musahar said inside the house, "but I am concerned for your safety. You are most welcome, no matter the circumstance."

Ram had likely filled him in on the risky border crossing. With each passing year, her lover seemed more comfortable sharing pieces of his life with his father.

"These terrorists are targeting everything. It's not only jihadists, but the Naxals, too. That is who claims responsibility for the rail crossing yesterday."

At the mention of Naxals Julie wondered if Jathia still collaborated with them. Within hours, she had her answer.

❧ She caught a cab to her reunion with Jimi and the newborn puppies that the Gupta family rescued from the street. The dog was nursing them as her own.

Out of habit Julie ended up on the beach and, other than the drunken bellowing and loud music seeping from the locals' gambling hut, the swish and tinkle of the waves were the only sounds in the midst of a sweltering summer night—until Jathia showed up. That hadn't changed.

"Booo!" Under his thick Hindi accent, it sounded like the wail of a lost calf behind her.

She knew Jathia's voice and took off at a trot along the hard-packed sand. "Get away from me."

"*Didi*, I am thinking it most excellent to see you, too." He cut a perky pace beside her, thrusting his imbecilic grin and heavily oiled mop of hair in her face. "Those ridiculous people at the border crossing. Quite a scene?"

Julie halted, undecided which maddened her more—everyone in town knowing her business within hours of arriving, or the blithe innocence of Jathia's demeanor. She reminded herself Jathia was a calculating killer. It burned a hole through her to have him act like they were brothers-in-arms.

She tugged him onto the sand between two fishing skiffs. "I'll tell you what was a scene. The rail crossing bomb. We were almost killed by those fucking friends of yours."

Jathia gaped. "They're not my friends. Never were." He tried to take her hand, but she pulled away.

"Look. I have to stay away from you. I haven't told Ram about us." Yet it was inconceivable Jathia wouldn't know about her and Ram since he was the one who sourced Julie's fake passport for his father.

When his shoulders sagged, despite everything they'd been through, Julie felt a tug of affection for this man who had ferried her to the Roman ruins in good faith. "Please tell me you've cut all ties with the Naxalites."

At the mention of the terrorist group, he fidgeted with the *beedi* cigarette in his hand. "It's set up so I won't be caught." He checked behind him and whispered. "It's a different group. They plant bombs in Delhi, not Kolkata."

Before Julie could protest, he notched up the volume. "*And* they're only targeting government things with no people."

"NO. It's still violent. Why haven't you done what I told you? Peaceful protest only." She'd never mentioned his father before. It was worth a try. "Oh, Jathia. Do it for your father, then. He loves you. I'm sure of it."

"Shut your mouth. I did not give permission to talk about family."

"You called me Didi—your sister," Julie said, returning his fierce stare.

With that, Jathia leaped up and stomped back to his card game, their meeting over as quickly as it began.

From the Musahar family dinner table Julie eyed Mayawati repeatedly poking at a nearby flower arrangement. This middle-aged matriarch's severe braided chignon and peacock-colored sari of the finest gold-trimmed silk lent her a long-legged dignity. Yet, rather than being the consummate hostess of her home, she seemed flustered whenever Julie was around. Did speaking English make her anxious? No, Ram said, his step-mother had always been insecure — except in the kitchen. She even had a personal maid dress her.

"Maya, your noble efforts are much appreciated." Mr. Musahar spoke from his seat at the table, unable to hide his peevish tone. "But I am asking we see to our guest's need to eat."

Mayawati scurried to the table and tried to placate her husband with a wave of her hand. "Ahchaa, ahchaa." She scanned the serving plates until she squealed — "Rotis!" — and sprinted to the kitchen, returning moments later with the steaming bread.

During the meal, the first dish Ram reached for was a sort of green mush shot thru with something white. Ram offered it to her first but Julie recoiled.

"Oh, but it is tasty," Mayawati cut in. "Spinach and goat cheese. Palak paneer from Bihar. It reminds us of—" Yet another odd Mayawati moment, she turned to Mr. Musahar in a panic. "I am Bengali. You taught me palak paneer. Yes?"

He smiled and nodded.

"We didn't have much time for home cooking," Julie said. "That soap factory took a long time to get through."

"Just to be clear," Mr. Musahar nodded to Ram. "I purchased the land where your mother's family lives, but none of the dairy was ever there."

"I know. We went there the day before the dairy ... to visit my aunt. We had to cross your field to see the shack where I was born."

Ram's father lost for words? Whatever the trigger, there was nothing subtle about the furtive looks he was giving his wife, either.

"You did?" Mayawati said. "How was it looking?"

Ram tucked in his chin and smirked. "Like a country shack with goats living in it."

Could this hut be where his mother was murdered and how might Mayawati be involved? Julie and Ram exchanged curious glances until Mayawati spoke up in an unnatural, high-pitched tone. "Ram, Julie knows your father becoming an engineer?"

"A bit. That it happened after I came from the orphanage," Ram said, turning to Julie. "We moved to a flat near the college campus. I was in shock with the luxury of having my own room."

She tipped her head into a calm waggle before responding. "All the time he was turning on the hot water. 'Auntie ... look.' Believing it a magic trick."

"It took many tries to get in," Mr. Musahar said. "I had to learn reading and writing. Actually, I had the gift for chemistry and physics. Some of the factory workers are also accomplishing this. I am very proud of them."

It occurred to Julie how flawed her theory was. How could someone so generous and kind also be a murderer?

"Julie wants to know all about Mo."

"I do?"

He poked his spoon at his father. "Well, yeah, without him you would have been beat before you started. Right?"

"That is correct." What must have been a youthful barrel-chest at one time now bloomed. "There were three of us. Me and my brother, the bachelor, the one you met, and Jathia, my older son. You—don't know him. We lived in that slum you saw and had three goats by then. So we made a cart from a broken-down bicycle rickshaw and went from house to house ladling milk out of steel urns."

She tried to imagine this portly man in a suit opposite her, pumping that unwieldy load uphill in plastic flip flops.

"We had to sell far away where we were not known to be low-caste. Then the wheel chain broke, so we pulled the bike from town to town and returned home in the dark."

"Early morning, we milked the goats. Sometimes with no sleep at all. It looked like the end for us. Harvest was coming, and we still owed the farmer our debt."

A long-forgotten delight tugged at the corners of his eyes. "We always stopped at Mo's chai shop before striking out for home and one night he laid out a business proposal—for a minor percentage he would sell some of our produce out of a fridge in his shop. That gave us rest time and kept us going. Soon Mo said he did not need to take a percentage anymore. He would do it for the glory of Allah."

Ram cut in. "This part's funny."

"'When you get rich you can buy me a house instead.' Mo was telling it as a joke, but we did buy him a house. That is how he came to move from Bihar and live down here on the ocean in Vakkali. We paid off our debt to the farmer. We never worked for anyone but ourselves again.

"Hard work alone will not make a business successful." A sly smile formed on his lips. "You need to put your whole heart and soul into it or have a friend who will. Mo was that person. He gave us his friendship and his generosity. After that we had so many goats we needed land for a dairy and some kind of cash crop to feed them."

Mr. Musahar put down his fork. His eyes sparkled. He took Mayawati's hand into his lap. "Then magic happened. Not as wonderful as the day I met Maya, or that of my children's births, but close. I walked down the farmer's road one last time. The *jamidar* was thinking 'this man is crawling back for work.' Prideful, at first, he was refusing to sell part of his land. But I held a bank loan. I was cunning. As the price grew so did this man's greed. By the end of that day I had procured the very land I worked on in bondage."

Mayawati tapped his arm as one would an overbearing child, but he barely noticed.

He stood, striking a pose, and raised his glass. "Let's drink to that."

Mayawati and Julie brought their water glasses up to join with his but Ram stayed seated.

"I think I've already had enough to drink," he said, rolling the stem of his wineglass between his fingers, each twist erasing the energy of the moment. "You guys go ahead." With that, he marched to stare at the sea through the terrace's glass doors.

There was a disjointed clinking of crystal and hasty scraping of chair legs across hardwood before Ram slid into his seat and, under his breath, said, "You missed a step in the story."

"All right," his father said. "You believe I have something to answer for. Julie is family."

Ram glanced around the table at everyone.

"Go on," his father said.

"Do you expect anyone to believe a bank would give the owner of a few goats enough money to buy hundreds of acres of farmland?"

Mr. Musahar sighed.

"You secured the loan with land the Naxal terrorists confiscated, didn't you? They stole it from another family at their kangaroo court and gave it to you instead."

"This is correct. And should I be refusing this help? Let it go to squander in the government's hands? What then of my vision to build the dairy and give the Dalit jobs. Free them from the squalor I myself lived in. Have you no gratitude, my son, for what I've done?"

"More fucking rhetoric."

Mr. Musahar charged to his feet. "I will not allow this foul language in my *home* and in front of ladies."

Ram rose, slammed the back of the chair into the table, and jabbed a finger at him. "And I will not allow you to pretend you didn't bribe government lawyers into giving you stolen land." His words reverberated throughout the hallways of the elegant home. "Or that a family of nine wasn't burned alive when they refused to abide by the terrorists' ruling."

Julie gasped and Mayawati silently retreated into the kitchen.

"I'm leaving," Ram said, after storming to the main door. He raked a set of keys from a hook before him and glanced over his shoulder.

"I'm not," Julie said, surprised at how readily she sided with Mr. Musahar. The world *is* rarely as black and white as we'd like, she thought, remembering what Mr. Musahar had said years earlier about the grey zone between right and wrong.

"I want to talk to your father and eat some of this food Mayawati worked so hard to cook," Julie said. "Send Ganesh back for me."

"I'll drive myself along the beach." He slammed the door on his way out.

Mr. Musahar's half-smile petered out while he raked a weary hand across both eyes. "He is crazy with grief over Goran. That is all it is."

Julie sat beside him and stroked his free hand with her fingers. "You must be, too."

"The gods have blessed both my son and I with strong women for times such as these." His eyes glowed.

"You still call on the Hindu gods?" This image of him worshipping a religion which propped up the caste system didn't make sense.

"I am nostalgic at times, I suppose. But you are right, Daughter. Never could I accept their attitude to castes. There is a quote in the book I gave you: 'He who shows no anger toward those who are angry; is peaceful toward those who are violent; is not grasping among those bent on grasping; is one I call a brahmin.'"

Mr. Musahar slumped into his chair and drummed his fingers along his lips. "It is not so easy to live by these Buddhist tenets. But I fear my own son is failing greatly."

"Ram would *never* hurt anyone," Julie said.

"No, he wouldn't." Mr. Musahar leaned forward intently. "But neither would he help them. A sense of charity is a gift I have failed to instill in my son. The fault is entirely mine. Ram has never been denied a thing in life. Always, I saved him from that pain."

"Mr. Musahar, the reason Ram went to find our driver's family was to compensate them for the ruined taxi and give their son a job in your dairy. Did you know that?"

"No, I … he did?" Mr. Musahar stood and stared at the door Ram had slammed moments before and his eyes grew moist.

❊ The next morning, Julie and Ram traversed the hard-packed sand for anything resembling a body, Ram's despair broken only when he spotted a figure carrying a surfboard in the distance. He gunned the gas as if it might be Goran. It made no sense, of course, having been over a week since his disappearance.

In the evening, Ram suggested a walk on the beach.

"I have a better idea," Julie said.

Suni jumped from his high stool behind the pastry counter the minute they walked in, shaking Ram's hand vigorously and embracing Julie. "You back." He clapped his hands in glee.

Even though Suni had finally slapped on a fresh coat of paint, the place echoed with an emptiness. She wondered what became of the pictures, especially the one of the Potala Palace but realized those things had their day.

"Drac." Suni shook his head sadly.

At the touch of Suni's hand on Ram's shoulder, his eyes fluttered closed, and in their moment of shared grief and stillness, Julie looked away, her heart tight-fisted and barren as in childhood.

Suni motioned to a table, but Ram pointed up toward the rooftop. "Closed, no peepo," Suni said. He opened his guestbook ledger dramatically to flip through blank pages. "You, yes."

They trailed after him up the first flight of stairs and down the hall leading to the rooftop.

Ram poked at a door and grinned as they raced to keep up. "My room."

"Then you better put your name on it," Julie quipped.

Without a single table or chair, the rooftop appeared massive and lonely; their only touchstone was the endless azure waves below.

A quartet of metallic collisions rippled from the back storage. Suni emerged triumphant, holding a round, rusted café table in one hand and two folded plastic chairs in the other. He arranged these front and center, nearest the ocean view, as if he intended them to be there for the next decade, then scurried away with their order for two beers.

Julie took a gander around her, enjoying herself. "This is where I sat while you ogled my breasts the morning we met."

"What? I wasn't ..." But his face flushed scarlet around a thin grin.

"Nice try. Women always know."

"Oh yeah? Well, men know, too. Remember the day you told me to burn my clothes? I walked out of my room in the morning and saw you at a table downstairs. Five hours later, you're still at the same table."

"So?"

"Hmf. We both know who you were looking for. Some people call it stalking."

"Thank goodness for dedication," Julie said, vibrating with a trill of giggles.

They sat in a comfortable stillness until Julie asked, "What was Goran like? I mean ... as a friend to you?"

As Suni emerged from the stairwell with their beers, a wariness eclipsed Ram's contentment.

"I'm not trying to start an argument," Julie said after Suni left. "I want to know." Her hand was shaking while she took a voracious bite out of her thumbnail. "Better late than never?"

He told her everything in his heart, starting from their childhood together at boarding school, and Julie listened, without interruption. At the end, while a single tear dribbled down onto his smiling lips, she blurted out the first thought to come to mind. "I was so jealous of him. Not because he was your best friend. Goran was everything I wanted to be, if I could just get it together."

He picked up his beer and, shifting his body, gazed out to sea. It was Ram's code for not only closing the discussion but stating: *If you think I don't know this already, then you don't know me.*

The day had been hot, even for India, edging to 40 degrees Celsius. Someone had taken the bold step of building a four-star hotel in the town's centre, and not relishing being cooped up inside their hotel with the air-conditioning blasting they decided to walk along the beach after all.

With the tide in, they skirted the fishing boats and congregations of exhausted dogs curled up under the hulls. Suni was right, not a single evening stroller except them. Most beachside restaurants were boarded up. Ram said he'd never seen it so slow before, even during the summer off-season with prices cut to attract locals.

At Julie's former seaside suite, they paused. No lights. No new lovers. No puppies tearing around. No Paula. And no Goran.

"Come on. It's getting cold." Ram pulled on Julie's hand.

It was still 20 degrees Celsius on the dark beach. He must be talking about his heart.

At Suni's, the shutters were still up with the Closed sign already out. A hulk of a policeman traipsed between the tables twirling a billy stick. From inside came a din of smashing glass mixed with loud voices.

Ram held Julie back. The door to the kitchen banged open. Two more burlies strode out and all three exited down the street in the opposite direction.

Inside the kitchen, they found Suni in a flurry of sweeping. Broken china and glass lay scattered over every surface. Only a hint of worry danced in Suni's eyes. "Ram. Good. You help?" His finger jabbed upward at the ceiling.

Ram nodded.

"What in hell's going on?" Julie said.

"I'm going to help Suni bring down the extra set of dishes from storage since it's obvious these are no longer usable."

"Two set." Suni said gleefully to Julie, holding up two fingers as if he'd won a prize.

"The resorts are the only ones who can afford a liquor license but I guess he didn't have money to pay off the cops this month. They always smash up the dishes if they don't get their bribe," he said, shaking his head. "I wish he'd asked me for it."

On the way back to their hotel, Ram hit on the idea to move into Suni's. "The room won't be up to what we want but he needs the money. And I can finish up his beer inventory for him." Ram would make the sacrifice.

They moved into Suni's the next morning. A decision which saved Ram's life.

J athia. What the hell?" He appeared by Julie's side, crouched low, his fingers gripping the edge of the ground floor table where she sat after breakfast. Ram had popped up to their room to gather his backpack before heading out to withdraw cash from the bank machine.

"Listen. I've heard something is going to happen," Jathia said in pitched bursts. "Move to my father's house down the beach. Get out of here. They're targeting the plant." Before Julie had time to even react, Jathia had bolted.

Why hadn't she told Ram years ago about her connection to his brother? Then she could confide in him. After Ram fell for yet another lie that she would visit Jimi and the puppies, Julie phoned Mr. Musahar — the next best confidant to Ram.

❈ Mr. Musahar sat hunched over documents inside his study when she entered. "I will ask for tea to be sent in."

Julie raised her hand. "Thank you, but we'll need privacy for what I've come to tell you."

He motioned for her to sit in one of the easy chairs by the ceiling-to-floor bookcase while he took the other. "Thank you for coming."

"But *I* asked you to meet *me*."

"Oh, I am most thankful when someone gifts me of their time."

He always seems so comfortable in his own skin. Still, how would he take the news of his own son's terrorist links, never mind the danger to the lives of so many in his care.

"Oh, yes," he said, after hearing Julie's warning. "My men received an anonymous call about a terrorist threat. We're at maximum security alert."

This wasn't the agitated response she expected.

She had carried her secret for almost five years. Time to let it go. "Then I should tell you my source was your son Jathia. He took me to the dive at the plant that night." She swallowed. "At the time, I innocently encouraged his group to trespass into the plant as a protest. They had a map which I assume came from Jathia."

"Yes, I have known all that. I am close with the police and, not only that, there are no secrets in this town. We knew that coast guard fellow breached security at the plant the night of your dive. I hired surveillance to follow him—right up until the police killed him in a shootout." Mr. Musahar smiled broadly. "Skilled police are such a blessing."

He's toying with me. All this time he knew his own son poisoned Arjun and that I helped dump the body. She jumped to her feet in a panic. "Does Ram know I helped Jathia and his group?"

"I doubt it. Otherwise don't you think he would have said something?"

"What I mean is … didn't you tell him?"

Lips pursed, he pulled in his chin. "What you and your husband speak about in private is not my business. What good would come of it? Ram was so young and full of opinions. I think you may find time has softened him to the deception."

She was struck dumb by everything he said, but by the amused expression on his face she wasn't doing a very good job of hiding it.

"I can assure you my son and I are very different. I certainly don't share this idea of his that technology alone can solve the staggering poverty of our country, much less annihilate the caste system. You see, I have the unenviable position of knowing everything which can go wrong at the plant." His face brightened. "Nevertheless, I sleep well at night."

He rose and tilted his head back in the direction of the upper shelves of his bookcase. "How are the Dhammapada contemplations going? Did the book perish at the rail crossing fire?"

"No. It's safe at home."

He edged his volume out of its slot. "Would you allow me to read my favorite verse?"

She nodded.

The dog-eared volume in his hands fell open to what he wanted. He cleared his throat.

> *"For many lives I have wandered, looking for but not finding,*
> *The house builder who caused my suffering.*
> *But now you are seen, and you shall build no more.*
> *Your rafters are dislodged, and the ridgepole is broken.*
> *All craving is ended;*
> *My heart is as one with the Unmade."*

He closed the book and ran his fingers across the cover. "It is a sad day when a baby is born. Poor thing is dropped into yet another round of suffering. Now death, on the other hand, is a joy indeed. It's our chance to enter the realm of the Unborn.

"Do you understand?" She didn't have a clue but smiled as if she did. Oh, how she wanted to please this man she once despised.

He moved behind his desk. "I know it was Jathia who phoned in. I took the call myself and recognized his voice." He leaned back in his chair with his palms pushed up against the desk's edge as if to buffer against something. "I don't move around the village much. I have not set eyes on him since he took the amnesty offered and came here to help build the plant."

Amnesty? Obviously, Jathia never intended to stop. That was her fantasy, alone.

Seeing her surprise, he said, "This movement must be like a drug because he went back. Are you surprised I can so easily forgive him?"

She was, but again said nothing.

"I forgive him simply because he's part of a humanity in which we all suffer." His voice wrapped itself around her. "Do you know a pearl starts as a parasite? Over time those foul innards inside the oyster release a protective coating around the poison. That becomes the pearl. If nature can create the strength and purity of a pearl from such ugliness, why not believe people can change no matter how far they've strayed?"

He looked away, lost in thought—but she wasn't entirely sure he was thinking of Jathia.

To Julie, it was like nothing she'd ever heard before. A horrific crack and growl shook the ground and she grabbed for the frame of the front door where she stood saying goodbye to Mr. Musahar. In the distance, a blood-red wall of flames spiraled into the clouds.

While these marbled mushrooms of fire and black smoke hurled themselves as high as tornadoes, she caught a whiff of gasoline fumes. "Oh my God," Julie cried. "It's the storage plant."

"No. It is not the fuel rods," Mr. Musahar said, his face ashen. "The town center is on fire."

Julie thought of Ram at the bank machine. "Please. Dial Ram's cell."

He held his cell phone in the space between them while they both listened to it ring. "Come on, Ram. For god's sake, answer," Julie said, but at the ninth ring Mr. Musahar lowered it and shook his head.

"Shit. I have to go." She whirled around toward her taxi but Mr. Musahar caught her arm and waved for Ganesh. "Take the jeep along the beach. It is faster and safer. I'm sorry but I must go attend to the plant." Cell phone still in hand he paused, his face rigid with torment. "She went today. Mayawati went into the central market."

The jeep jogged along the packed sand at the tide line and for now the wind continued to push the smoke inland. Within minutes they saw the first sign of what lay ahead. An Arabian mare, the kind the resorts paraded for weddings, burst from the underbrush onto the beach, its mane ablaze. With a piercing scream, it reared up and kicked until Ganesh chased it into the waves with the jeep.

The closer they drew to Vakkali's beach the louder the explosions became, one on top of the other.

-❀-At Suni's, Julie jumped from the jeep, almost piling headlong into him while he stood in Fishermen Colony Lane, transfixed by the firestorm a mere three streets away. "Suni. Are you okay? Where is Ram?"

"He looking for you at dog house."

"But—he's not answering his phone."

"Phone?" Suni ducked behind his pastry counter and held up Ram's phone, one end attached to a charger.

Outside, Julie gazed up the main tourist street which ran from the beach into the core and imagined Ram at the Gupta house, just fifteen minutes away by foot—if there wasn't an inferno in the way. She grabbed Ram's cell and charged up to their room to fill a backpack with water bottles and scarves.

"I'm going to look for Ram," Julie said to Suni outside the guest house. "Go to the Musahar's with Ganesh."

"No. I help you."

Suni was energetic and resourceful. Who better to help search? She showed Ganesh Ram's phone. "Wait here. If Ram comes, call me."

No more than a block away, zombie-like figures approached, their clothes burned away, leaving raw, bloody sores. On some the skin hung in shreds from their limbs.

She held out her arms to two young children who swayed from one side of the street to the other, but they screeched and shrank from her touch. "Suni." Julie pointed to them. "They need you more than I do."

Suni nodded, a sudden wrinkle of concern on his brow. Under his feet, the manhole cover had started to vibrate. As it rocked wildly side to side Suni jump free. "Rats!"

The iron plate exploded from the storm drain like a champagne cork and came to rest on the rooftop of the Ganga guesthouse.

But not a thing crawled out. They crept to the edge and peered in. Below, running to the sea, an underground river of fire ripped by. "What *is* that?" she said, but Suni had already retreated. It wasn't lava. At least, she didn't think so.

"Help the children, Suni." She turned on her heels and ran in the direction of the firestorm.

She could avoid the flames but not the smoke-filled streets and soon found herself stumbling along by feel alone. Shrieks and moans for help surrounded her, the pitched wails of children the most soul-searing.

Julie wiped her watering eyes with her mouth cover, bent over, and coughed until she vomited. If she didn't get out of this, she wouldn't make it to the Gupta's. Within a few steps she picked up the sickly-sweet smell of the bakery where she bought her cream puffs—and remembered the passageway beside it led to the temple with its panoramic view of Vakkali.

Except for a few dogs cowering from the commotion, the walled compound was empty. At the apex of its stone stairs she turned in the direction of the central bus station and sank to her knees at the scale of the disaster.

The shifting wind peeled back the smoke to reveal a field of charred and burning oil tankers crumpled one into another along the full length of the rail line bisecting the town. A red ribbon of burning crude surged down the town's main street. Only the Fishermen Colony neighbourhood remained—saved by a steady onshore breeze. She charged down the stairs into a maze of soot-encrusted concrete walls and metal skeletons.

A half-hour later, she pushed aside the blackened gate at the Guptas. Normally locked, it squealed in the wind. Inside the smoldering shell of a home two charred figures clung to each other under a set of blackened bedsprings. The grandparents, no doubt, knowing it would be impossible for them to keep ahead of the flames.

That's when she heard faint yelping from across the yard near Jimi's sleeping hole. A tiny nose poked out from under the remains of what she knew must be Jimi. Using a stick, she nudged the blackened dog aside and two pups emerged—unhurt. They survived in the cool earth of the hole, likely pulled or pushed into it by their surrogate mother. Jimi could have escaped but stayed to shelter her charges.

Julie's chest, already straining under the toxic air, quivered against a leaden sorrow, eased only by the memory of wrapping a towel around an equally helpless pup, broken and living in a refuse pile. Oblivious to the smell of seared flesh, Julie moved close. "You were a good dog," she whispered near what was once Jimi's ear. "You deserved something better than a life on the street."

Ready to scoop the pups into her backpack, Julie lifted her head to the howls of a baby and a woman on the street outside the gate. She gazed at the whimpering beings in front of her and knew she couldn't save them. They would only slow her down.

Julie rose and there he stood. Black soot covered his face and clothing. Tears dug pathways through her own grime as she buried her face in Ram's chest. Neither she, nor anyone else, ever heard from the Gupta family again.

They decided to save the children first. The ones they picked up on their way back to Suni's had the white leathery skin of third-degree burns; others resembled boiled lobsters. Suni's restaurant could be a triage center as long as the breeze kept the smoke and flames at bay.

While Suni ripped new sheets and pillowcases apart, Ram and Julie soaked them in bottled water and draped the wet strips over burns.

They laid a boy about ten years old on one of the tabletops. Brownish blisters covered most of his body and he shrieked when they touched him.

At least ten others lay nearby in eerie silence, staring at the ceiling through catatonic eyes, with blackened limbs and burns so deep their body's nerve endings were destroyed.

Julie tore off her mouth covering. "I don't hear any sirens. Why aren't they coming?"

"I *don't* know," Ram said, the whites of his eyes flashing. "Is anybody even aware of this?"

Julie headed toward Suni's television on top of his bar fridge.

"Don't bother," Ram said, "If you're thinking of the TV, the cable and electric lines will be gone." Ram spoke to Suni, who went in the kitchen and brought out a radio, batteries in hand.

A voice broke through the radio static and Ram stopped and listened, a sopping strip draped across his palms. His nostrils flared, he flung the cloth into a bucket, sending the bottled water splashing high into the air. "Naxals are taking credit. The target was the nuclear plant. Police think they cut the brakes on the tanker train last night. Got it rolling downhill but the assholes didn't account for the turn in the tracks at the cemetery. Burning oil from ninety-two fucking rail cars … all over town.

"How can anyone be so evil as to do this to children?"

"Give me those wet cloths," Julie said. "Never mind that. Keep working."

"They're sending in the army."

"It better be an army of doctors and nurses," she said. Surely help was coming. "Ram?"

He pulled a dripping strip from the bucket.

"If they let the oil burn off, how long will it take to go out?"

"Another week. Maybe two."

Good God.

Ram's cell phone rang. He flicked the water from his hands and pulled the phone from his hip holster. "That was my father," he said afterward. "Our old security guard took the limo and rescued Mayawati and a few others from the market. Smoke inhalation only. Baba's personal doctor and a nurse are at the house with medical supplies and stretchers. We need to transport all these kids with the jeep."

❖ After Ganesh returned from the first delivery, Ram turned to Julie. "He says there's so many bodies accumulating on the beach, soon we won't be able to get around them. You and Suni keep working here. I'll help carry the kids up to the house."

Twenty minutes later, Julie handed Ram a child, then watched the jeep zigzag around bodies on its way down the beach.

She spun around and there was Jathia, stumbling toward her, a baby on one arm, a woman with burns to her arms and hands propped up by the other.

Inside Suni's, Jathia eased the injured woman onto the zebra couch and Julie laid the baby on the table beside her, even though it was clearly already dead.

"From here, we take them in the jeep to your father's house."

Jathia nodded a few times, either to her or a broadcast on the radio. At the end of the report he squeezed his red-rimmed eyes shut.

"The boats," he said, bounding to Julie. "We can take the children by boat."

"Of course. All the fishing boats are in."

After Jathia beached his skiff in front of Suni's, they loaded the children and she climbed in opposite him while he yanked the outboard to life.

"How the hell did they do this?" she asked above the growling motor.

"Last night, they came to my door. Do I know about air brakes on trains? I do not. They wanted the oil cars to make an accident at the nuclear plant."

"But this oil *never* comes here," Julie said.

"Police found the crew and night watchman in a latrine beside the tracks." Jathia sliced a finger across his neck.

She glared at him. This connection to more murders, however thin, was too much to stomach.

"I phoned the plant before I saw you at Suni's. I did. But too late. Shit. Why did I not call last night?"

Bumbling Jathia. Along for the ride and headed down a dead-end road. "Maybe because you were scared of those guys?"

He averted his eyes from hers and didn't answer.

They rode in silence after that and Julie scanned the beach for Ram's jeep, hoping it would pass on its way back to Suni's. When it didn't, she felt sick. This was the worst possible time for Ram to run into his terrorist brother. What would he do when he figured out she knew him?

Jathia cut the motor and prepared to hop out of the skiff below the Musahar house. The task at hand, not the fear of running into Ram, appeared to be the only thing on his mind. Julie stayed in the boat and handed the children down to Jathia, who stood knee-deep in water.

As Julie was about to pass Jathia another child, Ram's jeep bounced out of the underbrush onto the beach. "Jathia, get in the boat. Hurry. Ram's coming."

"What?"

Julie pointed and Jathia turned to look—but too late.

Ram tackled Jathia. He held his brother's head under the water while Jathia's skinny limbs thrashed on the surface.

"No. You're drowning him. Stop it." Julie jumped out of the boat, landing heavily on her side in the waves.

Ram dragged Jathia deeper into the water.

Julie waded over, hitched her arms under Ram's armpits, and fell backward, bringing Ram along with her.

Jathia popped up, gasping and coughing.

"I'm going to kill you. Murderer!" Ram staggered in the waves, shaking his fists while Jathia scrambled into the skiff.

"Stop this." Julie pushed Ram toward the shore. "These kids need a doctor. Leave him. Take the jeep. Go."

Ram's sopping clothes clung to his body. He glared at her a moment, then clawed his way to shore, banged the jeep's door shut, and drove off in a whirl of sand.

After they carried the last of the children up, Julie told Jathia to escape Vakkali by boat. "Take this money. Find a bus into Kolkata. The army is headed here."

"Didi. I cannot take your money."

Mayawati's feeble voice called from a bedroom on the main floor. "Jathia ... Jathia?"

He glanced at Julie and frowned, then trudged down the hall into Mayawati's room.

When Julie looked in on them a few minutes later she witnessed a surprising scene with Jathia and his stepmother in each other's arms, weeping. Julie had assumed Jathia's bond would be as strained as Ram's. That's when she saw the blood-stained towel on the bed beside Mayawati.

"She is coughing blood," Jathia said, steering Julie from the room. "Bring the doctor."

Jathia spoke to Mayawati in Hindi and kissed her forehead as the doctor entered. In the hallway, he whispered to Julie, "It's the rocks. She doesn't like to talk about it."

Rocks? He must have the wrong word. "Jathia, you should leave before Ram gets back."

He hung his head and nodded, then took the rupee notes she held out, hugged her, and wordlessly left through a side door to the beach.

The doctor's diagnoses: Mayawati had lung damage from the heat and smoke at the market. He could make her comfortable with oxygen, but he didn't think her lungs would repair themselves at her age. "The main problem is the silicosis. It's not reversible. She told me it started bothering her ten years ago, but she wouldn't say how."

Laborers, including children, at Third World rock quarries contracted silicosis when they inhaled the crystalline dust from the stones they pounded. This Julie knew. But Mayawati's persistent cough was so slight, she assumed it was nerves.

❦ Julie was on the beach with Ganesh when Ram and Suni arrived with more victims in a boat.

Ram's eyes burned into hers just before he jumped out to pull it ashore.

He spoke in Hindi to Ganesh, who turned to Julie. "Madam, they abandoned the jeep. Too many bodies and more coming."

"No fucking medical help yet," Ram said to no one in particular as he waded ashore with a child in his arms. "In a few hours, it'll be dark. We need to eat, then we're going back. Work all night if we have to."

Ram and Julie carried the burn victims up the trail to the house on stretchers while the other two lifted them out of the skiff.

"There's something wrong with Mayawati," Julie said. "The doctor's worried. She's in one of the bedrooms." She hoped to dilute Ram's rage before the inevitable conversation about Jathia.

Ram said nothing but after setting down the last child, he shuffled down the hall to Mayawati's room.

The doctor and one nurse looked overwhelmed and exhausted. With bandages strewn across the carpet between the moaning children, the Musahar living room resembled a burn unit. Dozens of victims lay across every inch of the living room floor, hooked up to saline drips and layered in gauze.

Grief was etched into every line of Mr. Musahar's face when he arrived, but he acted oddly resigned to Mayawati's prognosis. It didn't seem the time to ask him about his wife's silicosis.

After emerging from Mayawati's room Ram dropped into the emergency response mode of someone used to mobilizing teams and thinking on their feet. But when he phoned for ambulances, he jammed his cell into the hip holster where he kept it and yanked Julie toward one of the stretchers. "Come on. We'll have to transport the kids to the barricades ourselves."

"Aren't the ambulances coming?"

He jumped at her. "For god's sake, just do what I say."

When Ram disappeared into the kitchen, the doctor tapped her shoulder. The hospital has informed us security forces will not allow medical evacuation."

"But why?"

"They want to prevent further attacks. Vehicles can leave, but they will not be allowed to re-enter. We must pray to the Gods for their help."

The Gods? Thousands—the entire population of Vakkali— were laying in excruciating pain, dying slow deaths on the streets a short distance away. Suni drove the family Suburban and Ganesh used the limo to transport the most critical children to the ambulances parked at the roadblocks.

Julie found Ram topping up the family's backup generators in an outbuilding behind the garage. A private space to speak about Jathia.

He glanced up when the metal door slammed shut behind her. "Go make yourself useful in the kitchen," Ram said from where he sat on a barrel examining generator gauges. "We need to eat. Especially the doctor and nurse."

"We should talk about what happened on the beach," she said.

He continued fiddling with the dials, the gas can in his other hand.

"Don't you want to know what my connection is to Jathia?"

He slammed down the can. "No. I don't. For all I care, you could be sucking him off from now until next Tuesday."

Julie stomped over and towered above Ram. "Apologize. Apologize." She drew her open palm back but before it could contact his cheek, Ram's arm darted up to grab her wrist.

He released his grip and pushed against his thighs. "I'm sorry," he said, barely audible. " It was a stupid thing to say."

"Your father has known about Jathia and I ever since he — ."

"Stop. I can't think about the never-ending dramas of your life right now." His words consumed the confined space they stood in. "I need news on this disaster."

It took no longer than one or two seconds. Ram rose to squeeze by. Forced to anchor his palms against Julie's shoulders, their eyes lingered on each other.

In a dog-eared la Boulangerie room of happy memories the previous night, they had grabbed two frosty Coronas from the bar fridge and carried the rattan couch out to the balcony where iron-hipped Malibu babes once posed. They joined their sweaty bodies, slow and easy, the way Julie wished it could have been the first time, and let the heat and night sounds off the Bay of Bengal roll over them.

That's the longing she saw in her lover's eyes as he pushed past to get the latest on Vakkali's destruction.

✦ Mr. Musahar smiled wanly as Julie entered Mayawati's sick room. How diminished he seemed bent and bowed over this woman he adored.

Wearing an oxygen mask, she lay in the middle of a labyrinth of plastic tubing, perhaps too weak to even open her eyes.

He glanced at the plate of sandwiches held aloft, then to his wife, and shook his head. "Thank you. I will try to eat. I need the strength to pick up more injured."

She gaped at him. "You're coming with us to the beach?"

"Of course. It is because of the plant that the emergency workers aren't coming. I feel responsible to those families." He placed his head in his hands and when he looked up, his lips trembled. "Some are the plant workers. The fishermen's families. Shopkeepers. They have all played their part in the happiest years of my life here in Vakkali. This town is finished. The plant, too."

Mayawati's eyes fluttered open. Shaking badly, she lifted her hand to seek his out. The fingers clasped his with more tenacity than Julie thought possible. A single tear rolled down her cheek.

The room filled with the unbearable finality of this couple's life together. Embarrassed, an outsider during an intimate moment, Julie turned from them and clicked the latch behind her. A mixture of low murmurs from Mayawati's feminine voice and his stirred along the hallway.

When Mr. Musahar emerged from the room, he carried the empty plate wedged between fingers tight with resolve. Otherwise, appearing as composed as usual, he announced, "Let us go find some neighbors to help."

Mr. Musahar, Julie, and Ram boarded the skiff to Vakkali's beach while Suni and Ganesh stayed behind to deliver the children to ambulances.

As the skiff closed in on the dead and dying along the beach, Mr. Musahar let out an anguished cry.

The mercenary soldiers patrolled, stepping over bodies and victims pleading for help. Some mothers held babies up to them, but they walked on, as if not noticing.

Inside the rocking skiff the three of them exchanged shocked stares.

With the tide out the victims were farther than ever from the boat. Having to slog through the wet sand, they'd only loaded three children by the time the sun dipped out of sight.

Julie waded ashore through ankle-deep water while Mr. Musahar's floodlight followed Ram's progress as he carried an unconscious boy along the beach.

At the water's edge three soldiers surrounded him and raised their voices.

It drew a string of agonized moans and weak cries from the darkness.

As the soldier doing all the talking stepped back and trained his assault rifle at Ram, Julie gasped, and bridged the final yard to his side.

"Julie, get in the boat. This is total bullshit."

After they climbed into the skiff he whispered. "Just wait until they've gone. The tide's coming in. It'll be easier to reach the kids. Then we'll start again."

"What is it? Are they trying to stop our rescue?"

Ram scowled in the soldiers' direction. "No one's allowed inside the town. We can be in the water but if we step onto the beach, they say they'll shoot us."

Julie's jaw dropped but Ram scoffed, "The fuckers are bluffing."

"Shouldn't your father tell them who he is and what we're doing?"

"They're private security forces. They say *they're* in charge now. My father has no status anymore."

The soldiers moved down the beach, but the cries in the dark grew louder.

While Ram swept his floodlight onto the beach, in search of the soldiers, the beams of cool light caught the top half of a quaking torso rising from the sand. Elongated strips of skin hung translucent as butterfly wings along outstretched arms. The hairless skull and face shone like boiled beets. The lips had melted away; two eyeballs darted around frantically in their sockets — the only human remnant left. That and bits of a blue-pattern sari seared as one within the charred chest and stomach.

Raw feet planted themselves in a slow march to the water. The figure toppled onto its knees. It crawled — a mechanical, relentless motion — leaving a snaking trail of blood and pus behind. Legs scraped along the gravel.

One by one, the soldiers entered the swath of light.

"For God's sake, help her," Julie cried, raising her hands to her head in disbelief. "Somebody help her."

The uniformed men stood, unmoved by the agony taking place in front of them.

At the tide's edge, the figure struggled to its feet once more. As it entered the water, arms reached behind shoulders to pull a crying baby high overhead.

It appeared unharmed.

In their sockets, the darting eyes stopped. *Please take my baby.*

Julie watched them flutter with exhaustion — and hope.

Please save my baby.

Then Julie found herself underwater and breaking the surface. She swam. Nothing existed except this woman's suffering. Not the echo of cries along the beach. Not the soldiers' shots over her head.

Waves were breaking over the woman's face when Julie snatched the baby from her grasp. Holding the infant high, she turned to call for Ram, but he was already there, lunging for the sinking woman. "Where is she?"

His father illuminated a body, face down, pushed by the waves to shore.

"She's gone," Julie said. "Help me with the baby."

They clambered into the skiff and no sooner had Julie sat down with the baby in her arms than she heard a splash.

"Baba, where are you?" Ram picked up the light and swept the skiff and water until he caught Mr. Musahar swimming for shore. "Come back. It's not safe." Ram called out in Hindi too, but his father's arms continued to slice through the waves.

The minute Mr. Musahar set foot on the wet sand a soldier pumped a bullet into his thigh. He staggered onto the beach, clutching the wound.

If Mr. Musahar cried out in pain, she didn't hear it above Ram's wail. He lurched, as if ready to plunge in after his father, but Julie caught the end of his sweater as a wave rocked the boat, sending him sprawling.

She heard another blast from a gun.

Ram raked the light across the beach. Its beams caught his father on his knees holding his chest. Then a third shot sent the top of his baba's skull exploding into tiny fragments like moths dancing along light rays.

He fell face down into the sand.

A high-pitched howl, as edged as a swirling typhoon, erupted from Ram. He struck at the side of the skiff with the flashlight.

"Oh. My. God. Nooo." Julie clutched her face. "Ram. Don't look. Give me the light."

"Baba. Baba, answer me." He cried out over and over to his father's body on the beach.

The soldiers rolled the body over, then abandoned it and moved down the beach.

"I'm so sorry." Julie rubbed Ram's shoulder.

Finally, Ram glanced behind him at the children then collapsed onto the seat nearest the outboard. He dragged the back of his hand across his nostrils and eyes and yanked the motor to life.

They rode in silence, the only sounds soft moans from the rescued children.

The baby in Julie's arms gurgled with contentment. She gazed at it, her tears rolling from her chin onto the fat cheeks of a perfect small being who survived such a horrific start in life.

In the blackness beyond the skiff, a yellow moon plumped, pinned to a satin curtain stretching seamlessly across the water and up into heaven. *Tsh … Tsh.* It caressed the hull.

Taaake it. Take it. She peered over the side, straining for the voice. Was it him? *Take the gifts and beauty of this day.* It's what he would say. *Sometimes, it's all we have.* Julie's lips trembled. She put a hand on the wooden seat beside her which held his gentle presence just moments ago.

She would never forget him—born an Untouchable, he left a Brahmin. Gone to abide with the Unborn.

❈ Once all the children were safely sent off to ambulances, Julie fell into a deep sleep but woke exhausted.

Ram hadn't gone to bed. It didn't surprise her. She found him stretched along one of the couches amid discarded bandages, basins, empty saline bags, and charred bits of garments.

He gazed out of dead eyes, not acknowledging the coffee she set down beside him.

"Is anyone sitting with Mayawati?" Julie asked.

Ram turned his back to her. "I just came out. The doctor is still sleeping."

She winced but understood his need to be alone.

In the kitchen, at the sound of her footsteps, Suni peered up from his station in front of a sizzling frying pan. On the counter, Ram's laptop broadcast online international news.

Suni raised the egg flipper in his hand at a cryptic angle and pointed at the screen; a headline under four head shots stated: "Suspects captured in connection with Bengali oil train terrorist attack." She didn't recognize the first suspect identified as "deceased." The last three, "in custody," were the two plotters from the Vakkali surf-shop—and Jathia. She drew her palms over her eyes.

*E*ventually, the never-ending waves rolling in from the Bay of Bengal failed to absorb the ashes of thousands, shrouding the beach pebbles with a dull gray powder as lifeless as the moon.

Julie imagined the bodies piled high in various stages of decay. Ghoulish faces, blue and bloated. The skin of the desiccated ones pulled back from the teeth and eye sockets in a horrific grin.

The doctor returned to the hospital with the burn victims.

Ram dragged himself around the house and grounds like a wounded animal in a leg trap.

Julie ached to touch him and comfort him, but he avoided her.

Four days after the accident, and the only thing he'd said to her was she could leave if she wanted. He was staying as long as the soldiers continued burning bodies, knowing his father's, and maybe even Goran's, lay below on the beach.

Night after night, in the home's silence, she heard him get out of bed and slide open the glass door to the stone terrace. A savage fascination with the burning pyres had overtaken Ram. More often than not she went to him, yawning, and offered to make tea.

One night, the bodies burned so incessantly the full moon beat red within the pyres' heat waves, as if it were a grotesque heart, impaled above a black sea. Wisps of gray ash swirled, stinging eyes and making it hard to breathe.

"It's bad tonight," Julie said. She brushed an ember from her shoulder. "Such an awful smell. Come and sit inside. I've put the tea by the window."

"No." A soft refusal. "I *want* to remember the smell. Everything … the taste of ash in my mouth … the stink of burning flesh. And the sounds … listen … do you hear that?" He cocked his head and waited. "Nothing. Not even a dog barking. It's all been obliterated."

The waves rolled into an outcropping below the house; they smashed up against his grief. "I owed Baba a friendly grudge match."

Ram stepped inside and picked up the rectangular chessboard from its reserved spot on an oak side table. He carried it to the edge of the terrace, raised it overhead and used his powerful arms to launch it high into the air. It spun downward into the void. The waves pulled back, and in the silent gap, a single sharp-edged *crack* echoed from the rocks below.

"I was sure it would be a radiation leak that took him." As motionless as one bowed in fealty, at the stone ledge he rested his forehead inside the crook of his arm. "Or a freak tidal wave. Then I could blame the Atomic Safety Commission, or the terrorists, or even the oil industry." He struggled up, his face tight. "But a soldier's stupidity? Who can I blame now?"

"Nobody," Julie whispered, tentatively placing her hand on his shoulder. "Your father's life wasn't about finding fault. And if it was you, and not him, who was shot?"

Ram stiffened and her hand fell away.

"He was human," she continued, "but he'd have compassion for the soldiers. Victims of a job which demands they put aside their humanity. Your father went on that beach out of love, not rage."

Ram turned away. "I'm so angry I can't see straight." He blinked at the ash-clogged air, thrust aside the glass door and charged inside.

Julie followed.

Back and forth he paced. "I don't even know if I want be a geologist anymore."

"Why would you say that?"

"What's the point? I was only doing it to please him. Imagine …" He cut short a flat chuckle. "Trying to please a murderer."

Julie stared, wild-eyed, at the dark turn in the conversation. She could well imagine trying to please a murderer. Not just the one she knew might be—but the one who *was*. Let the comment pass? Comfort him? Either would do.

Or she could ask the question she should have asked of *herself* a long time ago.

"Ram? If you knew, without a doubt, he killed your mother, would you still have wanted his approval?" In a remote outbuilding the gas generator thumped and hummed to life.

Ram sank onto the couch and remained there, unmoving.

She felt the heartbreak coming off him in waves.

He mumbled, "I would."

Julie sat on the armrest and caressed the back of his neck. "I know, sweetheart." She pulled his limp form to her bosom. "I know."

She had things in common with Ram. Some trivial, some not. But this shame-fueled childhood desperation to love, and be loved, no matter what, cut across the very core of who they both were. There wasn't a woman on earth who could understand Ram any more than the one who held him so close to her breast.

"You needed your father once," she whispered. "You still *do*. It's not too late to let him in." She released Ram and fetched the tea to a side table beside him. After pecking Ram's cheek, Julie turned down the hall to bed.

"Could you hit the lights as you go by?" he said.

She flipped off the main switch and glanced back. The only light flickering in his dark corner came from the pyres of burning corpses.

Early the next morning, she woke to tapping on her door.

Ram entered, his chin tucked in as if he'd been scolded. "I'm ready. I don't care about my brother, but I still care about us, so I need to know how you're connected to him."

She invited him to sit propped in bed against the headboard, knowing this intimacy might dilute any lingering resentment as she detailed the story—starting from Jathia offering his boat in return for help with the so-called protest.

He sat still, his face a blank until the part about Jathia phoning the nuclear waste plant. "Don't expect me to believe that."

"I do. It was your father who told me."

He pulled back to gape at her.

"Jathia warned me in Suni's less than an hour before the explosion. He couldn't have been with the Naxals at the same time."

Julie edged her thigh against his. "I'm not saying your brother had an epiphany, but he cared enough to put his own safety on the line as a snitch. He's getting blamed for something he didn't do and facing the death penalty in Calcutta Prison."

"Finally, a bit of good news."

Ram's sarcastic response sucked the last bit of energy from her. She let her head fall back against the pillow. They were speaking again. It would be easy to let Jathia take the fall and be the common enemy who reunited them. All she had to do was keep her mouth shut and get on with her life. But she thought of Mr. Musahar. He wouldn't desert Jathia, and he wouldn't waste his breath trying to recruit Ram to help. *Someone has to do the right thing.*

"I'm going to the prison to see him."

Ram sprang from the bed. "You *will* not."

"He needs someone on his side. What's wrong with you? He's your brother."

"What are you expecting to accomplish by going to see him?"

"I'll listen to what he has to say."

"Really. Listening isn't something you've ever been good at. I know first-hand."

"What's that supposed to mean?"

"You call yourself an activist and writer when you're only in it for your own ego."

"Fuck you."

"There's why you'll never find that artifact. If you're going after something that big you've got to feel it in your gut." Ram pumped his fist into his stomach.

He wrenched open the door. Before slamming it behind him, he turned and aimed his threat at her. "Go ahead, then. Go see that son-of-a-bitch. But don't bother coming back."

❈ She stood with a pair of scissors in her hand. Raising. Lowering. In what seemed like the tenth time, she brought the blades tight to her scalp, this time letting them slice through a long tress above her ear.

The only way was forward. Working from the crown, she snipped every last hair and finished off with Ram's electric razor, running her palm down the smooth indentation at the nape.

The relationship with her hair had never been close—more an obligatory one of keeping up appearances. What she felt now was utter emancipation from it.

Voices, including Ram's, drew her to the kitchen. Julie rubbed her sweaty palms and breathed into the beat of her pounding heart. As a concept, visiting Jathia was a faultless act of kindness. It was the reality which scared the shit out of her. Was she willing to lose Ram?

As she entered, all three stared at her bald scalp; Ganesh and Suni scattered. She lingered at the coffee pot, then deliberately sat directly across from Ram, which prompted him to methodically rise and leave without the slightest acknowledgement of her presence.

Julie placed her bags at the door. There could be no change of heart once she was on the other side of the barricades.

She slid the balcony door open and spoke to Ram's back. "I'm leaving now." No response. "I would appreciate if *you* asked Ganesh to drive me to the barricades." No acknowledgement again, but within minutes their driver appeared at the front door. She glanced back one last time before closing the front door and trudging to the limo; her shoulders sagged with uncertainty.

Julie slid her passport under the prison security glass.

"Julie Paglia. Spiritual guidance for Jathia Musahar. I'm Canadian. Staying in Vakkali, West Bengal."

From his stunned expression, she could see the clerk knew, officially, the town was uninhabitable.

She followed a young guard with a crisp gait through a metal detector, a maze of concrete passageways and crumbling stairwells, each with its own locked gate and danker than the previous, before exiting under a gray sky. Brick walls soared on either side of a narrow stone walkway. Along one side of the walkway a number of heavy wooden doors, some open, led into the open-air concrete spaces fronting each prisoner's cell.

Calcutta Prison still stood from colonial times. Barely. Retaining the name Calcutta rather than the newer Kolkata, there was a wing devoted solely to convicted terrorists where some said India's most famous freedom fighters were once held and tortured by the British.

During her week there, she learned the terrorists on death row couldn't leave the concrete cubicles, barely big enough to lie down in. Their only contact with the outside was when a fellow inmate dropped off their two daily meals through a cut-out in the concrete wall or if a human rights group came to investigate complaints.

Boiling resentment hung off every face she saw. For days after, it disturbed her the morning she waited for a guard to unlock a gate and felt an almost imperceptible tug at her shawl. She turned to a windowless cell, dark except for a row of sunlit fingers looped through the bars—and imagined the beings inside, penned together like farm animals.

No doubt, she seemed to them an apparition, this woman with a gleaming scalp and trailing white skirt and blouse which dimpled and flapped in the breeze.

Years earlier, during a call with her in Kathmandu Mr. Musahar had described how he and his teenage son, Jathia, had turned from Hinduism and converted to Buddhism at a monastery in Kolkata. To be a trainee in white meant she could masquerade as Jathia's spiritual adviser.

"I wasn't sure what you needed," Julie said, peering into the darkness of Jathia's cell beyond the courtyard and dumping toffees, a towel, soap, and a package of cigarettes from a cloth bag onto the paving stones in front of it.

Jathia squinted as he emerged into the sunlight, then stared, transfixed and wild-eyed when he spotted Julie. He lunged for the cigarettes, lost in the pleasure of them through half-closed lids.

As he did so, she blanched at the squalid cell behind him, pressing two fingers against her lips to muzzle a gasp. When her gaze fell on a vile toilet hole smeared with shit, out of the corner of her eye she saw Jathia hang his head. Here it was, the one thing she promised herself she wouldn't do—shame him.

Julie beckoned to the two guards hovering in the courtyard and while they worked to uncrimp Jathia's leg irons, they kept a close eye on the two five-hundred-rupee notes she held as a bribe. With the chains off, she saw the raw skin underneath and made a mental note to bring ointment the next day.

"You will have to pay them every time, my friend."

"Then I guess they're in for a windfall because I'll be coming every day for a week."

As soon as the guards were out of earshot, he asked how she got them to let her in.

Julie rubbed her scalp. "Haven't you noticed I shaved my hair off and I'm in white?"

He shrugged and offered her a glassy smile. His was the countenance of someone bobbing on a fantasy. His lower lip trembled.

It's possible he thinks I'm not real.

"The Buddha's five precepts?" Julie said, trying to jog his memory of the initiation ceremony.

He shook his head but continued to grin.

She laughed. "Nevertheless, I'm your spiritual adviser this week." She winked.

He winked back.

The bribe allowed them to sit in the compact courtyard outside his cell. When he first stepped into the direct light, he groaned and shielded his eyes.

Julie's heart ached as she imagined him sitting alone in the gloom day after day. "I've already contacted Amnesty International. It'll be harder to torture you under an international spotlight."

"I do not know about" — he took another long drag — "that Ampsty whatever it is."

She pulled Mr. Musahar's copy of the Dhammapada sayings out of her rattan satchel, thinking it would comfort him in his final days.

He stubbed out his cigarette. "If that is religious, put it away."

She jammed the book out of sight. "It's just a prop to get in. I'm obviously not family."

"Family is not allowed." He popped a toffee in his mouth and rolled it around. "Why do you come here? Really?"

"What I said. To be with you until the end. You don't have to be alone."

"And if I want to?"

When she reached over and slapped his hand in a playful reprimand, he jerked back, as wary as a trapped animal.

The blood pulsed at her temples. What *was* she doing here on death row?

"I told your father you tried to warn me of the terrorist attack. But he already knew it was you who phoned in. Nothing much got past him in Vakkali."

Jathia leaned in and clung to every word.

"He still wanted you to come home." Before it had passed her lips, Julie knew she was here to deliver Mr. Musahar's final message to his son. "You know he'd be here if ..."

Jathia must have sensed his father's death in her words. His bony limbs collapsed inward like a crumpled marionette. He buried his face in his knees while soundless sobs ripped through his body.

She waddled on her haunches, close enough to encircle both his legs and shoulders tightly between her arms. He smelled of urine, sweat, and now, tobacco. Would the sandalwood and eucalyptus on her linen shirt transport him to another time when a briny breeze sliced across the bow of his skiff, and night's final twinkling faded and died on the swells rolling into the mangroves of Vakkali?

Jathia wasn't an innocent prisoner of conscience, and it didn't matter to society whether he'd had a change of heart. To all seven charges, he had pleaded guilty.

"Mayawati's okay. Ram too."

He wiped the back of his hand across his eyes and scoffed. "When I swing from the gallows Ram will celebrate."

Julie tucked herself in beside him. "Look, I can testify you had nothing to do with that derailment. You can recant. It's not—"

"Stop. Stop." He placed his palm on her outstretched leg. "You know there were others."

Too embarrassed to let Jathia see her frustration with him, Julie looked away and muttered, "Why didn't you listen to me?"

"My beautiful Didi. It is okay." He squeezed her leg and when she raised her face to him, Julie saw nothing but resignation. Whatever fight the terrorist brought to Calcutta's jail was gone.

Julie nodded.

"Why didn't I know someone like you before I got mixed up in all this." He motioned across the cell as if it had been waiting for him all his life.

❀ Inside her hotel room, Julie checked her phone for anything from Ram. Nothing. She resisted the urge to call or email him, knowing what a mess she would be if he didn't respond. In this time and place, Jathia needed her more than Ram did. The fall-out from that decision could wait.

~❀~Mid-morning, a guard let Julie into the courtyard outside Jathia's cell. "Whoa." She scanned the scrubbed concrete and glanced past the bars into his equally clean cell. "Who cleaned?"

"I did," Jathia said, dragging himself and his leg irons from the gloomy cell into the sun. "A real bitch in these chains."

Julie handed over the bribe money and Jathia wiggled his eyebrows at her while the guard uncrimped his shackles.

Afterward, while they embraced, she took a voracious snort of the sandalwood essence dancing about his torso and remembered how clean and cozy his hut had been. "You smell good too."

"Anything for Didi. I was kinda' hoping for you to shack up with me."

"I'll run it by Ram."

Jathia sounded like his goofy self again. No. Better than that. He reclined with a lit cigarette and sent lopsided smoke rings up and over the top of his courtyard wall. "How is it with you guys?"

"Ram gave me an ultimatum."

"I do not know that word. But it cannot be good. Sorry about—"

"Hey, let's not talk about Ram." Julie was protecting her own raw heart, but what would be the point in reminding Jathia of Ram's rage? "Let's talk about your goat. Remember?"

"Sure," he croaked, midway through another smoky spurt. "I left my goats more satisfied than my women."

Jathia with a woman? Why not? She loved his cryptic, self-deprecating sense of humor. And except for the body under his bed, he'd been honest with her, never making Julie feel less-than. In a different time and place perhaps …

They sat against the same outside wall as the day before, close enough to reach out and touch.

"The Nubian goat changed *my* life. And *yours* too."

Julie chuckled. "A goat—I've never laid eyes on—changed my life? I doubt it."

"Didi, when you walk out of here for the last time, you will believe me."

"All right, then—shoot."

Jathia cocked his head and frowned.

"Sorry. That was dumb. I mean, *go ahead.*"

He shrugged. "In old-time India, a family name used to show your caste and job. Musahars started as rat catchers for the harvest. Actually, Mama had the worst job. Women in her caste scrape shit from dry latrines and carry it away in baskets on their heads. I can rightfully call myself Mr. Shit Disturber."

Julie smiled and poked him.

Still grinning, Jathia said, "Baba was a violent man."

"Wh—what did you say?"

"In the Patna slum, he beat me, but my mother got it most." Jathia paused and studied her expression. "My story is before he changed. Growing up in the slum, I had two jobs— finding something to eat; surviving a beating. When Baba was drinking, I searched for food. Always bringing my little brother."

"Wait. You have another brother? And Ram too?"

"Yeah. I will get to him. We owned no land or animals, so we ate snails from the bogs. And rats and cockroaches too."

Julie choked down a dry heave. "You're kidding, right?"

"Nope." His belly pumped in and out with laughter. "Better than being hungry. I started in bonded labor at eleven. There were lots of rats to eat near the corn fields, and Baba was too tired and too happy to beat me. The farmer paid him extra to force the crews to pick faster. One time, I saw a drunk worker take a knife and cut Baba's arm wrist to elbow."

Jathia sliced his thumb down an outstretched arm, ending with a triumphant flick of the wrist and a guttural cackle which made her scalp crawl. What did she expect from him? This was death row for a mass murderer, not wine and cheese for Citizen of the Year.

"He was mean but Baba taught me lots," Jathia said. "Like the rat traps. The first time I saw the arm whizzing by and cutting the rat in two, it scared me so much I laughed. Then Baba did too. He knew what I felt. The thrill of being tricky. Knowing how to take away someone's power."

Jathia rocked from buttock-to-buttock with the haughty grin of a child, his red-tinged teeth clearly visible. "And if no one was around, sometimes he even praised me.

"He told me why he loved harvest. How the *cool, spongy earth* felt between his toes, and *the sweet smell of corn on the wind at sunset.*'" Jathia wagged his chin, lost in thought. "Even then, in his crock-of-shit life, Baba saw the beautiful. 'Better than collecting body parts off the train tracks,' he said to me. I did that job too. We put together body parts, like a puzzle, and the government boss made a photo for missing persons."

"Why are they on the tracks?"

"Usually taking a shit. Sometimes drunk." He smirked. "Sometimes both.

"That first harvest I was a silly boy with big ideas for my ten rupees a day. My cousin used to work on a farm in Canada. I asked him how much I earned every day in dollars. He said twenty-five cents. Then he laughed like hell when I asked what twenty-five cents buys in Canada.

"'Leave the boy alone,' my father said. I could see his heart breaking. He wanted me in school, not the fields. Even now, the only thing I can write is my name.

"We worked hard but did not even feed ourselves. Baba knew we could never pay off the farmer's loan. That is how the idea to sell goat milk started. My uncle thought it would be easy money. Baba knew better. He said, 'A goat will cost a half-year of wages. Who will tend it? Everybody is working.'

"See, my uncle, the forever bachelor, needed one of Baba's sons to make his plan a success. Baba finally agreed. So, my six-year-old brother, Bir, quit school to graze and milk the goat.

"Poor Little Bir had the family's future on his scrawny shoulders. He was so excited to start school. Our low caste was not allowed at the local so Bir walked the five miles to the Catholic nuns.

"Every day, Mama stooped over the sooty pot, cooking the rice ration or whatever, so tired her eyes half-closed. Bir returned from the first day of school babbling about 'the white sticks he used to scratch his name on a black wall.' She put down her spoon and stared at him. I'm sure she saw the inside of a pretty house and a table full of delicious food."

Jathia cupped his chin. "That year my brother got murdered."

Julie grasped Jathia's knee. "No—"

"The goat was giving trouble since the start." His voice hoarse, he pointed to Julie's water bottle and took a deep swig after she handed it to him. "It was a dry year, the crops failed. Goats will eat anything, but it was wandering far to find food. When its milk stopped, the arguments started. Mama wanted to sell it and return Bir to school.

"'It is almost his time to help on the tracks,' Baba said.

"Mama argued, 'If Bir can read and write, he can apply for a government cleaning job. We will pay our debt to the farmer and leave bonded labor.'

"Baba shook his fist at her. 'He cannot return to school— ever.'

"Bir ran to her arms. They were crying together. Baba left the shack to a place under trees where the men were drinking hooch. For sure he had wet eyes, too. School was Mama and Baba's dream. Survival was the reality.

"That night, I heard Baba asking Lakshmi, the Goddess of Abundance, for guidance. But the next day, those prayers did not matter. I cannot recall why I returned home early from the fields. I was lifting the rice pot onto the fire. Bir's friend ran in, panting. 'Auntie, auntie. The goat.' Our family was fighting with higher caste landowners. They threatened to kill our goat if it ate their crops again.

Mama hiked up her sari and kicked off her plastic chappals. We followed the boy along a dirt path. I never saw Mama running like that.

"I remember a trail of smoke over the hill. The smell of burnt flesh and gasoline. Mama screamed. Kind of weird like. Not human at all. It went on and on, all the way to the flames.

"The blackish thing still was standing. The head rolling side to side. Its legs shaking like in a fit. Then it fell down. I heard the last air coming out. It never moved again.

"We looked for the men, but they were walking far away. One man pulled the goat by a rope. Police returned it to us but did not arrest any man for the murder of Bir. In India, twenty acres of crop is more valuable than one low-caste boy."

Julie waved him to silence and looked away. "I thought this was a happy story about a goat?"

"I'm getting there." He said nothing until she returned his gaze. "Okay?"

"Okay."

"Of course, Mama wanted to be rid of the goat. Not Baba. The milk started again. One day, she sent me for a big stick to kill it. I had to obey her. I was crying when Baba came home and asked why. I thought he would kill Mama so I ran between them. But after Bir's burning Baba was quiet. In a scary way. When he tried to beat me, his hand went white, and he threw away the stick.

"He had no power against the murderer. Every day the poison was growing inside him. That is why Mama ran away. I never blamed her. Baba cracked and yeah, it was bad."

Jathia turned his back to Julie.

When he edged up his cotton prison shirt, Julie's hand flew to her mouth. Amid the sweltering heat, her body went cold and Jathia pulled her to his shoulder and caressed her forehead. Julie's heart-rending moans weren't only for Jathia's red scars. She had her own to bear.

Inside his cell, a bare bulb hanging from a cord at the ceiling blinked to life, casting the walls in a purplish dreariness. "It is late." Jathia squeezed her shoulders and yelled for the guard. "Those dark stairways are dangerous."

Julie hung her head, still inside his story. "She had such a terrible life. First, her son is burned alive. Then she's abused and escapes, only to die in childbirth."

Jathia frowned. "Mama did not die in childbirth."

"What? Was she murdered? Did Mayawati do it?"

"My mama is still alive."

Julie arrived soon after the prison opened to visitors the next morning. "I hardly slept running scenarios through my head," she said to Jathia.

The afternoon before, he refused to continue his story, but now said, "Mama ran away pregnant, and Ram was born at her sister's house. She thought Baba might kill her for leaving. So, she decided to return home with her sister and brother-in-law after harvest time. She carried Ram on her back in the latrines but worried he would get ill and die. She only planned to leave him at the orphanage for a few months.

"One day, Auntie came begging help. Mama moved to be closer to the latrine dumps, but Auntie could not find her for three years. I was surprised Baba and Uncle wanted to look. Baba was full of energy like during the corn harvests.

"Mama's life was hard with Baba. Harder with no one to protect her. At the latrines a young girl pulled on my shirt-tail. 'Dadaji—older brother. Can I see your picture?' I was too tired to shoo her away.

"'I know her.' She pointed at my mother in the photo. 'My friend works with her at a gravel pit. I can take you.' She was jumping up and down to help. But we had to pay a bunch of rupees to her mother.

"There were mostly children at the pit. Some four or five-years old. They avoided us. Hauled rocks out of a stream then smashed them into pebbles and carried them in baskets on their heads to a truck. The girl ran to her friend and pointed at us but a guy with no shirt and a big belly hit both girls across the back with a baton. My father gave the fat goon some rupees and showed the picture. More and more rupees came out of his pocket. Fatty finally said my mama worked there but left and he did not know where.

"I felt like crying. After Big Belly drove off with a load, a woman sneaked over and looked at the photo. 'I know where she is. I need money.'

"Just three rupees were left in Baba's pocket. Still, she snatched them up and pointed to a plastic sheet. 'We lived under there for one year,' she said. 'Scavenging at latrines and breaking rocks here. We were tired and that man you saw yelled at her to hurry. She carried a huge rock on her head. She slipped. The rock rolled and struck her back. She didn't move. Then he dragged her onto the gravel pile of the truck and left. She was screaming.'

"Baba's face went white. He thought the man threw her in a river but the woman said, 'No, she is at the same brothel as these kids.'

"Baba asked why they were wanting a woman with a broken back in a brothel. 'Sir, you paid me,' she said, 'so I am reminding you whores spend all day on their backs.'

"The girls showed us the whorehouse near a Hindu temple where they were *devadasi*. Sex slaves of God for the priests. They said Mama was so beautiful the whoremaster kept her for his friends in his penthouse."

Jathia scoffed. "The place was a fucking hole like a greasy car repair shop. A low brothel for child molesters and rowdy men. That is when Uncle showed Baba a revolver so small and beat up it looked like a toy the goat chewed. Baba panicked. 'What, in the name of the Gods, is that?'

"'Is this a covert rescue or a picnic?' my uncle asked. 'We should rappel from the roof next door onto the upper balcony.' Baba pulled in his chin and peered at his pot belly, then took a gander at my uncle's flabby chest. 'You have been watching too many movies.' he said to Uncle. 'I will be a pretend customer with the money you brought and escape with her down those stairs to that field. That is safer.'

"We waited until the place was quiet and bastard brothel owner left. The guard was happy to pimp out my Mama for side money.

"I was lookout on the abandoned rooftop next door and my uncle stayed on the street with the gun. The guard had problem guts. When I saw him hurry to the latrine I gave Baba the signal.

"In he went to the penthouse. I heard a woman scream, then a gunshot. Baba burst out the door. The guard hopped out of the latrine with his pants down. Uncle shot at him to give Baba time to escape.

"Mama came out. I watched her side-stepping down the stairs, using her elbows to hold herself.

"The brothel owner returned in his limo. Wanna-be Pimp tried to delay him in a conversation but his boss waved him away.

"Mama had only two stairs left to the field. But the bastard was blocking her way. She did not flinch. She pulled a revolver from her sari blouse. Pointed it and pulled the trigger. Then cock-sucker's face looked like the ones dragged by trains. I was proud of her. She killed him with his own gun, holding it with the end of her sari.

"Mama thought Baba was doing an honor killing of her, but she returned to us and he found Ram too. It was the best day of my life. For a while, the four of us lived in a house beside the first dairy and milked two-hundred goats. His bitterness was gone. He had the energy of a young man. 'I have my family again. I must be the happiest man alive.' I remember him saying it all the time.

"But *I* was not happy." Jathia's breath quickened and a curl formed on his lips. "I could not forget what happened. I hated Ram. His privileged life. My father had my mother — and Ram."

Beneath Jathia's plodding tone Julie heard a boiling rage.

"What did I have — heh?" He jabbed his chin at her. "Jealously?"

She followed him into his silence, past memories of her own childish jealousies.

When Jathia emerged he stared with a sobriety so rarified she thought him incapable of it. "If only I had even a pinch of Baba's humility."

He rose. "When Naxalites came looking for recruits, I was first in line."

Jathia didn't have much on him at the time of his arrest in Kolkata: a key to his Vakkali shack, or what was left of it, his phone and wallet, a comb, and the bus ticket to Delhi. The police tracked him through his phone calls before he had a chance to go into hiding.

Only one thing remained in his possession. He pulled the wallet-sized photo out from the shoebox Julie brought him for his toiletries.

"We used this to find Mama. It belongs with Ram, now. Bir is in the front row. There." He pointed and rubbed the photo tenderly as if the piece of paper could make things reappear. Finally, he held it out to her. "You have heard all the stories."

As Julie scanned the photo in her palm, a memory appeared of a similar photo—one snatched from her hand in an altar room. It made so much sense.

—❈—Restless, Julie lay and stared at the ceiling of her hotel room. The next day was Jathia's execution at midnight. Despite what he said, she still ached for his father.

Every bit of Mr. Musahar's life story only served to push him deeper into her heart. *People can change no matter how far they've strayed.* He'd been talking about himself and the cruelty he overcame—both his own and that perpetrated by others onto him and his family.

Julie picked the Musahar family photo from the night table, examining the faces as if for the first time. Bir's fiery death not only changed the Musahars' trajectory, but Julie Paglia's path, too.

How strange that she would be the one to tell Ram about his mother.

Ram. She tucked the photo into her purse and pulled out her cell phone. It was time to send him an email. *Friendly and brief, or heavy and long?*

She typed:

Hi Ram, Tomorrow is my last day with Jathia. He's given me something that I know you will want.

Love, Julie.

The hotel clock showed three in the morning. Ram would have a full day to mull over his response—or whether to even send one—before she left the city. Julie switched off the lamp and lay in the dark a moment before pressing *send*. She was already lonely, but now she was worried, too. The perfect recipe for a restless night.

Her phone's notification dinged. Still clutching the cell, she raised the screen to her face.

I miss you, too. See you soon.
Love, Ram.

In the gloom, Julie's face stood out like an island of light. She imagined Ram, sitting at his window on the bay, his hands wrapped around a steaming chai. Under an infinite Bengali sky filled with sparkling blue Quasars and spinning galaxies, so, too, was his face shining. It might be the clearest night in many weeks.

❖ The guards arrived outside Jathia's cell to replace his leg irons with lighter chains for his walk to the holding cell off the execution room.

Julie and Jathia shared a smile. She'd worried he might fall apart, but his quiet acceptance kept her own tears at bay. There were no shackles in their universe, only the stories they'd told each other, floating up one by one like perfect, rosy apples in a barrel.

Jathia stared at the guards' hands moving around his feet, then asked her, "Can you forgive me?"

She thought of his father: *I forgive him simply because he's part of a humanity in which we all suffer.*

Jathia's face bore the same lonely longing for approval as when she caught him with Arjun's body under his bed. She wanted to tell him how right and brave he'd been that day and when he warned her in Suni's. No doubt, he saved *her* life, not once, but twice. Today wasn't the right time for that, though. Now, it never would be.

"Of course, I forgive you." She stepped forward and placed her hand at his heart and felt a goodness there.

The guard brushed her hand away, and the jangle of his chains commenced.

She followed behind as far as allowed. "I'll be here until the end, Jathia," she called after him. "Think about the Nubian goat in your arms and squeeze it as hard as you can."

She could see him one final time at midnight at the door of the gallows room. That thought calmed her.

Bir and the goat were both long gone from the earth.

Soon, Jathia would be, too.

"Miss, miss. The body is ready to view." A man's voice pierced Julie's sleep where she lay curled up on a bench outside what she had been told was the execution room.

"What?"

"The body is ready."

"But I thought …" What was this about a body? Jathia was supposed to pass down this hallway right past her.

The guard motioned to a rotund man in a sweeping white dhoti and checkered shirt of the kind heaped in any market and discolored by street grime.

He might be a weary clerk with papers for her to sign. His thick neck and arms slick with sweat, he seemed as lost as a wandering, wet puppy looking for a dry bed.

The man bounded forward and bowed, placing his palms together. "Madam, I am the hangman and I have done my duty." He held out a hand and Julie shook it in shocked silence.

These same hands killed Jathia just moments ago.

"May I ask your good name please?"

"Paglia … Julie."

"Miss Julie, I want you to know your spiritual devotee was in good hands tonight."

The good hands of a hangman?

"I am fourth generation hangman and my grandson has assisted me." He pointed to a sullen teenaged boy who slouched against a wall, the exhilaration of the family business seemingly all but evaporated. "Not all families can be hangmen." The man's chest puffed with pride. "We don't get spiritual advisers here often and I would like to show you the procedure, so you can see for yourself our methods are kindly."

He took Julie through the door of what she thought led to the gallows. Instead, she found a den comfortably furnished with a sofa, television, desk, and large glass case of books stretching ceiling to floor. In an anteroom, a spotless sink and toilet were visible.

"The convict stays here until moments before the drop."

Interesting word choice.

"I offered your devotee the chance to do *puja*. Offer flowers, drink water from the Ganges, but he declined."

He slid the bookcase aside to reveal a cell which was bare except for a metal bar extending from the floor at an angle. They both stepped in and the hangman pointed down between them. "My grandson guides the convict firmly until here, over the trap door. His hands are tied. Before he realizes what is happening, my grandson pulls the front flap over his face and slips the rope around his neck, here." The hangman sliced a finger under his chin. "I push that lever forward over there. The door releases and the body drops. We must not delay. It is over in ten seconds from the time the convict walks through the door."

Growing animated, he sucked in a shallow breath between his teeth. "I apologize for misleading you. Please understand I did the needful."

Julie shrank from his light touch on her arm.

His lips twitched, likely for where to resume his script. "Yes, it's all quite proper. We calculate the drop distance according to the convict's weight and find we can avoid unfortunate circumstances such as decapitations."

She jerked up, focused only on his moving lips.

"The body stops shivering in about ten minutes. I call the doctor over and he ..."

In about ten minutes. Ten minutes! A memory from her childhood flooded in. Julie's knees gave out.

She woke on the floor, a pudgy hand holding a glass to her face, and for a split second it felt like she was home in Cedarwood. Then she remembered—Julie pressed the tawny water away and shook her head. This could be the ghastly Ganges River water he'd boasted about. While she gulped from her own bottle, the fuzzy thinking subsided, and Julie remembered she hadn't eaten since morning.

The hangman's head began a relaxed waggle, another workday over, another man killed.

She thought of what Jathia said about his terrorism. *'It was a freedom fight, at first, but then it became about money. I had worth.'* Later, he conceded *'It was not much money, when I think of it.'*

"I must return home now, to light joss sticks for my parents and for the Gods. I won't talk to anyone for three days. Until I get drunk, I won't be able to erase his face from my mind. Would you like the guard to take you to the body of Jathia Musahar before it is cremated?"

Her brain barely fired. Would the rope still be around his neck? His jaw stretched? Eyeballs bulging like the dogs strangled by the fishermen? She nodded. She had promised to be with him until the end.

They led her down a flight of stairs to a bare concrete basement, past the rope, now coiled, to a gurney with a cardboard box and a body bag open at the head. A trick of the mind perhaps but Jathia seemed to be smiling in death. Moving to place the photo in his hand, she withdrew. No—its life was only beginning.

She bent and kissed his forehead. *Goodbye, Jathia.* Then left.

Behind her a metal pulley squealed, a fire roared. Only when she reached the stairwell did Julie look back to see the body bag slip from view into the flames.

As she exited Calcutta Prison, she saw the hangman one final time through the open door of an office, counting out a stack of thousand-rupee notes.

With the death penalty reinstated, bright days lay ahead for his family concern.

Isolated wisps of smoke still swirled along Vakkali's streets. A checkpoint soldier escorted her to the Musahar's home, and the first thing she did was look in on a sleeping Mayawati.

No sooner had she eased out the door than Julie was airborn in Ram's arms. He hadn't done this since the day he carried her like a naughty toddler up to his room at Suni's. Julie gasped, but before she could catch her breath, his lips smothered hers.

As soon as her feet touched ground, she staggered. "Are you trying to make me swoon?"

He wore the sly smile which told her she was part of a delicious secret.

"Tell me," Ram said, "I've never read one of those Victorian novels, but is crying part of swooning?" He stepped forward. "You're one gorgeous, pulsing heart." Ram flicked at the tears hanging from the corners of her smiling lips. "I could learn a lot from you, couldn't I?"

She slipped her arms around him and smiled. "Your father thought so, too." *Damn. Intentional or not, it was hurtful.* "Forget I said that."

He broke from her embrace, his face rigid. "I shouldn't have tried to stop you from seeing Jathia."

"We've *never* agreed over politics. I have my own opinions. That's just the way it is." Julie sighed. "It's a wonder we get along at all. Although … I don't remember it being such a big deal in the beginning."

Ram turned his head and mumbled, "The sex was better then."

What the hell? Where did *that* come from? "Don't you dare hold me hostage over sex. You've seen what I'm dealing with. I'm trying my best to please you."

"I *know* that." He faced her, his eyes moist and the saddest she'd seen since his father's death. For a second, she thought of holding off on her news, knowing the inevitable pain in store for Ram. "All right. We've both got stuff to deal with." She squeezed his elbow. "Come. I have something for you."

At the couch, Julie sat Ram down and stood over him. "Your brother wanted you to have this." She placed the photo on the table in front of him but he barely glanced at it.

"Who are they?"

"Don't you recognize them? It was taken the day after your cousin's wedding in Bihar. The goat's even there." Julie crouched. "See, here's Jathia at eleven. Your father is behind him. And this is your mother standing beside your father." She gave him time to think on it.

Julie now knew his cousin's odd behavior in the altar room was nothing more than an attempt to protect Mayawati's secret.

"But that looks like ... Mayawati as a young woman," Ram said. "What's she doing there?"

Again, she waited for him.

"Julie?" It was said as if he knew it was too late to put the lid on the box from which all manner of pain would soon flow.

"Mayawati is your real mother. She's raised you since you were five. But she's *also* your birth mother. She's loved you deeply since the moment she carried you in her womb."

He blinked rapidly but moved on to the next question so quickly it seemed to Julie he was grabbing at twigs as they floated by—any distraction possible.

"Who's he? The one with the goat."

"That's the thing. That little boy has determined the whole course of your life. His name was Bir. He's your brother. He was burned alive while tending that goat, a few days after this photo was taken. A higher caste attacked him when the animal wandered onto their land."

Ram peered, photo in hand. An avalanche of family history, which had teetered on edge for decades, broke free.

She sank down beside him, unsure whether to embrace him or let him be. "When your father wouldn't get rid of the goat, your mother left for her sister's. She didn't know she was pregnant with you."

As the story unfolded Ram digested the picture of his mother as if looking on an entity from another galaxy, his soul seeming to collapse in upon itself for what she endured. "Now I get why she checked in and out of hospital so much when I was young. Back surgeries."

"Jathia said your father was like a madman when he found out about you being left at the orphanage," Julie said. "He forgave her, though. And even agreed to go along with the lie she died in childbirth. She was ashamed of herself. I don't know why. Her intentions were always good. She was the one who wanted you overseas and away from danger, not your father.

"If he didn't love your mother in the beginning," Julie said, leaning closer, "he did at the end."

Ram winced at the mention of his father's death.

"Go to Mayawati. It's time to let her love you without the shame and regret from the past. Show her the photo. That's a good place to start."

⸙ When Ram emerged from his mother's room he was as shriveled and caved in as Julie imagined him to be the day he left everything dear at the orphanage.

While Julie held him, he whispered, "She wants to see you. I told her you've been to Jathia and he's going to be okay. I'm sorry I've done that to you."

Julie shrugged.

"She wants you to have these. My father gave them to her." Ram held up a string of pearls.

"But... Why?"

Ram cocked his head and Julie immediately regretted her senseless question. He looped the pearls around her neck before leaving.

Julie smiled as she sat at the woman's bedside.

Mayawati's withered hand found Julie's. "They suit you," she said, examining Julie off the tip of her nose.

Julie bit her trembling lip when Mayawati squeezed her hand. "You look after my boys. Ram is a good boy. Jathia, too." She sucked in sharply, her voice barely audible. "You saw him? They treat him well?"

"Yes, yes." Jathia's face in the body bag before it slid into the furnace's flames, danced before Julie's eyes. "He told me to say he loves you and he'll see you soon."

A thin smile formed along the old woman's lined lips. Perhaps she knew the truth.

❊ Ram appeared in the doorway of Julie's bedroom her first night back, lonely as a child. "Can I sleep with you?"

She lifted the sheet and he crawled in next to her.

Soon the bedclothes shuddered with his sobs. He rested his wet cheek against her shoulder. "I'm going to stay with her until the end no matter how long it is."

"Of course you are, sweetheart." She threaded her fingers through his hair, shorter now, but the familiarity of it reminding her of simpler times on Ram's balcony at Suni's.

In time, Vakkali's water and soil could be purged of seven-million litres of crude. The town rebuilt into an even more desirable resort than before. If only relationships were as predictable. Was this a new beginning for Ram and her, or the end of the line?

❊ It made the most sense. How incredibly proud Mr. Musahar would have been of his son. Ram gifted the limo to Ganesh and allowed him and his wife to live out their lives at the Musahar house with their children. He put his father's life insurance into a trust fund for any surviving workers and their dependents. La Boulangerie still stood but lacked water or lights; Suni joined his family in Kathmandu.

Julie returned to Nepal by land for a month-long meditation retreat in the mountains while Ram stayed by his mother's side.

When Julie entered the flat in Kathmandu, the sight of Ram's suitcase by the door meant his mother's death had taken a matter of weeks, not months. She clucked her tongue at what else it might mean.

"Ram?" Getting no response, she headed toward noises in the bedroom where she found him folding clothes into a suitcase. With a playful growl, she slid her arms around his waist from behind.

He stiffened.

"You're returning to work already?" Julie said. "We owe this time to ourselves."

She flopped onto the bed and opened her mouth to tell him about the retreat but stopped short. "Honey, you look terrible. Why don't I get some dinner going? We can sit down with a drink. Tell me how you've been. It might help."

"No. I'm fine. I've been here a week. I already ate." He turned from her.

"What's going on?" Her gaze darted to the half-empty closet. "Why are you taking two suitcases?"

The question stopped him cold, then he gripped the lid and slammed it shut. "I'm leaving in the morning for Stockholm."

His closet in Stockholm was jammed with clothing. Why take more?

Julie thrust herself off the bed. "Noooo. This is the worst possible timing. How can they expect us to move there after what we've been through? Talk to them."

"You've got half of it right." Ram snapped the suitcase locks. "I'll be the only one moving."

Julie cocked her head to one side and squinted. "Is this still about Jathia?"

"It's not that. It's ..." He lowered himself onto the edge of the bed and raked his hair.

"Wait. You're really leaving? For no reason whatsoever?" She bounded to her feet, a tightness building in her chest.

"I *have* reasons," he said, still avoiding her gaze.

"Good. I want the long version." She waited for him to say 'gotcha' and double over in glee. When he didn't she stomped from the bedroom and collapsed onto the couch.

Ram came and nudged up beside her, his gaze fixed on his feet. "First of all, I still love you. I'll always—"

"That's cliché crap. What the hell's going on?" Her voice shook, betraying her vulnerability. "Why would you do this now, when you need me and I need you?"

He studied her face a moment. "But you *don't* need me. Not anymore. I *know* you'll be okay, but that's not why I'm leaving. I'm doing it so you *can* be okay."

Julie said nothing and the Ram she knew came out of nowhere.

"I'm drowning. I can't deliver the domestic fantasy where you get every little need fulfilled."

"First I'm too strong. Now I'm too needy." Instead of virile, controlled Ram, Julie saw a lost boy.

"I don't even know how to make myself happy anymore," he said and retreated down the hall. Within minutes came the clink of glass and metal.

She gulped in calming breaths. Something else was happening. Julie strode into the bathroom and stood with her hands on her hips while Ram rummaged under the sink. "She's pregnant, isn't she?"

Ram rose, so calculated that in that moment she knew the answer. They stared at each other on opposite sides of a turbulent silence. At the bottom lay a moment they would remember the rest of their lives—pulling it out in times of doubt and self-loathing.

"Seven months."

Her fury dissolved. She offered her frame to the wall and sank down, swinging her head from side to side in negation of what she'd heard.

Ram crouched close and whispered, "You *know* I have to go to her." Ignoring his own tears, he dabbed at the tears which hung along the edge of her chin.

She brightened and clawed at her face. "*We* can have a baby, if that's what you want. It's not too late for me."

"No. You already know the story of how it happened. This isn't something I want, but it's here and I have to make the best of it. I'm so sorry."

Julie shot up and railed at him. "Now who's being controlled by the past. At least the people who haunt me are still alive. *You're* trying to please ghosts."

His stance told her there would be no changing his mind. "I've loved you so long," he said, "but you're so filled up with me there's no room in there for anyone else."

"Why do I need anyone else?"

"Because you're going to want to finish what you've started."

"What are you talking about? Finish what?"

"Once I'm gone, you'll know."

⁂ "Will you come and sleep with me in the bed?" Julie startled Ram where he lay staring into the dark on the sofa. Neither one of them had suggested he go to a hotel.

"Oh, that's probably not—"

"Just be there beside me. I promise I won't touch you. Anyway, I've never been good at seduction."

He smiled but quickly looked away, as she did. But they held each other during the night. Spooning. The warm curve of her back pressed against his chest and groin.

The sharp click of a door brought her to consciousness. His blunt departure at dawn meant he must be hurting as much her. She stood in front of the bedroom's French window, her bare body washed out by the sheer curtains.

Sometimes, when he left to a new project, she waited for him to appear below, outside the front door. He'd stop. Look up at her nakedness, then smile—descending the three-hundred stairs to the taxi stand, growing smaller with each step.

This time, he didn't turn nor smile. At the bottom, a gust sent the blue-black clump of a ponytail arcing across a sunbeam like a royal turn of the wrist. It was the last she saw of him.

❈Emails from Little Sara were rare. Even at that they were often the kind of useless, lowbrow jokes Julie despised. She hovered over delete without opening, unsure. It might be some news about Sam's appeal for early parole. She double-clicked.

Hey!
Light a candle. The old witch is dead.

Julie scrolled up and down, searching for something besides the punchline. *Oh, fuck it.* She tossed the phone on the couch and headed to the kitchen to face her leaning tower of spaghetti sauce-encrusted pots and dishes from the previous night. She waited while the suds turned blood red inside the white ceramic pot.

Before the water was even halfway to the rim, she cranked it off and stepped back from the sink.

Her mother was dead.

❈More than a year since Ram left and Julie still lived at the brick cottage. Each time Paula phoned, Julie pointed out he continued to pay the rent directly to the landlord. "He's coming back."

"No, honey. He feels guilty. Eventually, he'll stop. You might as well return to Canada and start writing again. I can't send you money forever, either."

She came close to leaving after a night of drinking with friends. Julie walked through the door and the loneliness of the place hit her. *Screw it, it's time.* She dialed Ram's home phone in Stockholm and asked the maid who answered if she could speak with Ram Musahar.

Another woman's voice came on the line. "I'm sorry but my husband is out of town right now. Can I help you in any way?"

Julie's finger hit 'end call,' her question answered. They got married.

On this afternoon, Julie's hands shook so much her fingers kept sliding off the numbers for Ram's satellite phone. Neither did it concern her that, wherever he was, he might be sleeping.

"Ram speaking." He yelled above roaring motors and something heavy hitting metal.

A twinge of nostalgia jabbed at her. She recognized the sound of hydraulic truck lifts laying down a row of seismic exploratory plates. Whenever he arrived home, pumped about a huge oil deposit he'd found for the company, she put on a smile—the shareholders likely sporting the broadest grins. All Julie ever saw in this news was another emergency air advisory for Beijing or Delhi.

"It's me. I'm sorry." Her voice cracked.

Ram's was equally anxious. "Good god … Julie? Where are you?"

"I'm still here."

"Has something happened to Paula?"

"No. Not that. My mother died in hospital last night."

"Oh." It was a small, anti-climactic reply.

"You met her. You saw how it was. I just needed to hear your voice." Julie sobbed softly. "This isn't how I expected it to feel …" She sucked in a sharp gasp, breathless and awash in watery sniffles. "The last time we talked was so awful and maybe I should have been nicer, but how could I …?"

The bangs at Ram's end reached a crescendo. "Slow down. Breathe. Breathe."

Something familiar and soothing. Ram's go-to solution.

"Your mother was sick. You don't have to do this to yourself."

Julie sniffled.

"Are you going to the funeral?" he asked.

"No. I don't know. Maybe."

"Go. Don't make the same mistake I did with Jathia. This isn't the time for that stuff from the past. Your aunt needs you. And stay with Paula. Okay?"

"Yup."

Someone called his name amid loud voices.

"I'll be there in a minute." Ram came back on the line. "Everything else okay?"

He tried to make it sound like a pleasantry but only a fool would miss his genuine concern.

"I guess. How's your baby?" She blurted it out to strip away the envy just below the surface.

"He's beautiful. He …" Ram halted. It sounded as though it dawned on him everything that needed to be said — had been said. One more step would land them both in a quagmire of pain.

Someone yelled the data was downloading inside the control trailer.

"I should go. The guys need me."

"Yeah, sure. Take care."

The line at his end went dead. Ram had done his duty to Alana, his parents, and society. He sounded content. Julie stood motionless, unsure whether the call she had fantasized about countless times had really taken place.

Julie, you don't have to do this to yourself, he'd said. But for a full year she had, embracing her pain like a duty, long after he had let go of his own.

In the bathroom she ran the water as cold as possible and pressed the wet facecloth to her eyes. "Oh, Ram." She sank down, the chill ceramic tiles against bare legs like a shot of adrenaline. "Won't you come and help me heal?" No, he would not. How long did she plan to wait for *that* particular fantasy?

During the evening, Julie lunged at her ringing cell, sure it was Ram. It was Paula again.

"Your sister asked me to return your mother's oxygen machine to the company."

Both women waited in silence. For what, Julie didn't know. "Thanks for that," she blurted out.

Paula snorted. "I have the two frames here in front of me."

Ahh. A quivering shame formed until Julie realized this wasn't her aunt, or worse, Little Sara. What could be better than Paula finding the coin and pay cheque?

"It's the gold coin I saw on your table in Vakkali, isn't it?" Paula asked.

"Yes."

"From your dive?"

"Yes."

"You sent it to your mother, and she framed it?"

"Yes."

Paula burst out bawling. "I've been praying for something like this my entire life."

Julie let her blubber along for a while. "This is why I love you, Paula." Her comment seemed to halt the sniffles at the other end. "Did you find the letter I sent her, too?"

"It was taped behind the one with the payment receipt."

"You read it, of course."

"When I saw it was from you, I knew I didn't need to. Whatever it said was probably the best goddamn fiction you'll ever write. You thawed the heart of a killer."

Julie giggled at this, the first curse word she had ever heard out of Paula. "I never thanked her. I regret that, now."

"You *did* thank her. You trusted her with that coin. What I wouldn't give to have seen her face when she opened the package and realized you still believed in her. After everything she did to you."

Julie struggled to speak through the lump forming in her throat. "But … that's not why I sent it to her." Her voice quaked. "I sent it to believe in *myself*."

"*She* believed in you. She just had no clue how to show it. *You* gave her that chance."

"I—" Julie tightened her jaw against a truth that threatened to overwhelm her.

"Your mother loved you, sweetie. You can stop wondering."

Julie wept softly.

"Can I leave you with that?" Paula asked. "Will you be okay tonight?"

"Mmm."

"Sweet dreams, my friend." Paula hung up.

When her hands stopped shaking, Julie carried a cup of chai to the trickling terrazzo fountain. She'd never sat there in the dark before. She'd never sat anywhere before and felt freedom from having to please her mother.

There was nobody left to please but herself. She was free to be whoever she wanted.

When it came down to it, she didn't want her mother to die a painful death. Just to be a better mother. That's all.

A terrifying thrill bubbled up, like being at the apex of a roller coaster. As the child of a killer, she'd been chugging up that slope of resentment for years. There was nowhere to go but down. Into what, she didn't know.

As during the Vakkali days, Julie woke at sunrise the next morning, gathered her purse and stepped outside to a spring breeze blowing, not from the Bay of Bengal, but off snow-capped peaks. Curious, low-lying fog shrouded the three-hundred stairs. She edged down the first treacherous step. *Take your mother's inheritance, be grateful for it, and do something useful with it.*

At Kathmandu's bus station she bought a ticket west to Kashmir, India. Julie had a book to deliver to a man in Srinagar. From there, Notovitch's monastery lay over the mountains.

V

Northern India, 2008

Some scholars speculated Srinagar was the mythical Shangri-la of ancient literature, portrayed as a seat of wisdom and harmony. On her first day walking around, Julie couldn't find a trace of either—just a typical Asian tilt-o-whirl of chaotic traffic and submachine gun toting paramilitary at every corner. The Muslim separatists who started their violent riff with India in 1989 were still at it.

Her destination, Shankara Hindu temple, felt more inviting, and not only because of the three hundred steps she had to climb to it. Each landing depicted a different stage in the life of the Buddha, from his birth in Nepal to his death, reclining on his left side. Historians believed Buddhist monks resided on the Shankara site when their monasteries peppered the hillsides instead of Hindu temples and Muslim mosques.

She began her search for Mr. Musahar's friend at the top, in a sprawling, domed, and pillared mosque of sandstone and white marble which reminded her of the tombs of India's ancient Mughal rulers. In every nook and cranny, aromatic incense burned amongst statues of Rama and his consort Shiva. White-robed Hindu priests sat cross-legged, their shaggy beards bobbing in time to their blessings before the Gods.

It was a boggling congregation of eastern religions, not altogether unusual for India, though.

On the ceiling of one domed antechamber a faded painting caught her eye. A Christ-like man sat on a knoll; his hands gestured before a small crowd. Christian motifs from past centuries were rare in India. Even more astonishing was the name of the man, translated into English—Issa.

Clang. Bang. She followed the metallic thunderclaps to an adjoining courtyard where a brown-skinned old man with spiderlike limbs pumped his forearm inside a cavernous steel cooking pot. She asked him to fetch the head priest, and when the man arrived, she bowed and pointed to the name on a page of her Dhammapada scripture, "Is this you?"

"If this is the man you are looking for," he said, "then you had it right to start." He motioned the pot washer over.

"A friend of yours living in Vakkali, uh … Bengal asked me to give this to you if I passed through here."

The pot washer stepped away from her outstretched arms. "What is it?"

"Just a book of wise sayings. They certainly won't bite you." She lifted the book to him. "It's a gift from Mr. Musahar."

The man frowned and shook his head.

"Your friend?" Getting no response, she pushed on. "He used to work at the nuclear plant in Vakkali."

He shrugged.

"He also owns the Musahar goat dairy and soap factory."

The man's eyes flew open. "Near Patna?"

"Yes, yes, that's the one."

He shrank from her. "Wh … what does he want?"

"Do you not know him?"

"I … I … know who he is but … he's not my friend."

"Well, just take the book, dammit. It's my favorite. I'd rather keep it, but he wanted you to have it after his death." She pouted. "I suppose I can buy another one."

At that, the pot washer ventured forward and took the book from her hands. He thumbed through it, craning his neck in and out like a turkey.

The language was likely too complex for him. She reached over and stuck her finger between two pages. "Something is written in Hindi on this last page."

The man scanned the words. His jaw dropped and the book fell from his hands.

Julie sighed. "Please be careful. As I said, I'm quite fond of this book." She picked it up, brushed it off with tenderness, and handed it back to him. "What does it say, if you don't mind me asking?"

"It's Musahar's will, witnessed by his brother." The man's words flew out halting and wild. "He gives his share of the family dairy … to me."

They exchanged startled frowns.

"You've never met Mr. Musahar and yet … You're telling me … Why would he do that?"

"Mr. Musahar and his brother stole my family's land to grow their own cash crops. Or, I should say, the Naxal terrorists did after they killed everyone — my wife, my children, my brother, and his family. They told me to go away or they would kill me, too. They gave the land to the two brothers. I heard they became rich raising goats on it." The man tripped over the word *rich*, perhaps realizing his fortunes were about to change.

"Mr. Musahar was a compassionate man," Julie said. "I can fully understand what he's done. Obviously, you've known nothing but hard times since then. You deserve something good."

"I do? Yes, of course I do. But *this* seems wrong."

"Why?"

"Because I'm the one who burned his son alive."

The priest spoke first. He thanked her for bringing the book with the will inside. "It's like a fairytale, isn't it?"

"Except this one is true." Julie shot him a hard look. "That makes it much better than a mere story."

She slept on one of Lake Dal's iconic houseboats for the next week, the rock and sway of it cradling her weariness. The one she chose lived up to its name — The Raj Palace.

Snow-capped peaks encircled Srinagar's Lake Dal. Most days she ambled along hillsides through carpets of wild roses, violets, and narcissus. She felt her heart expanding, her mind cooled by the torrents cascading over precipices.

She couldn't stop thinking about Mr. Musahar's startling act of generosity. How was he able to accomplish so much, with so little, and learn to forgive? The Hindu priest was mistaken. Except for a smidgen of luck, magic didn't play a role in this miracle, at all.

Ladakh, India, 2008

Julie sucked in a blast of cold air. At the top of the valley, the lights of Zongla Monastery twinkled, illuminated by a fresh sprinkling of late spring snow and the eerie glow on the horizon of an impending snowstorm.

Notovitch himself may have come this way. As did many others after him, also seeking the manuscript.

While the guides struggled with the tent under a rock outcropping, she tried to remember why she chose this three-day mud slog from Srinagar to Zongla in a jeep. She could have flown into the airport at Leh, a day-trip away. Doubtless, the adventurer's self-flagellation at work.

"I'm sorry, Miss Paglia, but the three of us will share one tent tonight. The snow is coming too soon."

The guide was spot on. Just as they finished their meal of freeze-dried stew and tea, chunks of snow grew into a howling wall of white. A half-hour later, warm and dry, she flipped the tent flap aside to see the jeep outside already entombed. If Julie was convinced these guides had scouted out every protective cranny along the road to Zongla, she was wrong.

"I have never been asked to take anyone to Zongla," the senior guide said. He set the kerosene lantern before him on the floor of the tent and struck a match to life. "It is not a favorite of tourists. Perhaps it is too remote."

His helper shifted toward her inside his bedroll. "What will you do there?"

Framed within the sudden glow of the wick, the senior guide cast a stern eye at the adolescent boy's intrusive question.

"It's okay." In this curious adventurer she saw her own childlike wonder. "How about I read you a story that will answer your question?" Even in the dim light she could see his eyes grow large.

The guide handed her the lantern. She pulled the dog-eared Notovitch book out of her pack and spread it open on her crossed legs. Julie read:

Paris, 1894.

The Secret Life of Jesus Christ by Nicolai Notovitch.

The story you are about to read will no doubt enliven your mind as to events pertaining to the so-called 'lost years' of Jesus' life. While it has long been suspected by many Bible scholars that much has been deleted by early church editors of the New Testament, the facts as here presented, remain an open book for the curious and sincere seeker of truth.

I was a gentleman adventurer, a scholar and a survivor of the Turko-Russian War when I decided in 1887 to make an extended sojourn into India and beyond to 'Little Thibet.'

This is my account as to the events leading to the discovery of a most valuable manuscript.

In a place called Ladak I began my peregrinations as fancy or curiosity guided until I reached a Buddhist convent where I learned by chance there existed ancient memoirs treating of the life of Christ.

At an altitude of 13,500 feet I came upon this white-plastered convent called Zongla. Seemingly glued to the face of a dull, rocky cliff and held there by miraculous intervention, it produced a strange effect in that half-dead country.

Assisted by my interpreter and servant, yellow-robed monks addressed themselves and questioned me closely regarding the object of my journey and concluded by inviting me to accompany them. The monastery is reached almost entirely by ropes being used to ascend and descend from one building to another; the only means of communication with the outside world, an endless labyrinth of passages and corridors.

At the top, I was greeted by a corpulent Lama with a fringe of scraggly beard and exceedingly ugly features but who received me with the utmost cordiality. He told me the monks much prefer European visitors to Mohammedans and when I asked the reason, the Lama replied: 'The Mohammedans have nothing in common with our religion whereas Europeans form part of the rank of worshippers of Buddha. Buddha did indeed incarnate himself with his intelligence in the sacred person of Issa who went forth to propagate our true religion through the entire world.'

When I asked: Who then is this Son of Buddha? The Lama's eyes opened in profound amazement.

'Issa is a great prophet. It is he who has instructed you. His name and his deeds have been recorded in our sacred writings. He arrived in the Sindh with merchants at the age of thirteen. Going north to the birthplace of the Buddha, he studied the ancient Pali language whereby he could read the Master's sutras. After returning to his homeland, he was assassinated by pagans who put him to the most cruel tortures, and whose descendants then adopted the doctrine which he taught. This is what I know.'

It all combined to make me think more and more of the career of Jesus Christ. 'Where are these sacred writings?' I asked him.

'The principal rolls,' said the monk, 'written in India and Nepal at different epochs after Issa preached there, number in the thousands. Our convent is of little importance, but we possess one copy in our own tongue of Thibetan. As his doctrine does not constitute a canonical part of Buddhism, he is not recognized as one of our principal saints.'

'Then it would not be an error to read these to a stranger?' I asked him.

'What belongs to God,' he replied, 'belongs to all men. I would gladly show them to you, but I do not know where these papers are to be found.'

A few days later, finally yielding to my earnest solicitations, the Lama brought out two big volumes with parchment leaves yellowed by time and read the biography of Issa while I recorded the translation of my interpreter. This curious document was written in the form of isolated verses which bore no connection to each other and which I could see it would be up to me to organize.

Upon my return to Kiev I was under no illusions as to the difficulties I would face in getting my account published but I didn't entertain the possibility of being publicly shamed and then arrested. Believing completely as to the authenticity of the narrative written by Brahmin historians and Buddhist monks, I addressed myself to several well-known ecclesiastics.

Monseigneur Platon, the celebrated archbishop of Kiev, believed the discovery to be of great importance but tried to dissuade me from giving it publicity, declaring it to be against my own best interest.

A year later in Rome I submitted it to a cardinal in high standing. 'Nobody will attach much importance to it, and you will create numberless enemies, whereby. You are still young, however, and if you need money, I can compensate you for your loss of time and expenditure.' Naturally, I refused.

In Paris, another cardinal opposed the publication under the pretext it would be premature: 'The church suffers too deeply from this new current of atheistic ideas and you would only furnish new food to the detractors,' he told me.

I took it to the great French philosopher Joseph Renan who wrote extensively on the origins of Christianity. He suggested I entrust it to him that he might make a report to the Academie. I feared I would be relegated to being just the discoverer rather than the illustrious author and told him it needed more work.

I held a public lecture in London and was ridiculed in the press by Oxford scholars as a fraud, but what happened next completely bewildered me. Returning to St. Petersburg, I found myself arrested upon entry into the country of my birth on a charge of literary treason and was imprisoned in Siberia.

And this, my dear reader, is where I now find myself.

> *Prior to my arrest my brother convinced me to keep a copy of the manuscript and my commentaries at his Kiev apartment for safekeeping and since word comes of my residence having been ransacked without mercy, I am forever grateful to him. I have long cherished the project of publishing a transcript of the manuscript I discovered at Zongla. On the occasion I am not able to do so, I give my consent to my brother and my inestimable gratitude for his help in bringing it to the world.*
>
> *There is one final request for those scientific societies which may be inclined to criticize my work as a fraud. And that is to organize an expedition to the locality in which the manuscript can be found.*

Julie thumbed through the warped pages of the paperback for a publisher's note which amazed her every time she read it.

> *Mr. Nicolai Notovitch died in captivity in 1893. Through his personal letters home, his brother published the full account the following year. Since then, explorers have journeyed to Zongla and found the scroll for themselves. Only a few are included in the following list.*

Her eyes settled on the pilgrimage of one Swiss matron. In 1939, one of the monastery's monks pressed the ancient manuscript into the hands of an astonished Madame Elizabeth Caspari, stating: "This scroll says your Jesus was here." Soon after, the precious artifact disappeared. The cogs on Julie's conspiracy detector spun madly.

The senior guide's voice filled the dark tent. "I've heard people talk of this man's visit. As a boy, my own grandfather acted as his porter, but I didn't know Zongla is where he went." Before she could ask the question on her lips, he said, "I'm sorry, but my grandfather died many years ago."

◆After depositing her at the office of Zongla's chief lama, the rental jeep left in a whirl of muck. A heaviness settled into her bones. Instead of alpine greens and endless blue sky, she stepped into a lifeless landscape cut with donkey-trails and lines of colored rags strung between every available hilltop.

The crumbling monastery reminded her of a monstrous, gaudy, carnival ride perched on the ledge of a soaring ravine. An army of ochre-robed monks bustled ant-like along log balconies of every colorful concoction imaginable.

Neither did the crotchety lama fill the shoes she'd laid out for him.

Born in America, he explained how he arrived from San Francisco in the sixties to meditate for the winter. He stayed and perfected his Ladakhi to become chief lama.

Many days later, when Julie explained what she really came for, the man became altogether tetchy. His warm welcome evaporated into the cracked earth outside his yellow-fringed window. He pushed his hunched form out of an equally decrepit chair to peer through the afternoon's fading light at the book Julie put before him.

"What does it matter whether or not Christ was in India?" he asked.

Hardly the response she expected at the end of her rambling explanation of Notovitch's discovery at Zongla.

"That story ended a long time ago." He squinted with eyes rheumy and blank. "I have more than enough work dealing with today, don't you?"

Julie persisted. "But Notovitch said the monastics revered Issa as one of your saints."

"The record of Issa is not a part of our canon." His solemn features softened. "I can rejoice the Jerusalem sage discovered the Buddhist sutras two-thousand years ago and gifted them to Israel. But I alone gain the merit of that joy. It's the only useful purpose for these intoxicating amusements."

Julie's jaw dropped. *Amusements?* The intervening silence seemed as monotonous as the mountain drafts which had whistled through the blackened rafters for half a millennium.

But when the lama spoke, he was gentleness itself. "Many people wonder why on earth I stay here. I graduated with an MBA. I suppose I could have stayed in America and become a wealthy stockbroker on Wall Street. At least I wouldn't have to subsist on so much yak butter tea and *tsampa* gruel."

He paused to pour his guest a dainty porcelain cupful of the oily tea and watched from the corner of his eye as the mixture of black tea, yak milk and rancid, salty butter, hit her confounded palate. "My spiritual journey would have been arduous, if not impossible, with so many temptations of the senses."

The chief lama squared his shoulders. "If you find this manuscript, it will become *your* Wall Street. The recognition and wealth you gain will peter out—or lose its fascination. And then what? However, you are welcome to look for it. I only ask that you attend all the daily *puja* prayers. I think you will find something here that will never run dry—if you care to seek it."

He assigned her one of the five crypt-like sleeping cells scooped out of the rock face above the monastery and reserved for nuns. With the heavy timber door closed, the only light and fresh air in her six-by-six-foot earthen-floored cave came in through an eye-level slot.

She could use the archives as much as she wanted after the final meditation ended at nine in the evening. But without the light from the other nuns' lanterns, climbing the scree-dotted trail to her cell was treacherous.

Under this so-called research privilege, she toiled in a perpetual state of sleep-deprivation. After rising at four in the morning to get to the first puja on time, both her and the robed archive librarian often fell asleep soon after arriving each night to their corner desk.

One morning, she woke with a start from where she sat slouched deep in her straight-backed chair. A sharp pain shot up her spine. Across from her, the keeper of the archive's pudgy cheek lay pancaked on the sun-streaked desktop, each snore vibrating the frayed pages.

Not only had they missed the morning chanting but the allotted time for chores was almost over. It became a competition to see whose forehead would be last to hit the table. The monk usually won.

Wrapped in silk between two wooden clappers, the papyrus pages soon covered every part of the desk's rough-hewn surface. At the end of the third week, Julie dumped an armful of manuscripts in front of the librarian and parked one hip against the desk where he squinted at a page.

"Will you complain to the lama for daytime hours now?"

He wrinkled his brow. "Com—plain?" The man might have been shaking his head. It looked like trembling.

Something had to change. It did. The Snow Leopard appeared.

The chief lama caught Julie's attention as she exited the puja hall one afternoon. "Have you seen our big cat during your nighttime hikes, yogi?

"I haven't seen any cats around, only the monastery dogs. Thank you for looking after them so well. I love all animals."

"Then you should be fine with the snow leopard if you happen upon it. Like any cat, it wanders at night."

She grinned at his sarcasm but soon sensed—this cat was no joke. For the next week, she trailed behind the four nuns and their lanterns, their continuous chatter and chuckles enough to scare anything away.

Without her late-night research, she no longer needed afternoon naps and looked forward to using the time to meditate in her cell. Other than working at morning chores, eating, bathing, chanting, and meditating, there wasn't much else for her to do. She was content.

Contentment got a lot of play at Zongla, she noticed, yet, that wasn't what she came for. For hours at a time Julie brooded and obsessed about the Jesus manuscript. With the time left—she practiced contentment.

In the midst of her first Himalayan summer she'd taken to leaving her wooden door open to gaze at the panorama of peaks as she re-entered the world from the absorptions. She felt no sense of body or mind, dropped as she was into a stillness beyond time or place: a spaciousness both concrete as rock and delicate as butterflys' wings.

A familiar hollow vibration replaced the tranquility. It was the peal from the rooftop long horn, the call to evening chanting. Outside, yards away, a sphinx-like creature reclined, its eyes closed. She delighted in its black-on-white spotted magnificence, no more threatened by it than the yaks she met plodding over dusty trails.

The leopard lumbered up and out of her view. It took over twenty minutes for the panic to set in, but when it did, Julie bounded to her door and bolted it. For the rest of the night she lay on the stone ledge serving as a bed and cowered under her woollen blankets, expecting the leopard to return. But nothing stirred except the jovial nuns returning from prayers.

In the morning, with the chief lama away on business, she waited until another monk who spoke English was walking alone toward the milking sheds. "I saw the leopard in front of my cell," she whispered, stepping in front of him. "I was meditating. I opened my eyes. There it was, a few yards away."

The old monk set down his wooden pail mindfully and clapped his hands. "You are indeed fortunate he has chosen you." He paused. "Oh, I see I must explain. This cat sits with people who love him. We think he gives protection.

"He prowls the monastery looking for rodents or marmots, but he has never attacked anyone. Monks walk safely within yards of him. He is harmless."

"Are you kidding me?" Julie said, her voice riding the panic. "It's a wild animal incapable of love."

The old monk merely grinned. "Excuse me, my yak is waiting." He scurried off, his wooden milking bucket bouncing in step.

A week later, Julie confirmed she'd stopped her research at the archives. "The librarian is delighted, of course, the head lama said, "Can you not help me to engage him once again in the evening sessions? We mustn't let him dwell in all that craving?"

What of her own craving to keep her throat from being ripped wide open? "I think I'll help myself this time."

"You've seen the big cat. So, fear stands between you and finding this manuscript even though we've assured you of your safety?"

"Sounds right."

He wrinkled his nose and sniffed a few times. "All right. I will allow you to use the archives at any time, except during prayers, of course, if you also resume your nighttime research until I say otherwise."

"You drive a hard bargain."

"Just a lifetime of looking into the faces of the deluded."

She'd try it for one night. What were the odds of running into the leopard?

Now in a foul mood, the librarian rejoined her. She climbed the ladders and brought the silk-wrapped volumes down while he thumbed through the Tibetan passages for anything mentioning the prophet Issa.

A week into the new arrangement, when Julie believed everything would work out after all, the leopard appeared once more after dark. The same sphinx-like outline loomed ten yards ahead, stretched out beside the trail. Should she take to the meditation hall until morning? Mere feet from the beast to her door, could she make it inside if it sprang at her?

She edged forward: "Om Mani Padme Hum, Om Mani Padme Hum, Om ..." The chant of protection rose and fell on a falsetto tone ... ten paces to her cell door ... five ... she spun and slammed the wooden door shut. Through the door slot she watched the white leopard amble to its feet and vanish into the blackness.

The next day, in the cavernous brick kitchen Julie sat humped over a metal vat of tsampa dough, rolling handfuls of it listlessly around her palms and pressing them into cakes. She'd left the meditation hall early, overwhelmed by the weight and texture of a depression she thought was gone for good. Repetitive tasks sometimes helped.

The chief lama entered but she pretended not to notice. He was certain to sense her mood. Yes, she had failed to find the scroll, but hearing herself say so would be too painful.

He stopped at the opposite side of the vat. "Yogi. I have decided you no longer need to continue the archive work at night. You can do it anytime you like."

One never knew what he was thinking but before she could try, he explained: "I thought you showed extraordinary resolve last night. I particularly liked your chanting."

"My what?"

"It wasn't the leopard. Just me sitting on a rock with my legs stretched out."

She gaped, speechless.

"You've learned a valuable lesson that can take others a lifetime. A mind filled with fear is not to be trusted."

On his way out, he paused, and spoke over his shoulder. "In case I forget, you can leave behind that heavy thing you're carrying. We'll put it with the others."

When he was out of sight, she peered around her feet. *What heavy thing?* If this old guy wasn't the oddest person she'd ever met.

❀ At the first snow, Julie decided to stay the winter. It had nothing to do with her search. Neither did she see Zongla as the epic journey she imagined. By anyone's standards, her life was tough.

Her dank cave-cell was heated and lit solely by a sputtering oil lamp. Rising in the dark, her back and legs cried for relief from hours spent sitting on the floor. She ate one meal a day, of which everything tasted like yak butter and barley tsampa. Other than climbing the archive's ladders, her only diversion that winter was learning to milk the monastery's yaks and goats. Even so, the nuns appeared to be the most entertained by Julie's tussles with animal husbandry.

Truth was, she couldn't see stopping her meditation while she continued to reach new attainments with each passing month. She rooted out her need to force outcomes. Meditation only progressed by letting go.

At Zongla, she finally found something she could love without having to control it.

❀ "Are you still thinking about the manuscript?" the lama asked Julie during a check-in.

Surely, he must know I am. She nodded.

"How valuable would it be if you did find it?"

"Priceless, of course. It would make me famous and probably rich, too, because of all the academic interest in it."

"And how valuable are these attainments to you now that you're along the path?"

Julie took her time. "Well, probably priceless, too. Either one would make me happy, I suppose."

"Ah, and how long would the happiness of the scroll discovery last? A week, a year, a lifetime?"

She hesitated, deciding against giving him the answer he wanted. "I wouldn't know if it could make me happy the rest of my life until I actually reached the end — but it's possible."

"And the peace you've found in meditation. How long would that happiness last?"

"Well, definitely until the end of my life, as long as I kept meditating. All I'd need is the will to do it until the last breath left my lungs. Nothing could interfere with that one."

"Say I gave you a choice of two doors. The scroll is behind number one and the attainments are behind number two. Which one do you choose?"

"I'd want both, of course."

"Walking through two doors at the same time is impossible." He arched his eyebrows. "The mental turbidity of fame and fortune would be immensely disturbing to one who has not yet reached enlightenment. And to one who is well on the path, this desire for it has long since been extinguished. Craving and ultimate happiness can no more exist together than water washing over hot coals. One will always annihilate the other.

"Serenity can't exist amid our natural predilection for ego gratification. If your aim is for true happiness, you won't get there by grasping after this manuscript."

Wise words, but a dilemma she might never have to face. With each passing day, the scroll seemed lost for good.

—✦—Julie trudged up the trail — only two nights left at Zongla. Outside her wooden door she spread out the straw mat she used for meditation, intending to watch the sun set one final time over the monastery she'd lived at for the past year.

When she opened her eyes, the valley lay in the milky-gray light of early evening. A gust whistled through a spindly web of underbrush. She stirred within her sheepskin cloak while a sea of baritones sent vibrations of happiness throughout the bedrock under her. Downhill, and to the side of the trail sat the Big Cat.

This time, she could easily retreat. *He sits with those who love him. We think he's protecting them.*

How practiced she'd become at retreating from those she loved. She revered Mr. Musahar, yet, when had she told him so, or even thanked him for the book he gave her? Julie rose, mat in hand, and took one tentative step, then another, in the direction of the leopard who loved.

When she was no more than ten feet from the cat, she edged onto her mat. "How's it going?"

The leopard bared his teeth and tilted his chin skyward as if to roar. His fangs glowed, but the only sound he made was the throaty moan of a yawn. He lowered his chin onto his paws and his eyelids fluttered closed.

"Don't you fall asleep on me. I've got something to say." She drew in a long breath and gasped as the snow-chilled air of springtime stung her lungs. "Thank you, Mr. Musahar. You were my first. The best teacher anyone could hope for. I miss you." Then she thanked Paula, and her aunt, and added her papa in an afterthought. Who else needed her love? Inside her head the old monk hissed, *Who else — indeed?*

Many years ago, Mr. Musahar handed her the key to her heart. At Zongla, she turned it and the door opened a crack. Through it she saw her mother, waiting patiently for forgiveness, suffering as all men do. She could forgive Jathia and his father, yet her own mother remained barred from her heart.

"Thank you … Mama," Julie said. "You were …" A melancholy she knew well demanded silence, but this time Julie ignored it. "You were the only mama I'll ever have. I know you tried."

The leopard let out another groan of contentment. Or was it the sonorous chanting from below, rising layer upon layer, outward to the hills and upward to the stars? She never felt farther from the narrow streets of Cedarwood and the bloated waters of the Kettle.

"I used to think you ruined my life, Mama. Now I see how your lies taught me to dream up my own swashbuckling tales of half-baked adventures. All this time, it's sustained me and made me who I am. But I've pulled that bullshit out and polished it up so many times the veneer is gone. God knows, I need a more honest version of my sorry-ass life to cure this bleeding heart. Who knew I'd have to come to the top of a mountain in the Himalayas to get it.

"I miss you." Her lips trembled. "I don't suppose I'll ever get over you." For all things unfulfilled between a mother and daughter. For everything which needed to be said, but never was—Julie wept.

She stood and peered into the dark but could no longer see the Big Cat. "So long, my friend." If a leopard could understand, and who's to say this one couldn't, he would have heard a faint refrain climbing the path with Julie. "I forgive you, Mama … I forgive you …"

Julie's final day at Zongla arrived but she had barely put a dent in the archive.

"Nothing yet?" Agile for his age, the chief lama stepped off one of the many ladders which trailed down from the archival shelving like ribbons in a young girl's hair.

Julie shook her head, pursed her lips, and thrust her palms up in the direction of a table stacked with manuscripts. Bound between wooden clappers, each one was then wrapped in silk, and stored in one of the cubbyholes which checkered the walls from ceiling to floor. "I'm sorry to take up so much of your monk's time."

"This is exactly what his job is—familiarizing himself with the ancient manuscripts."

Julie craned her neck; her eyes took in the collection. "There must be thousands of them in here. I keep rereading Notovitch's account for clues on where the original scroll might be filed. Listen to this. 'The Soudras were not only forbidden to attend the reading of the Vedas, but to gaze upon them even, for their condition was to perpetually serve and act as slaves to the Brahmans.'"

The lama peered over Julie's shoulder. "The Soudras are what we would call the Untouchables."

He reached across the desk and ran his finger along the text. "And down here is where Issa was run out of town by the Brahmins for telling the Untouchables that all men are created equal. I suppose that's why he returned Israel, but he didn't endear himself to the priests there either."

"Poor guy. A real rebel working out some nasty karma. Do you think he's still walking around as a reincarnation?"

"Could be. He was already a *Bodhisattva*. Might be some kind of teacher." He tapped one of the packages with his index finger. "Anyway, take your time." He turned down a corridor.

Late in the day, the chief lama called the librarian to the top of a ladder and handed him a thin scroll. The monk climbed down to the table Julie and he had worked at for almost a year, placed the scroll before her, then gathered up the other manuscripts. He grinned so broadly she saw most of his molars were gone.

Was this the end for her? Or was this the script she'd come for? Her hands shook as she unfurled the single page, divided into blocks of a script unlike the others they had read. A piece of modern-day paper lay on the top. Obviously, a translation, in English. It was the memoir of a man called Judas Thomas, in 99 AD.

It began:

This chronicles the final words Issa spoke to his followers as wrote down by Didymus Judas Thomas in the Year of Our Buddha 645.

I went up from my monastery in Madras to Srinagar to be with my Master, feeble with age and close to his end days.

'Thomas, you have served all these fifty-two years since Israel. I ask one final duty. Lay me in a shallow boat and release me to float on The Lake that my spirit will release as I pass into my next life. Then place my body beside my mother Mary's sarcophagus on the banks of the River Jhelum.'

I took my Master to The Lake and when we had arrived in the middle, I released his boat and all the people came to gaze upon him, and hear his final message. 'The days are passing endlessly. Do what I have instructed, and do not weep after me. Worship no idols for they do not hear you. Assist the weak and harm not a single, living being.

'The world is a bridge. Pass over it, but do not settle down on it.'

At this, the people began to encircle his boat with orchids and lilies until the waters to the horizon became carpeted with colors and fragrance. The people left to let the Great Master drift in blessed solitude under the stars.

At daybreak, we lowered my Master into Mary's crypt and followed his instructions to leave his sarcophagus unmarked.

The manuscript ended there, as if parts were missing.

"I had a heck of a time translating that. My Pali is so rusty."

Julie jumped at the chief lama's voice behind her, but she kept reading the sentences over and over, her eyes riveted to the page.

He sat across from her. "My Tibetan is flawless, but my Pali ... I found it on a shelf of Pali scrolls I've neglected. That was the language of India's monasteries during the first millennium. That scroll is an original. Probably brought to Zongla by monks on pilgrimage in India."

"Are you saying"—Julie jerked up and lifted the single page off the desk—"this ... could be two-thousand years old?"

"Uh huh."

She extracted her fingers one by one and let the manuscript recoil into scroll form.

"I'm guessing it came from Srinagar. It's on material made out of Himalayan Birch bark which was a common thing to write on during the first century around there. Not what you wanted but—"

"Is this saying Christ came to India after the crucifixion?" She cut off the senior monk in her excitement. "He survived."

The lama nodded. "I know of Tibetan monks who can go so deep into meditation their vital signs all but disappear."

"Christ lived to be an old man in Kashmir on Lake Dal?"

He shrugged.

"And Thomas is ...?"

"The Doubter. There's a cathedral dedicated to him in Madras, or Chennai, the modern name. It's all but certain he came to India after the crucifixion. This confirms that."

"So, this means Christ was preaching the word of the Buddha?"

"Seems so. Do you think you might want it?"

"What? Your translation?"

"No. The original. And I keep my translation. I don't trust the accuracy of my work. It needs an expert."

"But the manuscript refutes the resurrection."

"There'll be a lot of push-back on this. I'm not sure I want Zongla dragged into such worldly matters." On the way out, he called over his shoulder, "It's yours if you want it."

She sat mulling over possible scenarios.

How odd the thing surfaced the day before I'm about to leave, she thought. *Right after he warned me how disruptive this would be to my meditation. Is it phony? Is he testing me, again? How would I know? I don't read Pali.*

Her mind drifted. The artifact's energy tugged her into the past, then back to the present moment. She alone could possess it.

While she stroked the length of the scroll with her index finger a metallic grating startled her from the daydream. The Missing Molars monk shuffled between the stone window ledges opening metal hinges to light the yak butter lanterns. A dim glow illuminated the sooty panes.

She'd been sitting in the dark at least an hour. She picked up the scroll and wound her way through the tables and wooden benches, taking her time, until she reached the exit.

The monk stood with the lanterns, one in each hand, like scales. Riches and fame heaped on one side. On the other, her happiness. *Choose.*

Julie's eyes darted to the manuscript in her hand, then to the monk, then to a shallow rectangular basket beside him. This was the inbox for reshelving manuscripts. If she took the scroll, without doubt, a debt would need to be paid, calibrated in degrees of serenity.

The poisonous essence of ego hadn't changed. On this wind-scraped outpost there were still those trying to flee from its sticky grasp. Like them, she'd had a taste of the sweetness of living the life of a hermit.

She felt a stainless, moonlike quality of the heart, where the shackles of constant becomings are cut and thrown away. At Zongla, she put down all those identities she'd worn—the journalist, the adventurer, the activist—so sure at least one would bring contentment.

The search for Julie was over. There was no Julie.

There was no scroll.

Not for her.

It fell from her fingers into the basket.

Julie crept along the stone corridor in the wake of the monk's bobbing lanterns, giving the timeworn stones a shadow-play of heads nodding their approval.

In bed, she laughed out loud to think the old lama gambled on her and won.

❈The next day, while she waited for her few belongings to be harnessed to the donkey, she climbed above the monastery. From far below came the faint clang of a caravan's bells and the cracks of yak hooves plodding through an ice-encrusted creek. The valley pulsed with activity in the brisk spring air.

A wind raked her bare scalp. She ran a hand across it, remembering her arrival a year earlier. At the edge of humanity, in dim and dusty rooms of crumbling stone and tattered cushions, she had sat in contemplation and gone on the adventure of a lifetime.

She'd found everything she came for. The fame and fortune—in other words, *happiness*—was of the kind no one, nor anything, could take away. The same happiness Mo chose inside his dhal shop. With gratitude and love for his God, he shared the best of what he had before perishing in the Great Vakkali Fire.

She decided against tracking down the head lama to tell him—along the path to her cave-cell could be found "the heavy thing".

❈No surprise, on the main road the bus came late. All day, donkeys and rickety carts rumbled by, laden with cut barley, bundles of firewood, or sacks of raw sheep's wool. Inevitably, the Ladakh peasants stopped to engage her in an animated session of their language.

Hours later, from miles away, she heard the bus's grinding gears and blasting horn as it careened around blind corners. She stood and waved her arms. A bus resembling a dusty, one-eyed cyclops approached. The rusty crate teemed with people clinging to every available surface, including the roof. Passengers, who hung from the front and rear doorways, waved and laughed as they shot past.

"What the ...?" *Did the driver not see me?* Annoyed, but realizing the absurdity of thinking she had control over the bus, she chuckled until her mirth erupted into a rolling belly laugh. There would be no other traffic until daybreak. She set out her meditation mat and snuggled deeper into her bulky sheepskin coat in preparation for the long night ahead. Maybe the snow leopard would come to keep her company during her all-night meditation.

She hoped so.

VI

West Coast, Canada, 2012

Oceanview Hermitage is what Julie called the isolated treehouse she lived in for the next three years. Her shack nestled in the canopy of a rainforest overlooking the Pacific Ocean. A few hours north of Vancouver and down a rough logging road, it became the perfect place to record her experiences with meditation at Zongla Monastery. Her only connection to the outside world was through satellite Wi-Fi and her meditation blog.

She continued to live off her inheritance. Both her parents were never far from her thoughts—so filled with gratitude was she for this gift.

It surprised her when carloads of online followers showed up to meditate. They sat in the open and slept in tents at first, but soon started a covered meditation platform.

Arriving in a belching Volkswagen van, Paula fed the volunteers while a pot-bellied stove crackled night and day in the open-air kitchen under Julie's treehouse. When silence settled once again over the hermitage, Julie got busy stockpiling her winter wood.

As she felled a diseased stand of trees above the hermitage, a shiny convertible rolled to a stop. Seeing this, she yanked the chainsaw to life.

A figure in a business suit hopped out, waving to clear the cloud of dust settling inside the convertible. He scanned the treetops for the source of the high-pitched whines, then cut a dizzying course uphill through the choked underbrush.

Crack. Someone gasped. "Shit." A man, doubled over and looking like he'd wandered lost for weeks, burst into the clearing. His pants were soiled and torn, his hands scratched and bleeding where he'd likely tumbled into piles of deadfalls.

The saw purred to a halt on the ground. She pulled off one work glove and backhanded the sweat dripping from both brows. "You'd better get those cleaned up. Sepsis can set in quick around here." She nodded at his hands and chucked pieces of wood at his feet. Julie didn't want visitors to think the hermitage was one of those wilderness resorts.

"I came to—" he said.

"Since you're here, you might as well carry down a few of these logs."

He studied the cut wood being dropped into the crook of his outstretched arms as if the limbs belonged to someone else. He took one tentative step forward and slid.

"Hey, start now. Watch what you're doing."

Cross-legged on the planked meditation platform, Julie set a pot of chai between them. "I'll warn you, it's horribly sweet. A habit I picked up in India. Unfortunately, we can't cater to personal tastes or any nonsense like that out here."

Between rubbing his scratched palms and struggling to fold his long legs under him, he didn't seem to notice either the tea or Julie.

"No point in suffering needlessly, is there?" She got up, pulled over two chairs, and handed him a cup of chai. "Before you ask me questions, I have one for you. What do you hope to accomplish in meditation?"

The man's affable expression collapsed as if she'd insulted him. "I'm not here to meditate. I came here to negotiate a publishing contract with you. Did you not get the email? We sent it four weeks ago."

Julie's face lit up. "Has it really been four weeks since I checked my email? That's the longest I've been able to go so far."

The man ran a hand across his eyes but pressed on: "Your little book about meditation is in high demand. We'd like some background, like how you ended up at that monastery."

"I went to Zongla because I was obsessed with a theory Christ had spent his earliest spiritual years in India, the so-called Lost Years. Like all pastimes, I tired of that and moved on to the next adventure, which was meditating. Here I am, four years later, still at it. I thought I'd put something down on paper, or digital paper, I suppose, and self-publish."

"We'd like to get it into hardcover and distribute worldwide. We could have it translated right away. The Germans are eating it up online. We've already had a request for you to speak. Officially, we don't represent you, but there's been talk we're pursuing you."

"Well, certainly no one could say you're a slouch on that." Julie pointed at the muddy hillside.

She caught his mouth twitch before he leaned in and asked, "So, what do you think?"

"About?"

"Everything I've said."

"Sounds grand. Get the word out. It's not like meditation should be a secret only for the few. That ended in the Dark Ages."

"When the time comes, we can come out here to get you for your first speaking engagement. We'll bring a four-wheel drive next time, of course."

"Where would it be?"

"Stockholm, Sweden."

How perfect was that? Until today, Julie hadn't thought about Ram, Alana, and their baby in years. Ram's father occasionally came to mind. *There's no miracle to my success. How could I expect others to change when I myself wasn't willing to do so?* He had tried to tell her something important; she simply wasn't ready to hear it.

She kept the Dhammapada sayings of the Buddha by her bedside and read from them every night, just as Ram's father had. She dipped into them, especially when confused or low, but those days came so infrequently.

It surprised her Ram's family still lived at the penthouse. The place hadn't changed, it seemed, from Julie's only visit during the first year she and Ram were together. All cedar and pine, the home's ceiling to floor windows still evoked the outdoors.

Surreal was how her meeting with Ram felt. She decided not to add any expectations.

After she shook Ram junior's hand, he charged down a hall to get ready for an afternoon soccer match. Almost six years old, he was already the image of Ram. What a joyful life for her former lover — this precious child and his lifelong love, Alana.

"I'm so happy to meet you." A middle-aged woman of Indian descent extended a hand to where Julie sat on a sofa. Rather than a sari, the woman wore a lace blouse and straight-cut skirt to the knee. "I've been told you drink coffee," she said, her heavy Swedish accent so incongruous with what Julie expected. "Please excuse me." She left and reappeared with two steaming mugs on a tray.

Likely hired help, so the familiarity seemed strange to Julie. Then again, she could also be a close family friend. They smiled at each other and sipped their coffees until Julie finally asked, "Is Alana busy at the moment?"

The woman froze then pressed her hands to her chest. "I — I'm Alana. I thought you knew. I *am* a third generation Swede. Never so much as visited India."

Stunned, inside Julie's head, an epic movie played in reverse.

"We've shared so much over a lifetime, have we not?" With that, Alana straightened, hands sandwiched between her knees.

Not only was Ram's college sweetheart of Indian descent, but he'd married his mother after all. Alana was statuesque, formal. Not a trace of spontaneity. How odd, Alana and her. Mirror opposites. Yet Ram had spent an equal amount of his life with each.

"All that jealousy," Alana said, seeming afraid of the cumbersome silence. "I'm hoping we can be friends. It would make Ram so happy."

She was gracious—the kind of hostess timid guests might congregate around at a rowdy party.

"He was with you, though, when I became pregnant and for that I apologize deeply. I can't imagine how hard that was for you. I know Ram looked half-dead when he arrived here. It was obvious he still loved you. But a baby was coming. We both wanted it to work. And it did. You've seen Ram Jr." Alana went silent and sat back.

"I guess Ram always wanted a child. So did I." As the words escaped Julie's lips, she cringed, because this was one nagging desire she hadn't been able to shake off. "He didn't realize it until it was too late for us. How could I deny him a family?" Julie paused. "Despite everything, I only want the best for all of you. I mean that."

Alana's shoulders relaxed. "Here I thought you would confront me about whether I got pregnant on purpose."

"I don't need to know that anymore. But if it helps, I'm certainly willing to listen."

Alana swallowed hard. "Well. I did. Trick him into getting me pregnant. Yes. I suppose I did. I heard about the Nigerian bombing and how upset he was about his guys. I came here knowing he would take me into his bed for comfort."

Alana stopped and gazed at her hands. From her role as listener, Julie knew better than to stop someone at the cusp of shaking off the ill effects of shame.

"But I only wanted the baby, not Ram. I never intended to tell him. That's why I was over seven months pregnant when he found out. He came here after that horrible fire in Vakkali.

We literally ran into each other in the hallway when I came to the office to meet my friend for lunch."

It was incredible how one chance encounter in a hallway had altered the lives of three people.

"Everyone in the office believed I'd had a sperm donor," Alana said. "When Ram saw my huge belly, he knew it was his. After the baby came, he realized it was what he wanted. Just as you said."

With no sign of Ram yet, and Alana's confession complete, Julie kicked the visit into high gear. "I'm not here to steal your husband away. I only want to see him briefly. Is Ram, in fact, here in Stockholm? I have a flight to catch."

"No, actually, he isn't. I've become a single mother, after all. But there's nothing I would change; my son is my life and Ram is one of the great loves of my life."

Heavy footsteps approached in the hallway.

"Jon, come quickly! Here is someone you will want to meet." She enunciated each word for whoever was in the hallway.

A mammoth man with a shock-white ponytail clomped in. He had shoulders broad enough to take on a draft horse in a tractor-pull competition. The only feature to betray his apparent youthfulness was a fiddlestick pattern of facial creases.

"Jon, this is Ju—lie."

"Yul—ee," he repeated, crinkling his brow. "Ja," he blurted out. "Yulee. Ram Yulee."

"Yes, yes. Ram's Julie," Alana said.

Shaggy Mammoth Man's eyes scanned up, down, and all around Julie's body.

She felt like a monkey behind glass. A naked monkey, at that.

Alana let out a girlish giggle and jabbed him in the ribs. "You know how men are. He worked with Ram well over twelve years. Right up until two years ago when Ram left the company."

To be polite, Julie asked which oil company Ram switched to.

"He's in politics. Trying to become the chief minister of Bihar province in India."

"Bi—har." Had she heard right? "He no longer lives in Sweden?"

"Hasn't for two years. That's what I've been trying to say. Jon and I are engaged. As soon as the divorce papers are through, we're getting married."

Julie gripped the handle of her briefcase and pushed herself off her chair. "I should be going then. I wish you every happiness in your new life."

"No, don't leave yet. I have an envelope that belongs to you. You should take it. Please. It's this way."

They stepped into Ram's study. "It's exactly the way it was the morning he left. We had an argument the night, and I refused to move to India and subject our son to that place. Ram said if I didn't come, he was going anyway and that would be the end of us as a couple."

Julie circled the room, sensing Ram near.

The somber oak desk and mahogany paneling were what he liked. A small beer fridge, unplugged and open, stood in the corner, the bottles overlain with dust. She recognized the gold-plated Parker pens on the desk and the black leather briefcase, dog-eared from traversing the globe and still crammed with colorful charts of old seismic graphs.

His ribbed cashmere sweater hung from the desk's chair. It was the same one she'd wiped her runny nose on the night she met Ram in Vakkali. She traced her fingers along the threadbare sleeve; Ram's body odor drifted up. Spellbound by the memory of his dark skin against her own, she closed her eyes.

Her eyes fluttered open to find Alana gawking and red-faced, as if she'd caught Julie and Ram in a sex act.

Alana pulled a book from an upper shelf along the wall. "He left a lot behind in his rush to get out of here. I think that's why he forgot this." She placed a hardcover book in Julie's hands, titled *Tales Of The Unborn*. "He found your story about meditation on-line, retyped it, and had it printed. It's lovely, isn't it? I like that photo of you on the cover. Where is it?"

"It's the rooftop of Suni's," she said, stunned by what Ram had done. "Uh … India."

Alana nodded and smiled. "He always seemed to be reading it even though I don't believe he had any interest in meditation. You should take it." She placed it in Julie's hands.

"But that's not all." Alana reached over and spun the dials on a small safe and when it opened, she pulled out a manila envelope. "This has your name on it and an international stamp. It's sealed. He probably needed an address. I thought he'd come for it before this, but since you're here …. Would you like to open it now?"

When Julie nodded, Alana placed it on the desk and shut the door behind her.

Julie glanced at the date on the letter inside. Very close to the day she self-published her online manuscript two years prior. She read:

> *Dear Julie,*
>
> *Please find enclosed the original photo card you used on your dive in Vakkali. I had to make you think I destroyed it. But all this time the photos you took of the underwater city have been secure in my safe in Stockholm. They belong to you and always have. I send them now.*

Julie pulled her laptop out of her bag and popped in the photo card. As the crisp underwater images appeared, a longing as transcendent as the Roman ruins pierced to her core and choked off her breath. She continued:

> *I finished reading your book about meditation today. I often wondered how your life was going. Now I know. Do you remember what I said the day I left? 'You're going to want to finish what you've started. You'll know when I'm gone.' Now you do.*
>
> *I saw your heart of compassion and your strength when you couldn't. This is what I meant when I said you didn't need me. Yes, you needed my love, and no doubt I needed yours, but I stood between you and your life's passion. I was fairly sure it wasn't the Jesus manuscript. Unless I got out*

of your way, you were never going to find that purpose. You had settled for my life, my dreams. I ached for the Julie of confidence and conviction. Now that you're living that dream, I'm bursting with joy for you.

Finally, regarding the dedication in your book: 'To the memory of Patna's Ratcatcher, a special man who answered his own cry for help. With gratitude.'

It touched me. In so many ways you remind me of him, his humility and gratitude for everything life sent his way — no matter what.

So much time has passed but I hope you can also find it in that great heart of loving kindness you write of to forgive me for the pain I've caused you.

With love,

Your dear friend, Ram

There was a plane to catch. Destination: Washington, D.C. and the editorial offices of *National Geographic*. She had some photos to deliver, unknown as yet to the world-at-large.

Inside the taxi, she pulled Ram's version of her book out, curious what she might find. Tucked into the dedication page was the Musahar family photo from Jathia. Another thing Ram surely didn't intend to leave behind.

❦ With Ram's briefcase wedged under her arm, she mounted the outside steps at Hubbard Hall, stopping halfway to take it all in, letting her eyes rest on the words etched into the portico's marble: *National Geographic Society*. No doubt the four-story granite building had gone through numerous incarnations, but the Roman columns and cornices at the center spoke of a genteel time of curiosity and exploration long since out of style.

She smiled and stepped through the gold-rimmed doors as many other explorers before her. For Julie, there would be no fireside chat with a snifter of brandy in the assembly room of the Cosmos Club, but she could still deliver her bounty to the magazine's editorial offices.

At the receptionist, tucked behind a gleaming oak counter, Julie reached inside the briefcase and brought out the photo card, sealed inside a manila envelope with a *Fragile* sticker on each side.

She placed it on the desk. "I would like this delivered to the editorial department." Julie turned and stepped away.

The woman lunged across her desk and pinched the tail end of Julie's jacket. "Excuse me, ma'am. There's no name on this. Shouldn't you identify yourself?"

"No."

"What's inside?"

Julie paused and wrinkled her nose. She leaned in and rested her forearm close to the receptionist, as leery with this strange encounter as Julie was confident. "Might be a real fairytale," she said before leaving.

Outside on the steps, she pulled out the photo of the young boy with his face pressed against his Nubian goat. It reminded her of another boy with his whole life before him and the woman who took it, and so, suffered too. No creature, the old monk had said, down to the smallest ant, wants to suffer. Yet, we all do. It's what unites us. Then he challenged her to seek her own heartwood of compassion.

She opened Ram's copy of her meditation guide and flipped to the dedication page. *Also dedicated to my mother, a woman whose cry for help was never answered.*

Mrs. Sara Paglia lived her life the only way she knew how.

Julie had one final delivery half a world away. Her mother had been a tough but doable subject. Surely Ram would be easier.

Thank you for reading my debut novel. I hope you enjoyed it. A review on your vendor's site would be much appreciated.

Follow me on social media or join my mailing list:
    Facebook: AuthorLeeKaiser
    Website: www.leekaiserauthor.com